JAMES GREEN has been wri
commentaries to the worl
poetry. After leaving school
a miner for about a year. It scared the living daylights out of him and he vowed to never again do anything so dangerous or dirty. He spent the next thirty years with his wife Pat raising their three children and being 'the most ordinary people in the world'. Green's life took a turn for the extraordinary when he quit teaching, moved to Northumberland, and took up writing 'to keep the wolf from the door'.

Bad Catholics

JAMES GREEN

Luath Press Limited

EDINBURGH

www.luath.co.uk

First published 2008
Reprinted 2008
This edition 2009

The paper used in this book is neutral-sized and recyclable. It is made from elemental chlorine free pulps sourced from renewable forests.

ISBN: 78-1-906817-07-7

The publisher acknowledges subsidy from
Scottish Arts Council
towards publication of this volume.

Printed in the UK by CPI Bookmarque, Croydon CR0 4TD

Typeset in 9.5 point Sabon

This book is dedicated to Annie and Jimmy

Thanks to Gavin, Heather, Chani,
Jennie and Leila, who believed

Chapter 1

Kilburn, December 1994

THE WEATHER, AS usual, was trying its best to fit in with the general mood, cold and overcast, the rain driven by a sharp east wind. Traffic moved sullenly on the wet road and people huddled into their coats and averted their eyes from the shop windows. They were the unlucky ones who hadn't been able to flee the season of goodwill and enjoy warmth and winter sun.

The man on the pavement of Kilburn High Road had seen some of the lucky ones arriving at Malaga Airport that morning as he waited to board his flight for Heathrow. Now he stood in the rain looking across at a large Edwardian pub on the opposite side of the road. It was a beautiful façade, elaborate but not fussy or overdone, a London classic in its way, and fortunately never 'improved'.

But the name was wrong.

No one would have called a pub The Liffey Lad when that pub was built. If Kilburn was Irish in those days it wouldn't have wanted to advertise the fact. You might as well have come straight out with it and called it The Fenian Bastard.

He was middle-aged and carried a black holdall. An anonymous man, wearing a grey, lightweight suit. He held the collar of his jacket tight around his throat, a useless gesture given the thinness of the material.

Suddenly he stopped looking at the pub and seemed to

become aware he was getting wet. He looked up and down the street. Three doors up was a charity shop. He walked towards it and stopped, the display in the window told him there was a considerable choice of ill-matched crockery, hideous ornaments and improbable items of glass and kitchenware, but he went in.

It wasn't much warmer inside but at least the wind wasn't blowing and there was no rain, that was something. An elderly black woman was sitting reading a book behind the counter. She didn't look up as he went to the men's rail and put down his holdall. There were shirts, lots of shirts, a few cheap suits and a concise history of the polyester tie. The rail had three coats but they didn't look promising. He took the only overcoat and held it up. It had belonged to someone who had been seven feet tall, weighed twenty-five stone and had worn it every day for fifteen years. He put it back and took the next one, an imitation sheepskin, which he tried on over his damp jacket. It had belonged to a human pipe-cleaner and the buttons wouldn't touch, never mind fasten. He took it off and put it back. The only remaining coat was a blue anorak with a fur-fringed hood. He hoped for the best but when he tried it, it fitted. He kept it on, picked up his holdall and walked to the counter. The woman looked up.

'You really want that?' It was a genuine enquiry. 'Man, you must really need a coat.'

The man smiled.

'You don't have much to choose from and it's cold and wet out there. It was warm and sunny where I started from this morning. What's the price tag say?'

'One pound. You goin' to wear it or shall I put it in a bag for you?'

'I'll wear it.'

He handed over a ten pound note from his wallet. The woman gave him nine pound coins.

'We ain't got no fives.'

She took up her book again and continued with her reading, *The Christian Doctrine of God* by Emil Brunner.

The man pulled up the zipper on the anorak.

'Is it any good, your book?'

'I don't know, I just read it to keep warm.'

He went and looked out of the window across the street. The rain on the glass blurred the people and traffic.

'That pub across the street, when did it change its name?'

'What pub?'

'The one across the road, The Liffey Lad.'

'I'm from Antigua. Ask somebody else.'

It was the way she turned the page that told him their conversation was over.

The nine coins in his hand would be a real pain in the pocket of a lightweight suit. He thought about it. A couple of pints at London prices would lighten the load. It was just past twelve o'clock.

Outside he pulled up the hood of his anorak and crossed the road.

The pub was warmer than the charity shop had been. He pulled down the hood of his anorak. Why was it so empty? It always used to be a busy place. He stood just inside the door, feeling nervous. Kilburn was a bad place for him to be, and maybe the worst place in the whole of Kilburn was inside this pub.

He looked round. It was different, it had all been changed. They had knocked the old lounge and public bar into one big room that was set up for eating rather than drinking. And it was Irish, not the cheap comic Irish of the theme pubs, but as if you were in a good class Dublin pub. It had been very well done.

A voice called from the far end of the bar.

'Clear off, we're not open.'

The barman was young and big and as well done out as the lounge but his voice wasn't Irish, it was London, south of the river. The man looked at his watch, then he realised he hadn't re-set it for English time. It wasn't just past twelve, it was just past eleven.

'The door was open.'

The barman looked up from his paper, gave the visitor a steady, hostile look and then grinned.

'What are you supposed to be then, a fucking trainspotter?' Then the grin was switched off. 'Now fuck off, we're closed,' and he returned to his paper.

The man moved towards the bar, looking around him.

'This used to be The Hind, didn't it?' He carried on talking as he approached the bar. 'I liked it better as it was.'

The barman leaned forward with his hands on the bar.

'You fucking deaf or something, didn't you hear me? I said fuck off, we're closed.'

The man reached the bar, he put his holdall down and looked towards the range of beers and lagers which all came from a fancy continental-style set of taps, except for one black beer handle which was labelled Courage Directors. The man went and looked at the shiny brass array of taps then came back.

'What's Callaghan's Shamrock Ale? I've never heard of it. Is it any good?'

There was no reply; the barman was thinking, you could tell by the strain in his eyes.

'Anyway, I'll stick with Directors. A pint of Directors please.'

The man pulled the nine pound coins from his pocket and looked at them cupped in his right hand, when a new voice cut in from the end of the bar.

'Something the matter, Billy? Got a problem?'

A heavy-set man had come through the staff door behind the bar.

'Only I've told you before about your language, Billy, so I thought there must be a problem.'

'This bloke's making a nuisance of himself, Mr Doyle.'

'Well, if he's a nuisance throw him out.'

The man's hand closed tightly on the coins.

'No need, I'll go.'

'No you won't, you'll get thrown out, I want to see you fucking well bounce.'

The barman moved fast for his size and vaulted onto the bar, but the man stepped back and ducked low and his fist came up hard between the barman's legs as he jumped down and there was a howl of pain as they collapsed together onto the carpet. The man pushed the barman off him, got to his feet and dusted off his anorak. The barman struggled to his knees, bent forward clutching himself, barely able to breathe because of the pain. It was a simple matter to finish it by kicking him hard in the face.

Doyle looked over the bar to where Billy was lying on his back, bleeding heavily from his mouth and nose. He turned to the man.

'Have you killed him, Jimmy?'

'No, George, he'll live.'

Jimmy opened his fist, tipped the nine heavy coins into his left hand and flexed his fingers.

'Pint of Directors.'

Doyle pulled the pint and put it on the bar.

'On the house.'

'No thanks, I'll pay.'

'Come on, just to say welcome back.'

Jimmy paused for a moment and then poured the coins back into his right hand, slipped them into his pocket and picked up the pint.

Doyle waited until he had taken a drink.

'Been back long?'

'Arrived today.'

'Back for any special reason?'

'Just a short visit to see a man about a dog.'

'You're not here to cause trouble are you? We wouldn't want any trouble.'

'You know me, George, I never cause any trouble.'

'No, Jimmy, what gave me that idea? We all stood and waved you goodbye with tears in our eyes, as I remember, all so sad to see you go.'

'That was different.'

'Too true it was different. Everyone had to run for cover,

no one wants that sort of trouble again, no one.'

They paused as the young man sat up, blood from his mouth and nose spreading across the lower part of his face, staining his white shirt.

'You were right, Jimmy, he'll live. I'd have got rid of him anyway though, even if you hadn't given me a good reason. He couldn't control his fucking language, always fucking swearing in front of the punters. It's not the sort of image we want.'

Doyle looked over the bar.

'And look at that carpet. I can't have blood about the place can I, not real blood anyway? You're not back five minutes, and you're already costing me money.'

'This place yours then?'

'It's in my name.'

'It said Eamon Doyle over the door when I came in.'

'That's right, Eamon Doyle, that's me.'

'Suit yourself, it's a free country. What trade do you get in here now?'

'Tourists mostly, American, Oriental, all sorts. They bus them here to drink Guinness in a genuine London Irish pub. The Guinness and the others are all £4.50 a pint but they love it.'

'No local would pay £4.50 a pint in my time for Guinness or anything else. Isn't there any ordinary trade any more? This was always a busy pub.'

'There's a special rate for some of the locals, £1 a pint.'

'I'll drink here for £1 a pint, that's the cheapest beer in London.'

Doyle's accent changed.

'Can you do the accent, boyo?'

'Only North London, George. Pure Kilburn.'

'Do you know any Shaw, Yeats or Wilde?'

Jimmy shook his head.

'Can you look a bit literary? Can you be local colour?'

'No, George. I'm no colour at all.'

The voice was North London again. 'Then you'll pay £4.50

a pint like the other punters. We have a string of local talent who come and argue literature, the Troubles and religion. They know how to talk and dress. It's all very well done.'

'Religion and politics? Does it ever come to blows?'

'Nearly.' Doyle's London accent gave way again to the stage brogue. 'Ah God, Jimmy, doesn't myself put a stop to that? It's me, Eamon Doyle, you'll have to reckon with if you can't sort out your differences like gintl'min.'

They both laughed.

'I like the accent, very Victor McClaglan. And Eamon's a nice touch.'

'You know how it is, Nat always likes to give value for money.'

'Nat's still in charge is he?'

'Oh yes, Nat's still very much in charge. Hang on.'

The young man was now on his feet.

Doyle spoke with genuine concern in his voice. 'Alright, Billy?'

Billy wiped the back of his hand across his mouth.

'Yes Mr Doyle.'

'Right, then fuck off and don't let me see you near here again.'

The ex-barman looked as if he might do something but then thought better of it. He didn't look back as he left.

'You know, for a moment I really thought you were going to leave when I told Billy to throw you out.'

'I told you, I don't cause trouble.'

'Come off it, Jimmy, you wouldn't leave for the likes of him, I've seen you at work too often.'

'Suit yourself. Maybe people change.'

'People don't change, except maybe their underwear. You're the same alright, look what you did to Billy. He's not a mug but you made him look like one.'

Doyle folded away the newspaper and gave the bar a casual and unnecessary wipe. He had a question that needed an answer.

'Does Nat know you're back?'

'I told you, I just arrived, there's only you knows I'm here.'

'It won't stay that way long, you know how things work.'

Jimmy took a long pull at his beer.

'This is a private visit, I don't want trouble.'

'If you say so. Are you staying locally?'

'In London.' He finished his pint and put the empty glass on the bar.

'Well, I'll know just where to come and visit you, won't I?'

'That's right. Can't miss me in London, can you? Another pint of Directors.'

Jimmy pulled out the pound coins again and counted out five.

'Sorry, no more. One pint to find out why you're back and where you're staying will stand up with Nat but that information doesn't need two pints. I don't know what you're up to but whatever it is I don't want any part of it. A second pint and more chat puts me too close to you for real comfort.'

'How do you mean, too close?'

'The first thing you do when you get back to London is walk in here, which is bad enough, then you break up the staff, which is not a nice thing to do. It's very violent. If I have a heart to heart with you after that, certain people will start asking are we still close, like in the old days. Tell me, why do I feel that close to you is not a good place to be?'

'Have it your way, George. It's not a very good pint anyway, not like it used to be.'

'We don't sell enough to keep it really. We should take it off and put in another joke beer with a name like Kilkenny Cats' Piss.' Doyle brightened. 'In fact that's what I'll do, as soon as this barrel is finished. We'll get something cheap and fizzy, give it a real fancy name and ask £5 a pint for it. There you are, see what you can do when you try? You can still help people make a few bob as well as cost them money.'

'Always glad to help out, George. See you.'

Jimmy picked up his holdall, turned and walked towards the door.

'By the way, have you taken up trainspotting or what?'

Jimmy stopped.

'It does make a sort of statement, doesn't it?'

They both grinned.

'Jimmy, don't ever come in here again,' Doyle said. 'In half an hour I'll have somebody else behind this bar, somebody who could do more than just throw you out and make you bounce.'

'I know you will, George. Nice to see you again.'

'And you. Take care.'

Jimmy stepped into Kilburn High Road. It was still cold, windy and wet, but now there were white flecks of sleet among the rain. He zipped up his anorak and pulled up the hood. The coins felt heavy in his pocket.

It didn't use to be so hard to spend money in London. Things must have changed in three years. He paused for a moment then headed towards the nearest Underground Station.

In the pub George was on the phone.

'Yes, Mr Desmond, Jimmy Costello. I thought you'd want to know… By the way, Billy's given in his notice, can you get me someone over here? We'll have our first coach-load for lunch soon. I'd prefer Vic. I don't think there'll be any trouble but you never know, Costello making this pub his first port of call. It's not as if it makes any sense, not unless he wants people to know he's back… Yes, that's what I thought, so I'd be happier with Vic here until we know what's going on. No sense in taking any chances.'

George put down the phone and stood for a while. He was beginning to get worried about the health of his old mum. He worried about her sometimes. He didn't visit her as often as he should and right now he was getting a strong feeling that this was a good time to think about going away and asking after her health.

Kilburn, December 1952

In the pre-dawn dark of a cold December day two figures hurried along the empty Kilburn streets, a woman and a young boy. The boy's skinny legs poked out from the bottom of a long, belted navy blue mac and on his head was a school cap. The woman also wore a long mac and had a headscarf tied tightly under her chin. The boy had to hop and skip every few steps to keep up with her.

'Mum, if the Jews don't believe in Jesus, why won't they eat pork?'

The woman sighed. Sometimes she just couldn't make him out, he said the strangest things.

'Jimmy, what has believing in Jesus got to do with not eating pork?'

'Well, yesterday at Sunday Mass Father McGinty was telling us about Jesus putting the demons into the pigs. But if it was Jesus put demons in pigs, then only people who believe in Him wouldn't eat pigs, and if the Jews don't believe in Jesus they could eat pork if they wanted, couldn't they?'

He was a strange child.

'Did you work that out for yourself?'

'Yes, Mum,' Jimmy said proudly. 'It means the Jews are wrong, doesn't it?'

'Not really. I think Jews didn't eat pork for a long time before Jesus. It wasn't because of the pigs in that story. I don't think Jesus Himself would have eaten pork.'

'Why not?'

'Because Jesus was a Jew and the Jews don't eat pork.'

'But I thought Jesus was a Catholic, like us.'

'No, Jesus was a Jew. So were Mary and Joseph.'

They hurried on in silence. Jimmy thought about it. He didn't for one minute believe that Jesus was a Jew, or Mary and Joseph. If God was a Catholic then Mary and Joseph had to be Catholics and Jesus was God's Son so He had to be a Catholic. But he couldn't accept that his mum could have got things so wrong. That would be just as threatening as the Holy

Family not being Catholic. So he did what he always did, he put it away for the time being.

'When will I be a proper altar server, Mum?'

'When Mr Slavin says so.'

'Will it be soon?'

'It'll be when Mr Slavin thinks you're ready.'

'I nearly know what to do, and I can say a lot of the Latin.'

His mother intoned the priest's opening words of the Mass, '*Introibo ad altare Dei.*' Jimmy parroted the server's response, running the meaningless sounds together. '*Ad Deum qui laetificat juventutem meam.*'

They smiled at each other.

'Well done, that was very good.'

'What did we just say, Mum?'

'I will go into the altar of God. To God who giveth joy to my youth.'

He thought about it. Into the altar? The priest didn't go into the altar, how could he? And Mum wasn't young, she was old, so what was that about youth? Faith was full of mysteries, he knew that, so he put away the deep mystery of the Mass and moved on.

'How much longer, Mum? Maybe soon?'

'Maybe, but serving at Mass is a very great honour, you represent all the people who'd like to be up there with the priest but can't be. It has to be done well, because you're not just serving the priest, you're serving God.'

They walked on through the wet Monday streets towards the church and the first weekday morning Mass. The dark sky still showed no signs of dawn and the street lamps gave out a comfortless light. Christmas was only three weeks away but this was where the Irish working-class lived and when daylight came and curtains were pulled back there would be very little show in the windows to welcome the great Feast. Money was too scarce to spend it on entertaining passers-by.

Eventually they arrived at the parish church. Two other people arrived at the same time and they smiled acknowledgment at each other as they made their way out of the darkness into the light of the church. This six o'clock Monday Mass would last no more than twenty minutes. Other weekday Masses were more leisurely and began at the more comfortable time of eight o'clock, too late for most workers but as early as the new parish priest would permit. He liked the sound of his own voice and a quick Mass with no sermon was not something he approved of. The Monday congregation was always quite considerable, about forty to fifty people.

The brightly lit church was warm and welcoming after the wet, dark streets. Jimmy and his mother blessed themselves at the holy water font just inside the door and Jimmy snatched off his cap, tucked it in his mac pocket and ran up the aisle and into the sacristy.

A harsh voice met him.

'Don't you know better than to run in church? Have you no respect for God's house? Get out of here and go back and walk like a good Catholic and don't run like some wild animal.'

Jimmy turned and slowly left the sacristy. Father McGinty had shouted at him loud enough for everyone in church to hear. He walked slowly down the aisle, his head bent in shame. Those already in the church, sitting or kneeling, avoided looking at him and embarrassing him further.

He wasn't ashamed so much for himself, it was his mum he felt for. Everyone would see him walk down the aisle and then go back to the sacristy and know that Father McGinty had said he was a bad Catholic, no better than an animal. And Father McGinty was a clever and important man, a priest, so he must always be in the right. Jimmy added the shame his thoughtlessness had brought on his mother to his growing store of Catholic guilt.

Suddenly she was at his side, taking his hand.

'Come on,' she said in a voice unnaturally loud for the inside of the church, as if she was making an announcement, 'We're going home.'

Jimmy's brain turned slowly all the way home. This was

a completely new thing, a new and totally unexpected star in his private sky. He couldn't be sure, of course, but he had got the idea that his mum had defied Father McGinty, defied the priest, the parish priest, who had been to Rome and seen the Pope.

The only other person he had ever heard of who had done something as terrible as that was Tim Folan's father. He had heard his dad tell his mum that Mr Folan had sworn at old Father Shillitoe one night in the parish club and had never set foot in the club or the church since. Tim Folan and his mum now arrived just after Sunday Mass began and left just before it finished and always sat at the very back. Would that happen to him and his mum now, he wondered? Had his mum really defied the priest and would they have to sit right at the back of church on Sundays? And what about his altar serving, would he ever get to be a server? It took some thinking about. The seven years, eleven months and twenty-eight days of Jimmy's life had not prepared him for this.

'What will you tell Dad?'

'I'll tell him you weren't well so I decided you should come home.'

So that was it, he was right, his mum had defied the parish priest and now she was going to have to tell Dad a lie. Now she would have to go to Confession and if anything happened to her before she could get to Confession she would go to Hell for ever and ever and never see God. And it was all his fault because he had run like an animal in God's house. Jimmy's sense of horror, sin and guilt moved into an entirely new gear. Then his mind suddenly retrieved an earlier piece of information which was now ready to be dealt with. God had to be a Catholic or how could He forgive these terrible sins when you went to Confession, especially the mortal sins which closed the gates of Heaven and sent you to Hell for all eternity. And Jesus had to be a Catholic to be on the altar at Mass, because it was only Catholics who went to Mass. If Jesus and God weren't Catholics then none of the rest could work, could it? So God and Jesus were Catholics after all. Of course they were, and that meant that Mary and Joseph must be Catholics as well because they were Jesus's family, the Holy Family. Well, that was alright then.

Chapter 2

Paddington, January 1995

'PEOPLE NEVER CEASE to amaze me,' said Sister Philomena.

'Really?'

She laughed and continued in her thick Irish accent, 'Not you, Jimmy, you don't amaze me.'

'Is that a compliment or an insult, Sister?'

'A compliment if you're humble and an insult if you're proud.'

'I'll think about that. Where do you want this box of paper towels?'

She pointed down the harshly lit, institutional green corridor which ran between the staircase and the dining room.

'Down there, in the cupboard under the stairs.'

They walked to the cupboard.

'No, it's Lucy Amhurst who amazes me. It's not just that she gives her time in helping out here, it's that she's so good with the clients. She has no training or background in care or social work, yet she seems to know just what to say and do for them.'

'It's a knack, some people have it.'

'It's a gift. Here, I'll open the door. Put them on that shelf.'

Jimmy put the box on a shelf and closed the cupboard door.

'What now?'

'The toilets.'

'Again!'

'Sorry, but let those toilets go for a minute and we'd need to divert the Thames to get them clean again.'

Jimmy moved away to collect the necessary equipment. One bucket and one mop was never enough. Philomena's voice followed him.

'And plenty of Jeyes Fluid, plenty of that. I only want to get the smell of Jeyes Fluid when I walk past those toilets, that and nothing else.'

Bartimaeus House was a day centre run by the Sisters of St Zita. In a more than usually run down part of Paddington, it was a shabby, three-storey property, its main door halfway down a grim cul-de-sac. It had been many things in its history before being donated to the Sisters by its last owner, whose generosity had been amply rewarded by the tax benefits he had obtained on the gift. Known locally as Bart's, it had become an established feature of the neighbourhood. A welcome waited there for everyone who came through the doors. Addicts, homeless, battered women, the abused, the mentally unbalanced, all were offered warmth, safety, food, clothes and washing facilities. There was always someone to listen if they wanted to talk and medical help and a bed for the night could be found if required. Local residents also came during the day for companionship and coffee. Many were elderly people who survived alone and forgotten. At Bartimaeus House they found a place where they felt cared for and listened to. However, Philomena had been told that the enterprise would have to be self-financing after ten years, a target she sometimes despaired of achieving. If she failed, Bart's would have to close.

Jimmy had gone to his unpleasant task and Philomena stood, preoccupied by her usual worries, when the first of what she called the 'night shift' arrived.

Damn, she thought, as a hideously dirty, barefoot old man shuffled through the door, is it that time already?

'Hello Mac,' she called along the corridor, smiling. 'Are you well?'

'Fuck off.'

'Did you have a good day?'

'Bastard.'

'Where's Norah? You know Norah can come in with you.'

Mac's mad eyes glared at her, then he turned and went out to return moments later with a brown and white terrier as filthy as himself.

'Enjoy your cup of tea,' she said to his back as he pushed through the door into the dining room.

Philomena wedged the dining room door open then headed off towards the toilets. As soon as she could detect the smell of the disinfectant she called, 'Jimmy, it's later than I realised. Leave that and get to the front door. The night shift is coming on.'

Jimmy didn't answer. He just put the mop he was using back into its bucket, collected the other reeking bucket and mop from one of the toilet cubicles and took them to the nearby handyman's store. He poured the foul water into the low sink, put the empty buckets on the stone floor and left the mops in the sink.

There was a chair with a newspaper on it by the foot of the stairs next to the front door. Jimmy picked up the newspaper and sat down. From that position he could see most of the dining room and hear what was going on. Philomena was behind the tea urn at the counter talking to Mrs Amhurst, who was setting mugs out.

Mac sat at a table with a mug cupped in his hands. On the floor beside him, Norah looked up at him with simple and total devotion.

'Does Norah want anything, Mac?' Mrs Amhurst called. But Mac, in what was left of his mind, was far away. 'I'll get her a saucer of milk, shall I?' she added.

She poured some milk onto a saucer, came from behind the counter and set the milk down in front of the terrier, who immediately began to drink. She patted the filthy animal gently, then went to the kitchen to wash her hands.

Philomena's right, thought Jimmy, Mrs Amhurst is amazing, bloody amazing. Her appearance perfectly described her, a sixty-something lady who lacked for nothing financially. But she had a way of looking at people and responding directly to them. Maybe it was something to do with the eyes, she always looked at your eyes. And she listened, it was as if she was really interested. She was more popular with the regulars than Philomena or Janine, even though Janine had all the charm and vivacity of a young American as well as considerable good looks.

The front door opened and a young addict sidled in, glanced at Jimmy and hurried into the dining room. Jimmy smiled at him as he passed. The smile was forced, a requirement placed on him by Philomena. It convinced no one and was not intended to. He wasn't like Mrs Amhurst. He looked at people's clothes first, noticed how they walked or stood, listened to the way they spoke as much as what they said. He looked into their eyes last, if at all. He automatically judged them 'no problem', 'problem', 'big problem', or 'not sure'. It was the 'not sure' ones he watched with the greatest care. It was the 'not sures' he disliked most of all, but then, there weren't many people he did like.

Philomena came out of the dining room drying her hands on a tea towel. Behind her he could see Mrs Amhurst pouring tea for the addict and talking cheerfully.

'A slow start tonight.'

He nodded. Philomena was one he did like. It was a harmless indulgence he allowed himself.

'But it'll pick up. There's too many out there in need of this place for any night to be really quiet.'

'That's a fact, Sister.'

'It's good to have you here, Jimmy. I feel much better about Lucy and Janine with you here. Money and good looks are a terrible responsibility in a place like this.'

'I knew you had good looks, but I never knew you had

money. If you hadn't taken vows, I might have done something about it.'

Philomena laughed.

'Go on, you. I never had money and I never had looks and I never missed either. I never saw the one bring joy or the other last.'

'But you worry about that pair and not yourself? Couldn't you come to a bit of harm as well, or is The Man Upstairs looking after you?'

'I'll be alright. If you've done time in Idi Amin's Uganda, Paddington isn't so bad. And maybe I am being looked after by The One Upstairs, and if so, I think She's doing a good job.'

At that moment the front door crashed open and a drunk staggered into the hall. Jimmy was up and had him face hard against the wall with an arm twisted up behind his back before Philomena had moved.

'Easy Jimmy, easy. It's only Freddo.'

Jimmy moved back slightly and Freddo promptly vomited.

'Oh, God, sit him outside, then come in and clear that up will you? Some of our best nights started quiet.'

Jimmy took Freddo outside and sat him on the floor in the alley with his back resting against the wall. He was in no state to worry about the cold. Jimmy poked him hard in the leg.

'Don't come in again till you're fit.'

Freddo nodded without looking up, rolled sideways, and went to sleep. Jimmy went back inside, closed the front door and headed to the store room. This job meant cleaning one of the buckets and mops he had left there. He pulled on a pair of bright yellow Marigold gloves and, as he tried to clean the shit out of the mop head under the running tap, pondered on how Philomena took it all in her stride and never seemed to sit in judgement on the trash she dealt with. Maybe she was genuinely good, holy even.

As Jimmy put the mop down and reached for the Jeyes Fluid it was not the odour of sanctity that he felt was clinging to him. This was his third week as general odd job man and 'security' at Bart's. It was not what he had been used to but the work was easy. Some of the clients might be violent but never in any professional way, so they presented no real problem. He rinsed out the sink and poured some of the whitish fluid into it. Not hard work, but no one could say it was pleasant.

He put the mop into the bucket, half filled it with water and hoped they and he smelled more of Jeyes Fluid than anything else, then set off back to his next little assignment. He looked at the floor as he came back to the hallway. Someone had walked straight through the vomit and trailed it into the dining room.

'What the hell am I doing here?' he said to himself. But he knew exactly what he was doing here. Exactly.

Kilburn, June 1956

The group of three girls ran to where Jimmy was standing in the playground. They formed a line in front of him and chanted:

'Jimmy Costello,
he can't dance,
because he's got no underpants.
Jimmy Costello,
he can't sing,
because he hasn't got a thing.'

The last word was almost shouted so there could be no doubt what the 'thing' he didn't have was. Having finished their performance, they giggled and ran off to another part of the playground to annoy some other boy.

Jimmy was eleven and in his last year of primary school. Next term he would go to the secondary modern. Hardly anyone from his school ever passed the eleven-plus exam, at least, not often. This year Terry Prosser had been the only one, the first in a long time.

Another boy came out of the mass of noisy children and stood beside him.

'What you doing, Jimmy?'

It was Kevin. Kevin was a thief. That wasn't so bad though, because everyone knew Kevin was a thief so no one gave him a chance to steal anything. Jimmy disliked Kevin, not because he was a thief but because he was stupid. He was always trying to show off but had nothing to show off about. He loved to swear and show how bad his language could be but he had no imagination so he simply parroted the strings of obscenities which everyone knew, even if they didn't use them in school. He often tried to become aggressive but anyone who stood up to him, even a bold infant, could face him down. He was poor and he was dirty. At his First Communion he had been brought by his grandma and he had been wearing black pumps with a hole in one toe where the dirty grey sock showed through. He often tried to talk to Jimmy because Jimmy frequently stood alone in the playground. Kevin also tried to talk to him because he was one of the very few people who didn't humiliate or reject him as a matter of course. Sometimes, if Kevin was lucky, Jimmy would even talk to him for a bit.

'Do you want to do something?'

'Like what?'

A sly look came into Kevin's eyes.

'Let's go and shit on the floor in the toilets.'

Jimmy recoiled.

'What?'

'We could leave shit on the floor.' Then Kevin had a better idea. 'Or we could wipe it on the walls.'

He was grinning with enthusiasm. Jimmy was appalled. In his own home no one swore, ever. He had once said fart, and his mother had been visibly shocked, not angry, but shocked. Gently, with sadness, she had explained to him how a home was a place where the family were just that, family. You didn't bring the dirt of the streets in on your boots, your tongue or your mind. Everyone had to make sure the home was a place where the nastiness of the outside world didn't intrude. You couldn't always get away from that nastiness, but there were places where you didn't bring the dirt from outside in with you. Church was one and home was another, they were both sacred places.

At home elaborate language had been developed so that bodily parts or functions, if they had to be referred to at all, were referred to so that no suggestion of the rude or vulgar crept in. Jimmy knew the words others used, how could he not, but he never used them himself. Now, to have it suggested to him that he might go to the toilet on the floor, that was awful. But to touch it, to put it on the walls – he was physically revolted. He walked away from Kevin. Even standing next to him made him feel dirty.

About a quarter of an hour after the end of the lunch playtime, when everyone was back in their classes, the headmistress, Sister Augustine, sent for him. He went to her office, a forbidding doorway at the end of a dark corridor reached by a staircase of grey stone steps. He knocked and entered on her command. She sat behind a large desk. Her office was light, tidy and well-decorated, so different from the rest of the shabby, decaying school. Her expression told him something had happened, clearly not something good. He was glad he knew nothing about it and would not be called on to tell tales on anyone.

'You are a filthy little boy, Jimmy Costello, a disgrace to the school and a disgrace to your family, and if you were not so close to leaving I should certainly have expelled you.'

He was stunned. He had no idea how he had arrived in such a situation or even what the situation was. Sister Augustine got up, walked around her desk and stood in front of him.

'Don't pretend you don't know what I'm talking about.'

He didn't pretend.

Suddenly Sister Augustine slapped his face.

Jimmy had not expected that. He knew he would be punished for whatever he was supposed to have done but he had not expected anything so personal. In a way he was glad. That put her in the wrong.

'That awful mess in the toilets. I will cane you then you will clean it up yourself. No one else should have to clean it up.'

Then she became calm. She took her cane from where it lay on the desk. Jimmy held out his hand. He had never been caned before. His life in school had not been good or bad, it had been anonymous. The cane rose and fell three times. Jimmy winced. It hurt, but the pain somehow didn't seem to go past his wrist. It was a fierce pain, but it all stayed on the palm of his hand. He found that odd and interesting.

'The other hand,' demanded Sister Augustine. He held out his other hand. It was the same, fiercely painful, but localised. Jimmy lowered his arm and Sister Augustine returned to her chair.

'I have told the caretaker to put a bucket, mop, scrubbing brush and disinfectant in the toilets. Go and clean up your mess.'

'No.'

'What did you say?'

He knew all about it now. Kevin had carried out his foul joke and blamed him. He didn't mind being caned but he would not go among shit, especially not among Kevin's shit.

'No.'

'No one else will clear up your mess, Costello.'

'It's not my mess.'

'Don't try to blame anyone else. I know it's your mess.'

'It's not.'

If asked, he would name Kevin, but he had to be asked.

'Then why did Terry Prosser tell me it was?' Sister Augustine was playing her trump card. Terry Prosser's word could not be doubted. He was known by all to be as honest as he was clever. Jimmy couldn't understand it.

'You will clean that toilet and wash it down so the vile mess and smell are removed completely. If you do not do as you are told, I shall write to your parents and not only ask them to remove you, but to remove your sister also.'

To have to leave the school was of no consequence to him.

In just over six weeks he would be gone anyway. But his little sister loved the school and all her friends were there. Sister Augustine was using his little sister against him. He also knew that the shame would be massive for his parents, especially for his mother.

If he gave in now, the whole thing would be forgotten by tomorrow. He turned without speaking and left the office.

'Come back, you rude boy, and apologise.'

Her voice followed him down the corridor but she herself did not.

Jimmy went to the stinking toilet where he saw the ordure wiped across the floor and walls. How had Kevin managed it without taking the awful smell with him into his classroom? It wasn't a skill he wanted for himself but he was impressed that it could be done. There was a bucket of water with a can of disinfectant and a large scrubbing brush on the floor. He took off the disinfectant lid and recoiled, holding the can at arms length, but at once realised that only such a powerful smell could eradicate Kevin's handiwork. He looked at the label – Jeyes Fluid. It would be a name and smell he would remember. He poured the disinfectant into the water, took up the scrubbing brush, pushed it into the whitish liquid and began to clean.

After he had finished he left the bucket, the brush and the can and went back to class. He carried about him conflicting smells but the overriding one was Jeyes Fluid. His teacher, a kindly, gentle man, quietened the class on his entrance and continued with the lesson.

'Richard, called Coeur de Lion or Lionheart, was as brave as he was good…' his reading from the history book resumed. The girl who shared a desk with Jimmy fussily shifted herself and her books to the very far edge of the desk, held her nose and made a face. Jimmy sat very still. He didn't join in when the writing began and wasn't asked to. He was left alone until the end of the day, when the bell rang and the class stood, said prayers, put their chairs up onto their desks to make life easier for the cleaner and were dismissed. Jimmy went to the Infants' exit and met his sister, Mary.

'You smell funny, not nice.'

'Wait here, I'll be back in a bit. Wait and don't go anywhere.'

Mary was puzzled, but she nodded. Jimmy went to the main gate. As soon as he saw Terry Prosser he began to shout.

'*Proddy Prosser, Proddy Prosser, Proddy Prosser is a dosser.*'

It wasn't much but it was the best he could manage. Terry Prosser was an outsider, his family had moved to London from South Wales only a year before. The whole family spoke with a strong Welsh accent. His father was Chapel and it had been Terry's Catholic mum who had insisted on Terry going to the local Catholic school. Terry felt his strangeness very much among the London Irish of Kilburn and the taunt of 'Proddy Prosser' was enough. He ran through the crowd of children to confront Jimmy.

'A fight, a fight.'

The chant began as the two boys faced each other. Terry spoke in his gentle Welsh tones.

'What d'you want, shit cleaner?'

Jimmy hit him once, hard, on the chin. The blow jerked Terry's head back and tears came to his eyes but he didn't fall down like they did on the films. He touched his chin, then, suddenly and furiously, set on Jimmy. Jimmy didn't try to fight, he just wriggled and held on and, finally, fell down with Terry on top of him. Terry's fists were furious but only occasionally effective. Some blows landed hard but no real harm was done.

Jimmy had always, in a vague sort of way, felt afraid of pain and violence. He had avoided rough games and never been involved in the frequent playground fights. Now he found it didn't matter. Some punches hurt but it was just something that was happening to his body. He found he had gone somewhere else, somewhere deep inside himself where the pain didn't matter. The pain was there and it was real but it didn't touch the deep, inner Jimmy.

Terry Prosser stood up and looked at Jimmy on the floor, then he turned and walked away through the crowd. The fight was over and Jimmy was beaten.

The children dispersed, happy to have had a little extra thrill at the end of another day. Those few mums or big sisters who had been waiting at the school gates ignored the whole business. Most of them had been to this school or a school just like it and had seen it all before, it was just children coming out of school.

Jimmy got up and looked at the school building. On the first floor Sister Augustine was standing in her office window, watching. Then she disappeared.

He now knew what had happened. Kevin had told Terry that he was responsible, then told a teacher that Terry knew something about it. Kevin would have known that Terry, unschooled in the ways of Kilburn, would pass on his information. He had gambled, correctly, that once Sister Augustine had the information she would not enquire too closely as to its original source nor its truth. She would be satisfied to have a suitable culprit on whom to inflict punishment. Jimmy acknowledged that while Kevin wasn't good at much, some things he could do quite well. His were small talents but he knew how to make the most of them.

It was all over now. His parents need never know, or at least his mum could pretend she didn't know. He walked back to where his sister was waiting.

'I got a star for my writing today,' she chirruped happily as they walked hand-in-hand away from the school. Jimmy looked back at Sister Augustine's window. There was no one there.

It was then that he made a decision. He would join the parish boxing club, where he would learn how to make a fist and how to hit people. He would find out what to do to avoid being hit and what to do when you were hit. He would learn how to fight, and he would do it properly. The Church would teach him.

Chapter 3

Paddington, January 1995

EVERYONE WAS VERY upset when Lucy Amhurst was murdered, robbed of her handbag and stabbed whilst getting into her car at around eleven at night after the last clients had gone. Her body had lain on the far side of the car, which was parked by the kitchen window near the street. Janine had noticed the car from the kitchen window and asked Jimmy to see if anything was wrong. Jimmy had gone out, established she was dead, returned and told Philomena and Janine. Sister Philomena had phoned the police whilst he went back to stay with the body. The police had arrived and sealed off the alley. The Scenes of Crime team came and went. Evidence was collected and bagged, photos taken, witnesses questioned and notes made.

Shortly after the police, the reporters had arrived. They collected the details they needed about the victim and the crime, got the background of Bart's and decided what sort of story they would file.

It was not going to be a big story, a mention on the TV news perhaps, nothing more. It was probably drugs-related, an addict who needed to feed a habit, just one more knife-crime.

The reporters stood and chatted with the police for a while, sniffing around for other news. Then they left. Mrs Amhurst's body was taken away. Finally the last of the police left, having said that someone would return the next morning to continue the investigation.

In the dining room a terrible ordinariness had descended, that strange calm which surrounds those close to someone suddenly dead when they are finally left alone. Somewhere, Mr Amhurst would also have entered that awful, empty calm, where nothing looked different but everything had changed for ever. The world must move on and take up its daily business, the bereaved are left with their thoughts.

Janine stood beside Philomena at the serving counter. Slim and good-looking with thick, short brown hair, she wore jeans and a plain shirt with a nondescript cardigan. She wore no make-up, she couldn't hide her attractiveness but made no show of it.

'Those reporters were horrible,' she said, almost to herself.

'They were only doing their job,' Philomena said quietly. 'It's news even if we can't see it that way. I thought they asked their questions kindly enough.'

'But talking and laughing. It was…'

Janine began to cry. Philomena led her to a table. They sat down.

'We were Lucy's friends, we will grieve for her and miss her. And we will remember her and her poor husband in our prayers.'

Jimmy came into the dining room.

'Everything's locked up,' he said and looked at his watch. 'It's five o'clock.'

Neither woman moved, so he sat down.

'Tea, anyone?' asked Philomena.

'I think we all might benefit from something stronger, Sister.'

'Sorry, Jimmy, I don't keep anything like that here, the clients would nose it out no matter how well I hid it or someone would break in to get at it. We had twelve break-ins before word got onto the street there was nothing here worth stealing.'

Janine wiped her eyes with the backs of her hands.

'Tea will be fine.'

'Jimmy?'

'No thanks.'

Philomena went to the urn on the counter and felt it. It wasn't hot but it would do. She brought two cups back to the table.

'It doesn't seem real,' said Janine. 'I seem to be in a nightmare.'

Philomena took a sip of tea.

'You're in shock. Go off to bed and try and get some rest, I'll stay up.'

Janine stood up slowly.

'I'm not as strong as I thought, I don't seem to be able to cope like you two.'

'Nor should you, Janine. Please God it's not something you'll ever have to learn or get used to. I won't call you, get all the sleep you can.'

'Oh call me, please, Sister. I want to be useful and it will help to have something to do.'

'I'm afraid this sort of thing is something I've seen before,' Philomena said after Janine had gone. 'You don't get used to it but you deal with it. You bury the dead and care for the living and leave the rest in God's hands. And you, Jimmy, where did you learn to cope with this sort of thing?'

'It happens, and when it happens I can deal with it.'

'What am I to make of that? Were you in the Army or what?'

'Or what.'

'Well, your own business is your own.' Philomena looked into her tea, and then looked back up at Jimmy. 'It's been great having you here these last weeks.'

'I wasn't much use to you tonight.'

'If this was anybody's fault, Jimmy, it was mine. I should have made a point of seeing her to her car.'

'Sister, people get knifed for a packet of chips or the change in their pocket or for no good reason at all. It could have happened anywhere at any time.'

'But it happened here.' Philomena paused. 'Thank God I didn't have to tell her husband. Poor man, what he must feel like this night.'

It wasn't something either wanted to dwell on.

'The police were very good, considering, I've seen the woman constable before and the other uniformed one but I've not seen either of the plain clothes ones. They've never been here in all the times we've called out the police.'

'They'll be CID. It's not their work to sort out trouble among the clients.'

'Did the older one know you, Jimmy?'

'What makes you think that?'

'He just seemed to.'

'We've met before.'

'Is it anything you want to talk about?'

Jimmy sat looking at his hands on the table. It wasn't anything he wanted to talk about.

'When Father Lynch told me there was someone who wanted to come and help out for a while I wasn't expecting anyone like you. I asked him what he could tell me about you. Do you know what he said?'

Jimmy shook his head without looking up.

'*If you want someone to keep the place quiet, sort the trouble and help around the place then that's a job he'll do fine*. That's not exactly an unqualified reference, but then, the skills we needed here aren't taught in the better sort of schools or seminaries.'

'Sister, you're tired. I'll stay up in case anything's needed. Try to get some sleep.'

'You're right. I'm just talking to stop myself thinking. Before I go, Jimmy, will you say a prayer with me?'

'Sure.'

Philomena blessed herself for both of them.

'Our Father...'

Jimmy joined in the words of the Lord's Prayer. At the end she added, 'May her soul and the souls of all the faithful departed, through the mercy of God, rest in peace.'

'Amen.' The word left Jimmy's mouth automatically and they both blessed themselves.

'She's in God's hands now.' Philomena got up. 'As we all are. Goodnight, Jimmy.'

'Goodnight, Sister.'

When she had gone Jimmy again looked at his hands on the table, small hands with thick fingers, hands that could make strong fists. Hands that he knew could hurt people. Then he spoke quietly.

'Now that someone knows where I am I have a nasty feeling I won't be left to stay in God's hands very much longer.'

But there was no one to hear him say it, except God and the empty room.

Kilburn, October 1962

'You're a strange one, Jimmy, and no mistake. You're far and away the best boxer we have ever produced in my time at the club but you won't fight. You could turn professional. You're better than Stephen Gaines was at your age and look how well he's doing. He must be worth a pot of money now. I know you've had offers, I know there's been interest.'

Jimmy shrugged.

'Is it your looks you're worried about? Are you afraid a broken nose might not go with the Buddy Holly haircut?'

'It's a Tony Curtis, Father.'

'Is there a difference?' Father Liam grinned. 'These things change too fast for me. Why did you take it up at all if you won't go in for the contests?'

'Boxing was just a hobby, Father, I didn't like football or table tennis and there was nothing else. It kept me fit, I liked it, and I made some good friends in the club but it's time to pack it in now. Eighteen's too old for hobbies.'

The priest, himself quite young, nodded with mock seriousness.

'Yes, you're quite an old man now.'

'You know what I mean. It would have to stop sometime.

Now is as good a time as any.'

Father Liam put his hand on Jimmy's shoulder. Jimmy stiffened, he didn't like anyone except Bernadette touching him.

'We'll all miss you. Watching you box or boxing with you was like a university education for the lads, there'll be no substitute for you, Jimmy. You may never have boxed a match for the club but there's a lot of you in the cups and medals that have come to us through others.' He patted Jimmy's shoulder, then took his hand away. 'I've a lot to thank you for, not just the boxing but the serving at Mass as well.'

'That's for me to say thank you, Father. It meant a lot to me and my mum.'

'You've served longer than most. I suppose you got kidded about it?'

'I never let it be a problem.' Jimmy put out his hand. 'Well, goodnight Father. Thanks for everything.'

They shook hands.

Father Liam had come as a curate to Father McGinty five years ago. A keen and talented boxer himself, he had taken an interest in the parish boxing club. Jimmy had stood out immediately. It was the way he boxed, studying how to avoid punches as well as how to land his own. He seemed to allow himself to be hit so that he could study that as well. He had proved an apt pupil. But he resolutely refused to be entered for contests or take part in inter-club matches. It was as if he had some private agenda. With the effort and energy he put into his boxing, he was certainly going somewhere, wherever that might be.

It was nine o'clock, wet and dark. Across the High Road was The Hind, a big Edwardian pub. He decided to go in. The smoky bar was alive with conversation and laughter. Jimmy saw a face looking at him, a face he knew. He crossed to the bar.

'On your own, Kevin?'

'Sort of, I just stopped for a couple of quick ones then I'm off to meet some mates and we'll go on up West.'

The barman came over. He was about Jimmy's age. 'Well, you gonna have a drink, mate, or just admire me?'

He spoke cheerfully in answer to Jimmy's stare but no offence was intended and none was taken.

'A pint of mild.'

The barman began to pull the dark pint and Kevin resumed.

'But if you're doing something, Jimmy, then stuff them, I'll come with you.'

Kevin took a pull at the short he was drinking. It was like Kevin to drink shorts, if the barman would serve him at all that was. He looked anything from fourteen to eighteen if you looked at him carefully, but very few people bothered to look at Kevin, carefully or in any other way. There just wasn't much to see.

The barman brought Jimmy's pint of mild and was moving away to serve another customer when Kevin demanded loudly, 'Another Irish when you're ready.'

A short, fat man at the far end of the bar, wearing a flashy waistcoat and smoking a cigar, immediately got off his stool, went behind the bar and came to where they were standing.

'Did you bring him in here, mate?' he asked Jimmy.

Jimmy shook his head.

'No, he was drinking here when I came in a minute ago.'

The fat man called over the barman who had served Jimmy.

'George, did you serve this fucking lad here?' He nodded at Kevin.

'I suppose so, Mr Lonsdale.'

'That's it. Clear off, you're fired.'

Lonsdale gestured across the bar at Kevin.

'Look at the bloody little tosser. He doesn't look fifteen never mind eighteen. Even the friendliest bobby would have to do something if they found him drinking in here. I'm not risking my licence 'cos you're too stupid to look at the punters when you serve them. Get your coat and get out.'

He looked across the room and shouted to a group at a table near the window.

'Annie, want a bit of work tonight?'

A large, overdressed woman looked up from the table where she sat with another woman and two men.

'What, now?'

'Yes, behind the bar for the rest of the night.'

She rose awkwardly.

'Alright, Mr Lonsdale,' she said sullenly.

Lonsdale turned to Kevin.

'You still here?'

Kevin stuck his lower lip out.

'I'm eighteen. I can drink here if I want.'

Lonsdale leaned forward and lowered his voice.

'You can catch a fucking ambulance from here if you want to, sunshine. There'll be one leaving from just outside in five minutes.'

Kevin, with as much swagger as he could manage, drained his glass and turned to leave.

'Me as well?' asked Jimmy.

'As you please, mate, it's up to you.'

Jimmy decided he didn't like Mr Lonsdale. He turned and walked towards the door. Kevin joined him and they left together. As they came out onto the street, the now ex-barman came out of another door, saw them and walked up.

Kevin saw him and said hurriedly, 'Up West, then, Jimmy, pull some birds, what do you say?'

Before Jimmy could reply, the ex-barman was beside them.

'You lost me my fucking job. I think I owe you something for that, mate.'

Kevin was ready to run. This young man spoke with a confidence Kevin recognised. He rarely, if ever, meant what he said or delivered what he threatened, but he recognised others who would do exactly what they said and he was definitely one of these. All of his instincts told him to leg it but Jimmy's voice stopped him.

'You're wrong, mate. Kevin didn't lose you your job, you did it yourself.'

'How the fuck d'you work that out?'

'You served him. You should have thrown him out.'

'Yeah,' joined in Kevin, arrogant now he thought Jimmy would protect him, 'you should have fucking thrown me out. I fucking well would have.'

Jimmy and George looked at each other, then at Kevin, then they both burst out laughing.

'What're you laughing at?' Kevin asked, genuinely bewildered.

'You're right, mate. I lost my own job didn't I? You're right.'

'Yeah,' said Kevin, who never knew when he was well off.

'But why don't I kick the shit out of you just for the fun of it – something to do now I've got time on my hands?' and he stepped forward, but not before Kevin got Jimmy between them.

'Yeah,' said Kevin, 'you going to take both of us on?'

'Not me,' said Jimmy, 'this is between you two.' He turned and began to walk away.

With Kevin's prop gone, he obeyed the only god he truly believed in and legged it, shouting a string of obscenities over his shoulder. The ex-barman watched the rapidly moving figure for a second, then turned and joined Jimmy as he walked down the street.

'I'm George.'

'Hello,' replied Jimmy without interest.

'Got a name?'

'Jimmy.'

'Where are you going, Jimmy?'

'Home.'

'No.' George stopped Jimmy by catching his arm. Jimmy looked at him and he dropped his hand from the sleeve, 'Sorry, no offence. But it's too early to go home.'

Jimmy looked at George. He didn't know him, he was

certain of that. But the way George looked at him made him think George must know him.

'You know me?'

'Sure,' said George as they resumed walking. 'You're Jimmy Costello. I saw you fight once.'

'I never fought.'

'Yes you did, at that local Catholic club. I went there to see you.'

'I don't remember.'

'No, you wouldn't have noticed me. It was the night Joe Green offered you a contract. I was there.'

'You know Joe Green?'

Green was a manager with fighters like Billy Shiels and Larry Horgan.

'Not personally. Jack Lonsdale said Joe was going to see you, so I tagged along.'

'Lonsdale? The bloke in The Hind?'

'Yeah, it's not his name over the door but it's his pub.'

'What's he got to do with Joe Green?'

'If you had signed you would have been sold on to Lonsdale.'

'Is he a manager as well as a pub owner?'

'He's all sorts of things.'

'And where do you fit in?'

'I get around. I'm getting to know the right people. That's how I got the job in The Hind.'

'Didn't last though did it?'

'That's nothing. I made a mistake and got the elbow. If I'd made a real mistake,' he smiled, 'Lonsdale would have broken my elbow or some other bits.'

'What are you telling me?' asked Jimmy, stopping. 'Are you saying Lonsdale is a crook?'

'No, no,' laughed George, 'he's just a poor unemployed bloke who lives in Swiss Cottage and owns a Jag for weekdays and a Daimler for Sundays. He's lucky with the horses, I guess, or got rich relatives or something. No one, and I mean *not anyone*, will ever hear me say Jack Lonsdale has ever broken any law, never.' Then he winked. 'Look, we're nearly there now, let me show you something, somewhere special.'

'No,' said Jimmy firmly. He wasn't interested in strip joints, dives or girlie bars. He was still as uncomfortable with public sex as he was with obscenities in mixed company. His soul had never quite cast off its altar boy's cassock and he always felt his mother would somehow be there, appalled and ashamed. He was attracted to sex but never comfortable with it.

George made a guess. He was a good guesser, that was one of his talents.

'No, Jimmy, nothing like that. It's a jazz club, next on the left, just a few doors down.'

Jimmy had heard jazz on the radio, but a jazz club was a new idea.

The club wasn't in some smoke-filled basement as Jimmy had expected, it was over a launderette. They went up some stairs towards the sound of music. George insisted on paying for them both and they went inside. It didn't look like Jimmy had expected either. It was quite well lit, but toned down to make an atmosphere and it wasn't very smoky. The tables had blue gingham plastic tablecloths and the customers were of all ages from thirty to sixty. The age group missing was Jimmy and George's, who had no time for jazz because they had discovered rock 'n' roll. They were the youngest there. On a small stage in a corner of the room was a trio: piano, double bass and drums. The music was also not as Jimmy had expected and certainly wasn't trad jazz. George led him to a table where a man and a woman in their thirties were already sitting. They nodded as George and Jimmy sat down.

'Know them?'

George shook his head.

It was a friendly place then, thought Jimmy, and he began to listen to the music. The trio played for another twenty minutes. Apart from the clapping and shuffling of chairs between the pieces there was little movement. Then the lights went up to full and the pianist announced an interval. George got up.

'Want a drink?'

'No.' Jimmy didn't drink shorts and he didn't think they'd serve mild.

George left the table and returned with a bottle of Coke and a glass.

'No bar?'

'Yeah, but it's all wine and shorts, Dubonnet, stuff like that.' He poured out some Coke and took a drink. 'I don't like alcohol, it gives me a headache.'

Jimmy found himself taking to George.

'Like the music, Jimmy?'

Jimmy nodded.

'The group's not great but, then, they're not expensive either.' George poured the rest of his Coke. 'Got a job, Jimmy?'

'Yeah, I'm a bus conductor.'

'No, you're kidding me. You, a bus conductor? That's a joke, isn't it?'

'No, my dad's a bus driver. He got me a job when I left school, at the depot as a cleaner and odd job man, then I got to be a conductor. One day I'll be a driver.'

George looked at him in amazement.

'The best middleweight prospect from this part of London in years and he leaves it all to clip tickets? Go on, pull the other one.'

'I don't want to fight.'

'Use your talent, Jimmy, don't let it just go to waste. There's always money looking for talent.'

'How do you mean?'

George paused for a moment. He made another guess about Jimmy. He was still a good guesser.

'Well, if you ever want a few quid, I could probably put you in the way of getting it.'

'Not interested, George. I don't know any Joe Greens or Jack Lonsdales and I don't want to know any. I like the buses. I'll stick with them.'

'Just as you say.'

Over the next few weeks George and Jimmy began to get to know each other. Jimmy sometimes found himself drinking with people who accepted him because he was with George, but who made other strangers unwelcome. Jimmy liked George. George introduced him to music he had never known, black American stuff by people with daft names like Duke Ellington or Count Basie, and even to some classical music.

George was a never-ending source of interest, he didn't fit into any of Jimmy's limited set of categories. His schooling hadn't been Catholic but in other respects it had not been so very different. George actually bought and read books and sang the praises of a writer called PG Wodehouse. He lent Jimmy one of his Wodehouse books and said if it didn't make him laugh then he was dead already, but he just hadn't noticed. Jimmy couldn't understand the book never mind laugh, but he made out he had enjoyed it because George liked it. He visited George's flat, where they talked and listened to records and he sometimes met George's girlfriends. He began to feel he knew George, even though George never volunteered any information about himself and Jimmy never asked. George never asked to visit Jimmy's home and Jimmy never invited him, but at eighteen Jimmy had encountered a new and enjoyable experience. He had a friend.

Chapter 4

Paddington, January 1995

A GENTLE KNOCK at the door of his small room in Bart's woke Jimmy. He looked at his watch. Ten o'clock. He had only been in bed one hour. Philomena's voice came through the door.

'Sorry, Jimmy, the police are here, I think they'll want to talk to you.'

'I'll be ready in a minute.'

Jimmy lay on his back looking at the naked bulb suspended above his bed, trying to force himself awake.

Who will it be? he wondered.

Then he decided he didn't care. Now they knew he was here, he didn't care who came. He would deal with it if he could, and if he couldn't... well, somehow it would be taken care of. He got up and took his washing and shaving things along the corridor to the staff bathroom.

In the dining room two detectives were talking to Janine. The older of the two had been there the previous night. He was the one who had recognised Jimmy. They both had cups of tea in front of them.

'I didn't see her leave. I was in the kitchen. I didn't even say goodnight.' Janine paused. She was finding it difficult to talk without crying.

'In your own time, Miss.'

The older detective was a paunchy man, lived-in with a worn and shop-soiled look, but there was kindness in his voice. Janine sat twisting a damp handkerchief in her hands and looking across at the window which gave a view of the blank brick wall on the other side of the alley where Mrs Amhurst's car had been parked.

'You okay, Miss?'

Janine nodded but remained silent.

The other detective lit a cigarette and asked, 'Can you see where the car was parked from...'

'I'd rather you didn't smoke.'

He ignored her remark. 'There's a kitchen window that looks out on to the alley. Could you see her car from it?'

The cigarette smoke drifted across the table towards Janine. She moved her chair to one side and then looked at her questioner. He was thirty-something and quite unlike her idea of a policeman, even a detective, but he wasn't untidy or seedy like the other one. He looked like someone whose business was at the edge of honesty and morality. He wore light slacks and had an open-necked shirt. His jacket looked expensive but the colour was wrong, it was too close to yellow. He had short, curly hair and a handsome face. He looked the expensive end of what she had heard called 'common'.

'In your own time, Miss.'

The older detective was still being kind.

She looked down at her hands and suddenly it seemed to dawn on her what she was doing. She tucked the handkerchief into her cardigan pocket.

With a visible effort she tried to become calm and business-like.

'I was in the kitchen, heating soup. The cooker is at the other side from the window. You can see the car if you're near the window but I didn't see anything. Then I spilled a pan of soup and Sister came in to help me clean it up. Later, I saw the car was still in the alley so I asked Mr Costello to see if anything was wrong. When he came back he told us...' She paused, tears again formed in her eyes. 'I didn't even say goodnight.'

'You didn't look out of the window at all?'

The detective seemed unconcerned about Janine's obvious distress.

'Not that I remember. I don't usually. There's nothing to see.'

The detective put his cigarette out by dipping it in his tea. He dropped the soggy remains into the saucer then leaned back in his chair and stared around the dining room. The kind detective picked up his cue.

'Thank you, Miss,' he smiled, putting his notebook and pen on the table. He stood up. The interview was over. 'You've been most helpful. Could you ask the Sister to come in now please?'

Janine rose, her handkerchief back in her hands and at work again. She nodded and left.

'What d'you think?'

The kindness had gone from his voice. The other detective shook his head.

'Nothing there. Let's see what the nun says.'

They sat in silence until Philomena came in. She walked to the table and the older detective stood up politely.

'Sit down, Sister, please.'

Philomena sat down.

'Do you remember Mrs Amhurst leaving last night?'

The tone conveyed that he didn't like having to intrude, but the job had to be done. He hoped she would understand.

'I don't know. She usually came through the dining room to say goodnight to everyone. I can't remember her doing it last night. I must have been in the office when she left.'

The other detective lit another cigarette and joined in the questioning.

'Could you see Mrs Amhurst's car from the cooker in the kitchen, if you were heating soup, say?'

'Don't smoke, please.'

He repeated his question, blowing smoke into the air.

'Would the car be visible from the cooker?'

Philomena stood up.

'Let me know when you have finished your cigarette,

Sergeant, and I'll come back if I'm free.' She turned and walked towards the door.

Kind cop got up quickly and followed her.

'Excuse me, Sister.'

She paused.

'Please, come back and sit down.'

Philomena looked pointedly at the policeman at the table. He drew on his cigarette. Their eyes met. Philomena didn't move. He dropped the cigarette into his tea cup. Philomena turned to his colleague.

'Very well, Inspector.'

They returned to the table and sat down.

'By the way, Sister, I'm a Sergeant. This is Inspector Deal.'

Philomena scrutinised them slowly, one at a time.

'I have my own ways of deciding seniority,' she said.

Inspector Deal leaned forward. 'Wasn't it irresponsible to let a woman like Mrs Amhurst come and work in a place like this? Weren't you inviting trouble?'

The Inspector's question was meant to sound exactly as it did, an accusation. He wanted her to know who was in charge and that he was in a position to allocate blame.

When Philomena replied, her Irish accent was more pronounced, deliberately comic.

'Now what would you be meaning, Sergeant, by "a place like this"?'

'You know exactly what I mean. And it's still Inspector.'

Philomena dropped the elaborate brogue.

'I do not know what you mean and I don't care what rank you are. I don't like your question and I don't like you.'

The Sergeant was worldly-wise enough to see that the Inspector could very well get the sticky end of exchanges with this woman and if that happened the fall-out would certainly land on him.

'Please, Sister, we're only doing our job.' He was vainly trying to keep the peace.

'Are you? And what job would that be at all?'

The comic accent was back and with it a sweet, innocent

smile. Then the brogue and the smile were gone and the voice was serious.

'Is it your job to put the blame on us at Bart's for Mrs Amhurst's death? We shouldn't let the refuse of the street gather here to be fed and rested? We're part of the problem, are we? The best answer would be for us to close down and move on because we're not wanted. Is that your job, to get rid of us? Would the best answer be for me to say that I was to blame, and for us all to pack up and go?'

'Of course not, Sister, no one is saying…'

'It's one answer,' cut in the Inspector, leaning forward. 'At least that way no other innocent volunteer gets knifed.'

Philomena leaned back and relaxed. She had the measure of Deal now. He was a blusterer and a bully, a nobody.

'Do you think that might work? Maybe you're right, it's been tried before.'

'To close you down? I never heard that, nobody ever said…'

There was genuine surprise in the Sergeant's voice.

'Not here, it was in another country, and it was a long time ago.' Philomena turned to the Inspector. 'But then it was handled by a really dangerous bastard, not some pocket-edition desperado,' she looked at his curly hair, 'with a nice perm.'

There was a moment's silence, then the Inspector spoke in a flat voice.

'Okay, we got off to a bad start and if it helps, I apologise. Can we get on now? Could Mrs Amhurst's car be seen from in the kitchen?'

'You can see the car from the sink by the window. But not from the cooker, you'd have your back to the window.'

'Did she always park it in the same place?'

'Yes, near the entrance, because there's a light over the door so we could see it even when it's dark.'

'Even so, it wasn't really safe, was it? It's not the sort of neighbourhood where unattended cars are just ignored.'

'There's nowhere else. And it was quite safe there, for that car, I mean.'

'How can you be so sure?'

'The first time Mrs Amhurst came, she arrived by taxi and the next time her husband brought her in his Bentley. So I warned her about the neighbourhood. It's not the sort of place where people travel in Bentleys. One day, someone would have been waiting.'

'It looks like one day someone was. Anyway, what did she do?'

'She got an old Skoda, a dreadful old heap but she was proud of it.'

'She was proud because she'd bought a heap?'

'Can you see anyone bothering to hot-wire an old Skoda? Who would want it? She even left it unlocked so no one needed to break a window to get in, not that there was ever anything inside. That car could have sat there unlocked for ever. The worst thing that might happen would be somebody sleeping in it, but only if all the local doorways were already occupied.'

Inspector Deal sat back. The nun was dead right about the car, of course, but she was still wrong for all her cockiness. The car may have looked right, but the Amhurst woman didn't. She looked money, quiet, smart and understated, which meant a lot of money. He didn't like interviewing people who were in control. They only told you what they wanted you to know.

'But she must have stood out round here, even if her car didn't.'

'Well, she certainly never had any trouble with any of the clients. They all seemed to like her.'

The Sergeant joined in.

'I'd have thought they'd resent the Mother Teresa sort.'

'Still looking for your killer among the clients?'

The Inspector took over again.

'They knew her movements. It would have been easy for someone to wait for her coming out one night and grab her handbag.'

'And kill her?'

'She might have recognised whoever it was. Or it might

have been someone on drugs. That sort kill for anything they can get, sometimes for no reason at all.'

'I won't pretend one of our clients couldn't have done it. But any regulars, those who knew what time she went home and where her car was, also knew there's never anything on these premises worth stealing, and the same goes for the staff. She would have had nothing of value on her, no money, no jewellery, not even a watch.'

'That's right,' said the Sergeant, going back a few pages in his notebook. 'We were going to ask you about that. She had no watch on her when she was found. We thought it might have been taken.'

'No, she never wore one while she was here.'

'Can you give us a list of those who were here yesterday?'

The Inspector wasn't giving up.

'I can try. When do you want it?'

'In your own time, Sister,' said the Sergeant, 'but the sooner we get it the more help it is. Tell me when to call and I'll collect it.'

'I'll have it ready tomorrow morning.'

'I'll be here at 9.30, then.'

'I'll be at Mass, come at 11. By the way, did you find her handbag?'

'Not yet.'

The Sergeant stood up. 'Thank you for your co-operation, Sister.'

The Inspector pocketed his cigarettes and lighter.

'I've never questioned a nun before.'

'You still haven't. I'm a Religious Sister, not a nun.'

'There's a difference?'

Philomena smiled her sweet smile.

'Not one that you would be able to understand,' and went on with mock seriousness. 'I could try to explain if you're really interested in the Religious Orders of the Catholic Church but I...'

'Could you ask Mr Costello to come in now, please, Sister?' the Sergeant interrupted. He didn't want hostilities to be resumed.

'Of course, Inspector.'

Deal watched her leave the room.

The Sergeant looked up from checking his notes. 'She didn't mention cleaning up the soup,' he observed.

Deal shrugged. He didn't like his Sergeants to point things out to him.

'That wasn't relevant. If they were cleaning up soup they couldn't have seen anything.'

'So what do you think?'

'I doubt there's going to be anything here for us. But let's see what this Costello guy has to say.'

A minute or so later Jimmy walked in and came over to the table. He looked at the Sergeant. There was no hint of recognition in their faces, but they both knew that they knew each other.

'Sit down, Mr Costello.' Inspector Deal pointed to the chair. 'Do you mind if I smoke?' he added with exaggerated politeness, taking his cigarettes and lighter from his pocket.

Jimmy indicated that he didn't care one way or another. The Inspector placed his cigarettes and lighter on the table without bothering to light one up.

'It was you who found Mrs Amhurst?'

'I was asked to go and see why her car was still there. She was lying by her car.'

'Who asked you?'

Jimmy shrugged.

'Janine or Sister Philomena.'

'And when you went out you found Mrs Amhurst had been stabbed?'

'No. I found her lying by the car outside.'

'You didn't see she'd been stabbed?'

'She was lying face down and no blood was visible when I first saw her.'

'She might have fainted or been mugged or it might have been a heart attack or something, and yet you didn't try to help or revive her? Why was that?'

Jimmy remained silent.

'You went out and when you saw it was Mrs Amhurst you came straight back in and told the Sister and she called the police?'

'If you say so.'

'You made no attempt to find out what was wrong with her? Were you already sure she was dead, is that it?'

Jimmy remained silent.

'In your own time, Sir.'

Jimmy looked at the Sergeant. Clearly it would be a very long time indeed.

'When you came in, what did you say to the Sister?' the Inspector continued.

'I told her Mrs Amhurst was lying outside by her car, that she should phone the police. I can't remember the exact words I used.'

'You asked her to phone the police, just the police, not an ambulance?'

Jimmy nodded.

'Why no ambulance?'

Silence.

'In your own time, Sir.'

Silence.

'Mr Costello, this is a serious investigation. We need a clear picture of everything that happened last night. You seem reluctant to give us your full assistance.'

Jimmy remained silent, so the Sergeant took up the questioning.

This was turning into a hard morning.

'After you told the Sister about Mrs Amhurst, what did you do?'

'She asked me to go outside and stay with Mrs Amhurst. I went and stayed until the police arrived.'

'The Sister asked you to go, or you decided to go?'

'I don't remember.'

'Who was in the dining room last night?'

'I don't remember.'

The morning wasn't getting easier. The Inspector took over again.

'Come on, Mr Costello, are you telling me you can't remember anyone who was here last night?'

'Sister Philomena, Janine, Mrs Amhurst, me. I can't be sure about anyone else.'

'Did you see anyone outside when you first went to the body?'

'Not that I remember.'

'Or when you went out to wait for the police?'

'Not that I remember.'

The Inspector sat back. He hadn't liked the nun and he didn't like this guy.

'You seem to have a very poor memory, Mr Costello.'

'I know, I worry about it sometimes.'

'Do you think your memory would be better if we talked to you at the station?'

There was no mistaking the threat in the words. Jimmy leaned forward and put his arms on the table with his hands together and examined his thumbs.

The Sergeant didn't like the way things were going, the threat was a mistake. Not for the first time he wondered how Deal had got to be a Detective Inspector. He tried to move things forward.

'When did you find out she had been stabbed?'

'When I went out the second time, I could see blood just under the edge of her coat.'

'Anything else?'

'Her car keys were on the pavement.'

The Inspector took over again.

'Close by her?'

'Yes.'

'Anything else? A handbag?'

'Not that I can remember.'

'Your memory again.'

Jimmy went back to studying his thumbs. He gave the very strong impression that there was nothing more he had to say and now, please, he really did want to get on with the study of his thumbs.

Inspector Deal stood up.

'We may want to speak to you again, Mr Costello. Please don't leave the area, and inform your local police station if you change your address. Alright, Sergeant.'

The Sergeant put away his notebook and pen and stood up. At the dining room door the Inspector turned.

'Let the nun know we've finished, for the time being.'

Jimmy nodded but didn't look at them. He was still busy with his thumbs. Philomena came in a few minutes later.

'I heard the front door. Have they gone?'

'They're gone.'

'What did you think of them?'

'They'll do whatever has to be done.'

'What about the Inspector? What did you think of him?'

'Nothing in particular.'

'I think he was not a nice man, Jimmy.'

'So long as he does his job, does he have to be nice?'

'I suppose not. Will they find out who did it, do you think? There's police in the alley looking round but there doesn't seem much to go on.'

'They might get someone. Mrs Amhurst wasn't like our clients, she wasn't a nobody and her husband's very well-off isn't he? He'll want a result, so they might get someone.'

'But will they get the right one?'

'It'll be close enough to suit most people.'

'You sound a dreadful cynic.'

'I just know how these things work. I'll go upstairs and lie down for a bit, Sister, if that's okay.'

'Go on, then. Janine needs to keep busy, so she and I can use today to catch up on cleaning and the like. God knows there's plenty of it to catch up on. When will they let us re-open do you think?'

'Couple of days maybe. When there's nothing more to be got from the scene of crime.'

Jimmy went up to his room and sat on his bed and thought

about the Inspector for a moment, then the Sergeant. The Sergeant hadn't told the Inspector that he knew him. Now why was that, he wondered. He kicked off his shoes and lay on the bed. Did it matter one way or another, he asked himself, and fell asleep thinking about it.

Philomena sat alone in the dining room. There would be trouble, maybe a lot of trouble, she knew it for certain, but she couldn't tell how she knew. It was like the rains coming in the African bush, the signs were all there long before the clouds could be seen.

All you had to do was look for the signs.

Soroti Diocese, Northern Uganda, 1974

Soroti diocese was remote from Kampala, situated in the far north of Uganda. But its remoteness had not saved it from the terror of President Idi Amin's regime. People in many parts of the diocese had suffered, but the small convent school of Our Lady of Pity, close to the Sudanese border, had so far been spared any violence. The school served a large and sparsely populated area and the hundred or so girls it educated were all boarders. There was a staff of four teaching Sisters, two Irish, one Belgian and one, the youngest, a Ugandan.

It was just after dawn. Sister Philomena, the headmistress, was already up and about, directing the few lay workers who cleaned and cooked, when the Land Rovers arrived. She went out to meet the visitors, whoever they might be, as soon as she heard engines. Visitors were rare and anyone who passed the school always stopped. Places to rest and refresh yourself were few and far between in this part of Uganda, so hospitality was a necessity rather than a courtesy. In the early morning light Sister Philomena watched the dust drift away as the two Land Rovers stopped on the dry dirt road in front of the school. Father Schenk, a Dutch Mill Hill missionary priest, got out. This visit meant trouble. To have reached the school so soon after dawn they must have set out in the dark, and to travel the roads across the bush at night, however slowly, was an act of pure madness. Whatever had made it necessary would be very bad news indeed.

'Sister, we've come to take you and the other Sisters away. Just gather what you can get together in five minutes, then we must go. Tell your locals, if they're still with you, to get away into the bush, and spread the word.'

His Dutch-accented English was flat, without alarm or emotion. She realised that the occupants of the first Land Rover were the three Medical Missionary Sisters who represented the only medical presence for hundreds of square miles and if they were leaving, staying certainly meant dying. At the wheel of the second Land Rover was Brother Thad, an Australian.

'Is Brother Thaddeus going?'

Father Schenk nodded.

'We needed a driver-mechanic to be sure of making it all the way across the border, but he'll come back when we are safely in Sudan.'

Sister Philomena didn't really need to be told Brother Thad would come back once his job was done. He had long ago decided to die in what he now regarded as his home. Whether his death would come about by disease, accident, old age or violence he left in God's hands. His job was to keep the vehicles running. He supervised the workshop-school that serviced and repaired all the vehicles for various missionary orders and trained local boys to be mechanics. He had been in Africa for twenty years, the last sixteen in Uganda.

'What about my girls?'

The priest stood silent for a moment.

'That's your decision, Sister. We can't take any of the girls. You will have to decide what to tell them. It would be better, I think, if they didn't stay here.'

'Where can they go? We're not near anywhere. If they walk away from here they'll die in the bush.'

The other Sisters were now standing together by the door. Sister Philomena turned to them.'

'Collect only what you can carry in one hand and come out to the Land Rovers.'

'And you, Sister, are you coming?' asked the priest.

She wanted with all her heart to go, but leaving the girls alone to face whatever was coming would haunt her for as long as she lived and destroy finally and forever the small idea of faith she fought daily to keep alive. To leave would be to kill even a pretence of belief. It would, in a sense, kill her as surely as a bullet in the head. Yet she feared death, the kind of death that might be coming, and she feared even more what might come before death. A good driver in the bush, she had sometimes gone out with the Medical Sisters. If she did the driving, more people could be seen. Twice in the past year they had come upon evidence of where the soldiers or police had been. The shock had lasted days. It was not just death or the dead. She had seen the dead and the dying before, but only from old age, disease or accident, not from butchery. She always blotted out these scenes, refused to remember.

But now a memory came, the crying baby sitting in the dust next to its gutted mother, who had no face. The other bodies, women, children, babies or the old, all in odd and awkward positions and all mutilated in some way or another. Only this one crying baby left unaccountably alive. She didn't remember much about leaving that place of horror. She vaguely remembered the Sisters helping one or two survivors who had crept out of the bush and she remembered being given the baby to carry. They had left the place as quickly as possible, because the scene was quite fresh and the perpetrators would still have been nearby.

The next time it was a family: mother, father, two young children and a baby. The heat, flies and scavengers had had about two days to reduce the corpses to what they found by the roadside. The Sisters took the spades from the top of their Land Rover and buried what there was. She had been able to help bury the bodies and join in the prayers and drive on.

The Medical Sisters, who saw such things more often than she did, had told her that they were prepared to take calculated risks with their lives. They knew the army or police would come for them one day, but they would stay and work until that day came.

Now that day had come.

Finally Sister Philomena spoke.

'I'll stay, Father. I'll try and get as many girls away as I can. After that, we're in God's hands.'

The Irish and the Belgian Sisters came out of the school, walked past and got into the second Land Rover. The young Ugandan Sister came and stood beside her.

'May I stay also?'

'Would it do any good to talk to you about this?' the priest asked her in a resigned voice.

The young Sister shook her head and looked at the ground.

'I'll pray for you,' he said and looked towards the school, 'pray for you all.'

'I hope you all reach somewhere safe,' Sister Philomena said. 'Goodbye Thad,' she added fondly.

Neither smiled. It wasn't that sort of farewell.

The Land Rovers pulled away and were almost immediately lost to sight in their own dust. Silence returned. The heat of the day was beginning to make itself felt.

The two women turned and went back into the school.

Sister Philomena sorted out a group of about sixty from places which could be reached by three days' walking and split them into four groups, according to the direction of their villages. She allocated the most sensible girls to be in charge and added five of the very youngest from the distant villages to each group, bringing the total to eighty. She briefly instructed them in the rudiments of direction-finding, explained about resting and spacing food stops, and made very clear the importance of avoiding any vehicles which might carry police or soldiers. She equipped and provisioned them as best she could, prayed with them and sent them on their way. She knew that groups of twenty were far too big, but by sending eighty girls away and keeping twenty at the school she had balanced the probabilities as best she could. Now all she could do was wait.

It was soldiers who came, not police. They arrived at dusk on the same day, about thirty of them in an open Land Rover and four lorries. Sister Philomena went out and stood in front of the school as soon as she heard them coming.

The soldiers jumped out of the lorries and stood silent, looking at her. She had come out alone, instructing the young Ugandan Sister to stay with the remaining girls in the dining hall. The soldiers were heavily armed. They were quiet but it was the quiet of interest and anticipation, not of discipline. An officer got out of the Land Rover, dusting his uniform as he walked towards her. He came to attention in front of her and, surprising her, gave a smart salute.

'Good evening, Sister. I am Captain Nduma. We will be requisitioning equipment from the school and staying for the night. We will leave tomorrow. I trust we will have your full co-operation?'

He spoke very good English and gave her a beautiful smile. His combat uniform was clean and smart, his leather belt and holster highly polished. He was a big man in his early to mid-twenties. He gave no impression of malevolence, rather the reverse.

Against the odds, she began to hope.

'You may take what you need. Will I get something in writing to show what you have taken?'

He laughed. He had an attractive laugh. 'Of course, Sister. This is the army, not a group of bandits. Everything will be properly done. May we go to your office? My Sergeant will take the men and look over the school and see what we require.'

She turned and walked towards the school. 'Come with me please.'

The Captain motioned to a Sergeant who in turn began to give orders to the men. Captain Nduma went with Sister Philomena to her office, where he took off his cap.

'May I use your desk, Sister?'

This was not what she had expected. His correctness unnerved her.

'Of course.'

Captain Nduma went to her chair, put his peaked cap on the desk, undid his belt and put his holster next to his cap. Sister Philomena noticed that the holster flap was undone.

'Will you have a chair, Sister?'

She brought a chair from a corner of the room and sat down, facing him.

'Is your school well equipped?'

'Yes, I think so, all things taken into account.'

Captain Nduma smiled again.

'Everything is always taken into account. You understand, we will have to take many things. We have a wide area to cover and we must be as well equipped as possible to round up the insurgents.'

'Insurgents? There are no insurgents here.'

'Indeed, Sister? You sound very sure. Is that because you have specific information?'

She recognised at once her incaution.

'No, I have no specific information, no information at all. I don't know anything about insurgents.'

'So often, people tell me that they know nothing at all about insurgents, assuring me that there are none in their district. They fail to see the essential inconsistency of that position. That is because they are not educated people like you and I.' His smile disappeared and his voice changed. 'If you know anything, Sister, it would be better to tell me now. If you do know anything, you will certainly tell me before I leave.'

'Is that a threat, Captain?'

She was trying hard to get the headmistress into her tone. Captain Nduma smiled again.

'Very much so, Sister. Would you like me to give you some demonstration of just how much a threat it is?'

He pulled his automatic from its holster and laid it in front of him. The Sister and the headmistress both disappeared at once and Philomena, the frightened, powerless woman, was in their place.

'No, I need no demonstration.'

In the pause that followed, she became aware of a confused noise beyond the office door, bangs and crashes and, further off, screams.

'What is happening, Captain?'

She had stayed voluntarily. Now she must do her duty. If she had nothing else, she still had her duty. She was a professed Sister and knew and respected the discipline of her order. Her voice now carried some authority, without confrontation but also without fear. She had a right and a duty to ask. She asked again. Captain Nduma fingered his pistol and kept his eyes on her. He was thinking, making a decision. Then he made up his mind.

'My men are taking what we need, everything else will be rendered useless. Nothing,' he continued pointedly, 'will be left which might give aid or comfort to the enemy, nothing at all.'

She understood perfectly.

Suddenly the door burst open. It was the young Sister. She was breathless.

'They're breaking everything, *everything*, and taking everything they don't break. They say they'll take the girls when they go.'

Sister Philomena stood up. The Sergeant appeared in the doorway, casually pointing his automatic rifle in their general direction.

The young Sister came to the desk and faced the Captain.

'Make them stop. You can't do this.'

Captain Nduma picked up his pistol and shot her once through the face. The noise of the shot exploded off the concrete walls and filled the room. Philomena was only vaguely aware of the way the young nun's head was thrown back, pulling her whole body into the air before she fell dead on the floor. As she recovered from the noise, Captain Nduma rose and, still holding his pistol, came around the desk. She tried to think of a prayer but nothing came, only the echoes of the terrible bang. He strode past Philomena and shouted at the Sergeant, who left sullenly, then returned to the desk and sat down, putting his pistol back in its holster.

Sister Philomena looked at the body on the floor. A dark red pool was forming under the young nun's headwear, which was already blood-soaked. There was a hole between the bridge of her nose and her left eye, out of which a small amount of blood oozed.

From the desk, Captain Nduma spoke calmly.

'Please, Sister, be seated again, everything is in order.'

Philomena obeyed. Captain Nduma smiled and pulled his chair closer to the desk.

'I'm afraid my Sergeant will now be more brutal than is essentially necessary. I had to tell him that if he ever points his weapon in my direction again it will be him I kill and not anyone standing between us. He does not take reprimands well.'

As he spoke the screams, closer now, began again. Philomena, lonely and afraid, sat staring at her hands in her lap.

'What will happen to me?'

'You will be killed, Sister. But don't worry, that is all that will happen to you. You have my word. In fact,' his voice became softer, 'I will do it myself. You will feel nothing. I don't make a mess of such things.'

It was as if thanks were expected.

'Are you taking the girls?'

'The men need them.'

'And what will happen to them?'

'What do you think?'

'But after, what will happen to them... after?'

'If we are in a position to sell them, we shall. If not, we will leave them at some village or other. If we are in the bush,' and he shrugged, 'we will kill them. It would not be an act of kindness to leave them in the bush alone, without resources.'

'Just like...' she inclined her head towards the body.

'That was quite different. She was young and pretty and certainly a virgin. There might have been trouble sharing her out. Sometimes it is necessary for me to assert my authority by depriving my men of something they want. I knew I would have to kill her as soon as I saw her. She was kind enough to co-operate, however unknowingly. She was what the Sisters used to call "One of God's good little acts".'

'Sisters? What Sisters?'

'I was educated by Sisters like yourself until I was eleven, I have fond memories of them. They were among the few really kind people I have ever known. They gave me a good education, love, they even gave me their faith.'

Philomena sat still and listened. Captain Nduma was disposed to talk. He seemed oblivious of the noises coming from outside the office. It was as if they were friends chatting together.

'Are you a Catholic?' she asked him.

'Oh yes. Does that surprise you?' He didn't wait for an answer. 'I became a member of the Catholic Church when I was a small child and it played a very important part in my early life. Perhaps it will again, one day. The Sisters taught me about God's love, His unconditional love. After I was eleven, I was taught by priests. But they taught me all about sin and another Christian God, an angry, vengeful God. The priests were very frightened of Him and they tried hard to pass on that fear. Their fear and guilt were their faith.'

'Did they succeed?'

'I might have become a priest or brother myself, but two things combined against that. The memory of the nuns' God, and then there was the foolishness of it. I saw and have seen many cruel, even very wicked acts, but I never saw God's hand perform them, always men's hands, Sister, always the hands of men.'

'Your hands?'

'Yes, nowadays sometimes even my hands.'

'Are you still a Catholic?'

'Oh yes. If I survive all this I shall go to Confession to a suitable priest, say my penance and then begin again to be a good Catholic.'

'Could you not have continued to be a good Catholic despite everything?'

'And go to heaven as a martyr? No, Sister, neither I nor my soul are ready to face our Maker yet. I would have liked to have stayed a good Catholic but, very quickly, I would have been a dead Catholic. So, for a time, I must be a good soldier and a bad Catholic and do what I have to do.'

'Including killing me?'

'Yes, Sister, that as well.'

'How can I be of use to the insurgents, even supposing there are any?'

'Oh, there will be insurgents, Sister. If there are none now, there soon will be after we have begun our work. And, yes, you could be of great help to them.'

'How? I couldn't even help my school, my girls, or even, God forgive me, that poor dead Sister.'

'But you know things.'

'What things?'

'You know how many of us there are. How well armed we are. What vehicles we have. And you can identify me personally, even by name. Now, or perhaps in the future, when accounts come to be settled, what you know may be very important. You have seen so much. I'm sure you understand.'

She understood.

'Do you still believe in God?'

'Yes, Sister.'

'And do you feel you will have to answer to Him for all of this?'

'Let me put it this way. I believe in God, in His justice and His mercy. I would have liked to have walked in the paths of righteousness all the days of my life. But now there are no paths of righteousness. The times require that in order to survive it is necessary to be, how shall I put it, company for the Devil. Mine was not a completely free choice, therefore it does not count as a mortal sin. Even if I die, God, in His infinite love, will give me mercy.'

'Even though you give no mercy yourself?'

'I am not God, mercy is too expensive for me. Only the most powerful can afford it.'

'So you will go on like this?'

Captain Nduma picked up his holster and cap. He got up.

'God's good little acts, Sister,' he gestured to the body. 'Would you rather I had let my men have her? The Sisters were good people even though they knew how wicked the world was. They told me how educated Western people often called floods, earthquakes and the like, Acts of God, and saw God as indifferent to the suffering He caused. But the Sisters said that for every flood or earthquake there will be millions of unnoticed little acts of God which will have brought comfort and help. That may very well be true, but for all God's little acts of kindness the world is wicked. The educated people are right and the Sisters were wrong. God's good little acts have to take place in a wicked world and, unfortunately, they are powerless to change it.'

He moved to the door.

'I will make sure that you will be safe if you stay here in this room tonight. Think of it as one small act of kindness from one Catholic to another.'

And the door closed.

Sister Philomena sat listening to her school being destroyed and her girls becoming the property of the soldiers. Suddenly the door opened and the Sergeant was striding in, his automatic in his hands. He walked past her, reached up and, with the muzzle of his gun, smashed the single bulb that hung from the ceiling. She froze. In the darkness she heard the Sergeant's boots on the concrete floor. Then the door closed.

After what seemed a very long time she realised she was again alone in the room. She began to cry quietly. A quick death, a bullet in the head and nothing else, one of God's good little acts. Then, still crying, she got up and felt her way to the the young Sister's body, knelt down and began to pray.

'May the souls of the faithful departed, through the mercy of God, rest in peace. Amen.' Then, 'The first Sorrowful Mystery of the Rosary, the Agony in the Garden, Our Father who art in heaven...'

The buzzing of the flies swarming on the corpse woke her. At that moment, the door opened and Captain Nduma came in and stood over her.

'Good morning, Sister. We will soon be leaving. The lorries are being loaded.'

'Is it time?' She got up awkwardly.

'Time, Sister?'

'For me.'

'I have been thinking about that. One dead Sister, more or less, matters very little. If I am ever called to answer for my actions, to someone other than God I mean, then a Sister alive here when I leave may turn out to be more useful than a dead one.'

'You are not going to kill me?'

'On balance I think not. But don't be here when I return. I will be back in a week, two at the most. Don't be here then.'

'Isn't that information of value to the insurgents, Captain?'

He grinned.

'What insurgents? There are no insurgents in this area, everyone knows that. You reassured me of that yourself.'

'Why are you letting me live?'

Captain Nduma paused.

'The Sisters who taught me all spoke like you. They were Irish, I think. Let us just say you have reaped where others have sown.' He snapped to attention and gave a smart salute. 'Thank you for your co-operation and hospitality. You have the government's thanks, you have done your duty. Stay in this office for at least one hour after you hear the last truck leave. At least one hour. Do you have a watch?'

'Yes.'

'You shouldn't have. The Sergeant should have taken it. Give it to me please.'

Philomena took off her watch and handed it over. Captain Nduma took it, smiled, gave a casual friendly salute and left.

A few minutes later the noise of the flies was drowned as the engines roared into life. There was some shouting and clattering of boots and then the convoy moved off. Then there was only the noise of the flies and silence everywhere else. Philomena put the chair back in the corner and went and sat behind the desk. She opened the top right-hand drawer and took out a worn, black-covered book, opened it at a page marked with a thin blue ribbon and began to say the morning prayers of the Divine Office of the Church.

Four days later, Brother Thad returned in his Land Rover and found her unconscious on the floor of her office. She was lying next to a large dark stain. Over the next two days he nursed her back to sufficient health to travel. Little water and no food had weakened her but had done no permanent damage. They left what remained of the convent school in the early morning. Nothing in it was unbroken, every door, pane of glass, partition, piece of furniture was smashed, the corrugated roofing had been removed from every room except the office. What couldn't easily be broken, like blankets, had been burnt. When the rains came the building would begin an irreversible process of decay and quite soon it would be cheaper and easier to build a new school than repair this one. Brother Thad and Philomena said prayers together where she had buried the young nun on the day the soldiers had left.

As the Land Rover rocked and bumped along the road she reflected on the fact that he would have had to bury her as well as the young Sister, had Captain Nduma been as good as his word. Then perhaps she would have been still and at peace, in a blessed and blank oblivion, with no more duty to do, no sickly half-belief to protect and no empty faith to follow into an uncertain future. She would be at peace and, if it was true after all that there was a God, perhaps at home.

Chapter 5

Paddington, February 1995

AFTER HIS VISIT to Bart's Inspector Deal sat with his Sergeant in the car thinking about the interviews he had concluded.

'What do you think, boss?'

Deal stared in front of him for a moment before replying.

'There's nothing, no witnesses except those three in there and they know bugger all. If there's no forensic, there's nothing. Some thief or addict knifed her for her bag. No story, no mileage. Nothing in it for anybody.'

'What about Costello? What was all that needle about taking him down the nick? Do you think he's involved?'

'No, I just didn't like him. I didn't like the nun either and all the girl did was cry. But Costello, there's something about him.' He thought for a moment. 'But why would he kill the old lady? Why would any of them? No, it's all straightforward stuff this. But I didn't like him, and my gut tells me he's wrong. The way he acted, he's got to have form. You can't tell me he's not seen the inside of an interview room, and more than once. I don't like him and I don't want him anywhere on this patch. I want him gone.'

'Boss, I didn't say anything because I wasn't sure but I think he rings a bell.'

'I thought so. He's a villain, is he?'

'It's just his face. I think I've seen it, but I can't place it.'

'That's enough for me. Sort him out, find out who he is

and mark his card.'

'Make another visit or pull him?'

'Just a visit to let him know the times of trains and buses out of this patch. Tell him Paddington has an unhealthy climate.'

'Okay boss, if that's what you want. Back to the nick now?'

Deal looked at his watch.

'No, drop me at Bertani's, I'll have a coffee then I've got a meet. I'll be back about two.'

'Any hurry with Costello?'

'Not really, he's nobody, just move him. Let the man know he is not loved.'

Soon after the police had left Philomena knocked again on Jimmy's door. Jimmy dragged himself from sleep.

'Yes, Sister?'

'Sorry, there's another visitor I'm afraid.'

'Police again?'

'No, definitely not police.'

'A big man, black, well dressed, good looking?'

'Is he a friend?'

'I know him.' Jimmy felt like shit.

'He looks like a businessman, but he has the manner of a politician, all smiles and insincerity. Has he come to sell you something or get your vote?'

Jimmy came out of his room, rubbing the sleep from his eyes.

'Maybe both. Maybe I'm rich and influential, maybe working here is just an eccentricity.'

'Whatever he is, is he trouble? That's exactly what he looks like, trouble with nice manners. I've seen the type before.'

'Yeah, he might be trouble.'

Philomena held Jimmy's arm. They stopped at the top of the stairs.

'Then have your trouble somewhere else. There's to be no more trouble here.'

She let go of his arm.

'Thanks for your support, Sister.'

'Sorry, but that's how it is. If I could help I would, but there's no sense in beating around the bush. Do you want me to call the police?'

'No, definitely no police.'

'That bad? Well, God go with you, Jimmy, but go you must if you have trouble coming. Remember, there's to be no more trouble!'

'Don't worry, nothing will happen here. I'll see to it,' and he began to walk down the stairs. Philomena noticed his feet.

'Your shoes, where's your shoes?'

Jimmy looked down. 'My mind was elsewhere,' he muttered, and went back to his room. Philomena watched him as he came back and went down the stairs.

'God go with you, Jimmy,' she said, but this time she said it so that only God could hear.

'The lad!'

The voice was loud, cheerful and South London. The big man came towards Jimmy as he entered the dining room. Immaculately and very expensively dressed, he wore a fawn overcoat like a cloak over his broad shoulders, with a white silk scarf hanging loosely round his neck. He looked like something from the fashion section of a glossy magazine.

'The boy looks well, though shabby, and the boy hasn't lost his touch, you retain the old skill, Jimmy.'

'What do you mean?'

'You know what I mean.'

'The barman at The Hind?'

'The Liffey Lad, Jimmy.' The big man looked pained. 'The Liffey Lad, please. It hasn't been The Hind for years now. No, not the barman, a modest talent could have taken him. No, this place. Who would think of looking for you in a place like this?'

'Have you been looking for me, Nat?'

'I let it be known I wanted to say welcome home. Sit down, my boy, sit down and tell me all about yourself.'

Nat pulled a chair out and sat on the edge of the table.

'I've been alright.'

'I'm glad, Jimmy. I'm glad of that because, if you remember, we never got to say goodbye last time, did we?'

'No, Nat, we never said goodbye.'

'Dead, and never called me mother,' Nat laughed. 'What am I to do with the boy?'

Jimmy sat hunched in the chair.

'You shouldn't have come back, it wasn't a clever move. And you're only back five minutes when there's blood on the carpet, my carpet, and then there's a dead body alongside you, and it all happens in my sphere of influence. I don't know, what on earth am I to do with you?'

'Your sphere of influence reaches as far as Paddington now, Nat?'

'Oh, Paddington is well within my sphere of influence. I've never regretted emigrating over the Thames. Going north agreed with me.'

Jimmy changed the subject.

'Who was the Inspector? He wasn't here in my day.'

'New lad, been here eighteen months, two years. He's doing well.'

'Your man?'

'No Jimmy, doesn't take yet, he's clever. He knows what he's worth as an Inspector and he knows what he will be worth higher up, so he's staying clean. I respect him for it.'

'That's why you waited till they'd gone.'

'That's right. No fuss needed.'

'Is there going to be a fuss?'

'If I wanted a fuss it would have been Vic and Sammy visiting, not me.'

'Vic still with you?'

'Always, Jimmy, always. No one like Vic.'

'And Sammy?'

'Since your time Sammy's the only one who could take Vic and Vic's the only one who could take Sammy so naturally I put Sammy and Vic together.'

'What about you? Could you take them?'

Nat laughed.

'What a boy! Perhaps I could but I don't do that kind of work anymore. I haven't come to talk about me, pleasure though it is. I've come to tell you what I'm going to do about you.'

Nat was no longer smiling.

'I don't like you, Jimmy. I never got to say goodbye last time, but as I had no good reason to go looking for you when you skipped, I left it alone.'

Nat stood up.

'Goodbye, Jimmy. This time I do get to say goodbye.'

Jimmy's surprise must have registered.

'That's right, I'm going to let you leave.'

Jimmy put his arms on the table, put his hands together and looked at his thumbs.

'Urgent, my going?'

'No, not urgent. You're not important any more, just not wanted. Take your time, my lad, but let me see you once before you go.'

Nat adjusted his coat.

'Why should I see you before I go?'

'So you can say goodbye to me, and give me a little something before you go.'

'Do I have something of yours?'

'Let's say I have a moral right to it.'

'Do I know what it is?'

'It's what it always is, Jimmy. Money. You see, when I heard you were back I was going to kill you. You knew I would, because I don't take chances, not even little chances like you, so you made sure you disappeared. That was good but it gave me time to think. It must be a lot of money you left here for you to take the risk of coming back. I suppose you took plenty last time but now you're back for the rest, and there's no way you could get in, get the money and get out without me nailing you. So, you make an entrance, you pop in to see George and he tells me. You knew he would. Then you come here and you lie low while people are looking, looking all over. When no one sees you around everyone figures you've gone, got what you wanted and got out so they stop looking. Then, when nobody expects it, you pop up, get your money and run and all anyone has time to do is watch your dust. A good plan, Jimmy, no chances, you know how things work so you make them work for you. But I worked it out, so maybe it's not so good after all, because I set about finding you and then I sent you a little message before I came to call.'

'What message?'

'The one I left on the pavement last night.'

Jimmy shook his head.

'That's no good, Nat, it doesn't fit. I don't think you found me. I think I was recognised and you got tipped last night, so I don't think the body was down to you.'

'You're right, I did get tipped last night and that was quite handy, although I was half-expecting it, and I paid enough for the tip to make it look good to the law. They think I only found you 'cos I was tipped and that was after the old lady was iced. They think they were the ones who told me where you were so, the old lady can't be anything to do with me, can she? I always think a good police alibi is worth whatever you have to pay for it.'

'Sorry, Nat, I don't believe you.'

'And I don't give a fuck what you believe. You'll give me a hundred grand if you don't want to leave in five different directions at once. Get the money, get it to me, and get out.'

Jimmy resumed the study of his thumbs.

'That's a lot of money.'

Nat relaxed.

'Don't pretend you haven't got it stashed somewhere. I won't believe that. You were always good, and you were always careful, you didn't splash it about. And you made plenty, we all did.'

'How long have I got?'

'Take your time. I know where you are now and I'll keep an eye on you, so there's no hurry. But my advice is, don't linger. It won't be long before everyone knows where you are and I won't work up any sweat to keep you alive, not even for a hundred grand. Now you know how it is, I'll leave you to it.'

Jimmy watched him go. Now he knew how it was, and he didn't like how it was. He got up and went to the store and collected the buckets and mops. The toilets needed cleaning. He'd managed to sluice them down but you could still smell something that wasn't Jeyes Fluid when you went past.

Two days after the murder Detective Sergeant Eddy Clarke was drinking coffee in the Police Station canteen with a uniformed Sergeant. The uniformed man looked agitated.

'Bloody hell, Eddy, what did he want to come back for?'

'Search me. But I'll tell you this, he won't be staying long. Boy says he wants him gone. I've got to tell him to go.'

'Boy? He doesn't know him, Jimmy was gone before he came here.'

'I know, but Boy's taken a dislike to him so he wants him away. He told me to find out about Jimmy and then tell him to go.'

'Find out? You know about him as well as I do.'

'Yes, but Boy doesn't know that and when Jimmy's gone it won't matter.'

'And you think he'll go just 'cos Boy says so? It doesn't sound likely to me. And if you think you can make Jimmy leave, you must have stopped taking your medication.'

'He'll go alright. Boy's not the only one who knows he's back and won't want him to stay around.'

The uniformed Sergeant nodded.

'I see, earned yourself a few quid have you? Was that why you didn't let on to Boy straight away.'

'Somebody would have told Nat. It might just as well be me as anybody else.'

'Sure, the money's got to go in somebody's pocket and a favour done for Nat, well, you can't do too many of those can you?'

Clarke stood up.

'I'll go and break the news to Jimmy. Boy says he'll be back at two. Tell him where I've gone, will you?'

'Sure, Eddy.'

There was the buzz of conversation in the dining room. Philomena was at the urn and Janine was sitting at a table with two old ladies when she saw Sergeant Clarke come in. She excused herself and got up.

'Hello, Sergeant, did you want anyone?'

'Mr Costello, if he's around.'

'He's in his room. I think he might be asleep. He looked terribly tired when he went up.'

'Well, Miss, I'm afraid I'll have to disturb him again.'

He looked around the dining room. It was crowded with elderly people.

'Are you always this busy at lunch-time?'

'I'm afraid not, very few of these are regulars. The word got out that we could open today and I think a lot of these are...'

'Sight-seeing, I know. We get a lot of that in our business. Never mind, they soon get bored and go back to their TVs. Could you show me to Mr Costello's room, it would be better if we spoke there.'

Janine led him upstairs to Jimmy's door.

He waited till she had gone and knocked.

'Jimmy, it's me, Eddy Clarke.'

Jimmy's weary voice came through the door.

'Oh Christ, I'm asleep, clear off.'

'Sorry, Jimmy, I have to see you.

'Okay, come in.'

Clarke went into the room where Jimmy, shoeless, was sitting on his bed. There was no chair, so Clarke sat beside him. Jimmy had his head in his hands.

'Tired, mate? That girl tells me you've been looking a bit ragged. Haven't been getting much sleep.'

'No. After you and Inspector Dick Head left Nat turned up

and since then you could say I've had one or two things on my mind. What do you want this time, Eddy?'

'He came himself, did he?'

Jimmy nodded wearily.

'That's right. Did you think he'd send Vic and Sammy?'

'I didn't think anything. How would I know Nat would come round?'

'Because you told him I was here, last night, as soon as you could get rid of your Inspector.'

'Somebody would have told him, wouldn't they?'

'That's right, Eddy, don't worry about it. As soon as I saw she was dead I knew Nat would turn up. Someone would tell him I was here, it just happened to be you, that's all.'

'What'd he say?'

'Not much. He asked me how I was.'

'Didn't seem to mind you being back, then?'

'No, why should he?'

'Well that's okay then. I just thought that if there was a problem maybe I could help.'

'Thank you, it's nice to know you're on my side.'

'Just for the record, why are you back?'

'Whose record?'

'Just asking.'

'Well, I'll tell you, Eddy, since it's you asking and since it's for the record. It's none of your fucking business.'

'Have it your own way, Jimmy. I can see how you wouldn't want to tell me but you can see how I had to ask. Now I can say I don't know anything and you wouldn't say anything. Come on, let's get out of this dump and I'll buy you a pint. The Falcon's handy from here, it's quiet and no coppers get in there.'

'Alright, if I'm not going to get any sleep at least I might get a drink. How far is it?'

'Fifteen minutes in the car, five if we walk.'

Jimmy smiled.

'London bloody traffic. It never changes does it?'

He put on his shoes, opened a cupboard, and took out his anorak.

'You're not going to wear that, are you?' laughed Eddy, standing up. 'We're not going fucking trainspotting.'

Jimmy was beginning to like his anorak. It really did make a statement.

'It's camouflage. In this I become invisible.'

'Please yourself.'

Downstairs, Jimmy stopped at the dining room door. Janine was deep in conversation with an old lady. He went over to them.

'Sorry to interrupt, dear,' he said to the old lady.

'Don't you "dear" me,' she snapped in a half-crazy voice. 'Bloody cheek.'

'Now, now, Mrs Lally,' said Janine, 'it's only Jimmy. You know Jimmy?'

'No I don't. He's no right to creep up and listen to what people are saying, wherever he works.'

'He wasn't listening, were you Jimmy?'

'Didn't hear a thing. I'm off out for a quick pint.'

'It needn't be a quick one. Take your time, we all need a break.'

'You know, I might take your advice.'

He went back to the corridor, joined Eddy and they both left.

Clarke was right about The Falcon, it was about a five minute walk and it was quiet. They took their pints and sat at a corner table.

'How long's that Inspector of yours been here?'

'Boy? About two years, he came from Kent, somewhere like that.'

'Is he any good?'

'Depends what you mean. His clear-up rate is alright.'

'Is he going to give me trouble?'

'I was coming to that. He doesn't know anything about you but he's taken a dislike to you, he'd be happier if you moved on. Will you be moving on, Jimmy?'

'Last thing he told me was not to go anywhere, stay put and keep the nick informed of my address.'

'That's just form, it was afterwards that he thought about moving you on.'

'And did you plant that bright idea in his head?'

'Not me, it's nothing to me whether you go or stay.'

Jimmy drank his beer thoughtfully.

'Will you be going, then?' Clarke pressed on.

'It's still none of your fucking business.'

They sat in silence.

'Nothing changes, Eddy, nothing fucking changes.'

'Don't you believe it, nothing's the same. Different faces, places opening and closing, you never know where you are or who's doing what.'

Jimmy took another long drink. It was good beer.

'Nat's the same, though, he hasn't changed. He was always smart and clever.'

Clarke nodded.

'Yeah, I remember.'

Jimmy finished his pint. He had enjoyed it and felt a bit better.

Clarke finished his pint. 'He's about the only thing that is the same though, everything else has changed. I'm not saying it's not for the better, but I don't like changes. Another pint?'

If they were drinking together they might as well do it properly. Jimmy nodded. Clarke went to the bar and came back with two more pints.

'Cheers.'

'You know, Eddy, a clever bloke once said everything in life has to change, that's what it's all about, living is changing, and if you change often enough everything can be okay.'

'I know the sort. Some up-and-coming smart-arse university copper, like Boy, had an education and lets everyone know it. Do it right, do it my way.'

'Sort of.'

'Who was it?'

'Who?'

'Who said all that about change.'

'Bloke name of Newman.'

'Which nick did the smart-arse work out of?'

'Oxford.'

'Oxford! What were you up to in Oxford? No, I know, it's none of my fucking business.'

They both sat and drank, each with their own thoughts.

'You know, Jimmy, I sometimes think I should get a transfer to Oxford or somewhere like that. Go for something quiet.'

'Why don't you?'

'Well, you know how it is, all the bother of the move, new faces, it would be just another change. Anyway, I'll be able to retire in two years and then me and Sharon will make a proper move, somewhere warm and sunny.'

'Still with Sharon?'

Eddy nodded.

'You're too young to retire, and a copper's pension won't keep you warm in the sun.'

'We'll do alright.'

Jimmy laughed.

'I was right, Eddy, nothing changes. Somewhere quiet like Oxford might be nice but London's where the money is. You'd never get rich working out of a nice quiet nick in Oxford.'

Clarke grinned. 'Here's to crime, Jimmy, and fair shares for all.'

'I'll drink to that.'

And they both lifted their glasses and drank.

Kilburn, December 1962

'Look Jimmy, nothing can go wrong, it's just sitting there asking for someone to pick it up. It's a sin to leave it.'

George sipped his Coke. Jimmy was thinking it through. It was a sin to steal. Even if you didn't get caught God would see you, God always caught you because he knew as soon as you did what it was you were up to. But, then, God always gave you a way out. You did your sin, decided you were sorry, really sorry, went to Confession and everything was alright again. But you had to be truly sorry. Jimmy decided he would be. After all, it wasn't as if the money was for himself, at least, not all of it. Trying to save on the wages of a bus conductor was impossible and Bernadette's wages from her job at the post office mostly went to her mother, a widow with two children younger than Bernadette and still at school.

'How much?' he asked noncommittally.

'Don't know, but definitely no less than a ton.'

'Each?'

'Each.'

The money was in a locked drawer overnight. No one would be on the premises, so no one would get hurt. Getting in and out was no problem. The place and the money were insured and hardly any damage would be done forcing a window and a cupboard door. Jimmy could understand how George saw it. The money was almost being given away. If George knew about it, others would, if not now, then soon.

Someone would do it.

So why not them?

But if they got caught, during or after, it would definitely mean prison. He could accept that as a risk but what he was not sure he could accept was how going to prison would affect his family and Bernadette.

Bernadette had long ago told him what she called her awful secret. Her mother was not a widow. Her father was alive, somewhere. The police had come and told her mother that her father had been arrested. The rest was straightforward but vague in her memory. A trial, a twelve-year sentence and her father was gone, sent to prison somewhere in the north, Manchester or Durham, she thought. Her mother visited at first, took Bernadette twice while somebody looked after her brother and the baby. But it wasn't any good. Her father swore at her mother and it always ended in tears.

The visits used up far too much of what little money they had. They had moved and her mother had begun the fiction that she was a widow. Nearly all the women in their new community of Kilburn came to know it was fiction, but no one ever challenged it. They all knew only too well it could just as easily have been their husband, their son, their brother, their father. No need to make the shame worse or last longer. To all the women at Mass, at the shops, in the street or market, Mrs Callaghan was a widow whose fine husband had suffered an early and tragic death. The men accepted the women's decision and minded their own business. Children old enough to know something was not quite right made no jokes or comments, it was a grown-up thing, of no interest.

Bernadette had not been humiliated in the playground, or anywhere else. She never tired of thanking God for his goodness to her. Others might have survived the humiliation but she knew she never could. God had spared her and in return she would devote her life to God.

At fifteen she announced what she had long ago privately decided, she would become a nun when she was old enough. She talked about it first to her mother, then to Sister Angela, the headmistress at her school. Both were delighted. Bernadette was shy and somewhat awkward in company. She was a great help and friend to her mother, a good listener to her kitchen chatter.

In another age, not long ago, but utterly gone all the same, her domestic accomplishments, her skill at looking after the two younger ones, her carefulness and ingenuity, all of these things would have made her a desirable wife. But now it was hairstyles and makeup, stylish clothes and dancing that the boys wanted, and whatever else they could get.

It was explained to Bernadette that nuns lived enclosed lives in communities, apart from the world. Theirs was a life of prayer. Sisters took vows and belonged to communities but they worked in the world. Theirs was a life of service, showing God's love by serving people in many ways. Bernadette's mother was happy to be guided by Sister Angela who told her that while Bernadette was healthy and strong, she didn't have the brains or aptitude for any serious academic training, so becoming a teaching Sister was out of the question. But she might make a very good nurse and as a nurse she could go on the foreign missions. Mrs Callaghan thought long and hard about what Sister Angela had told her.

'I don't know, Sister, all those black people. I know we're all God's children and He loves us all, but it would be terribly different in Africa, wouldn't it?'

'It wouldn't have to be Africa, it could be South America or India, anywhere she was sent. Nurses are needed all over.'

'But it would be somewhere foreign. You know what I mean, it wouldn't be like being among your own, would it?'

Sister Angela nodded in agreement. She knew what Mrs Callaghan meant. Hadn't she left Donegal to come and live and work in London? She knew all about being an alien in a foreign land alright.

'You know, they say that when God created mankind, first He made black people, but He wasn't satisfied, so then He made the white people, but still He wasn't satisfied, so then He made the Irish and said to Himself, *Well, I'm glad I've got that right at last.*'

They both laughed.

Eventually a decision was arrived at.

'So, an enclosed order, Mrs Callaghan. Well, you can't do better than one of the Benedictine convents. I'll talk to Bernadette about it and we'll see what happens. In the meantime, pray for her. A vocation is a very important thing and needs lots of prayer.'

But God's plans for Bernadette, if indeed He had any, lay in quite another direction, the direction of Jimmy Costello.

A few years before God, according to Sister Angela, was providing for Bernadette Callaghan, God, or at least His Church, was also providing for a young woman in the West of Ireland beginning her novitiate with an order of missionary teaching sisters. Her vocation, however, was less a response to God's plan than an escape from a weak, worn-out mother, a drunken, violent father and a brood of younger brothers and sisters. The convent was a haven from rural dirt, poverty and brutishness.

She had decided on her vocation at the age of sixteen in the kitchen of her home, when she had stabbed her father with the big carving knife.

It wasn't a serious wound but it was bad enough.

Her father had stood sullenly holding his arm while the blood seeped through his fingers and his daughter shouted at him, 'I swear by the Holy Mother of God if you ever touch me again I'll kill you. You'll never lay your filthy hands on me again.'

Her father had left the kitchen muttering.

He would go and get drunk and he would come home and knock her mother about and maybe some of her brothers and sisters. But he wouldn't touch her again. He was big and violent but he wasn't stupid. He knew she was as good as her word. Nothing was worth getting a knife stuck in your belly for.

As she sat in the kitchen with the blood-stained knife on the table she had made up her mind. She couldn't protect her two younger sisters but she could save herself. They might be black savages in Africa but they could be no more savage than what she had already seen and experienced.

Next day she announced to the parish priest she had a vocation to become a missionary Sister. The priest knew the family and understood. It wasn't the best reason to become a Sister but it was better than anything he had to offer or suggest. The arrangements were set in motion and the girl who was to become Sister Philomena left her home and cast everything about it from her mind.

It was early Saturday lunch-time in The Hind, things were still quiet.

'Show me,' said Jimmy.

'What do you mean?' asked George.

'Let's go round the back, look at the windows, hang around and see what it's like.'

'What for? Why queer it by messing about. In and out is what we want.'

'If it's safe, a visit won't do any harm, will it? Or is it not so safe?'

'It's as safe as sitting in church.'

Jimmy waited. He was careful. He wasn't going to take any chance he didn't have to. So he waited. Then George said, 'Okay, we'll visit, you can have a look.'

'We'll both have a good look,' said Jimmy, 'and if anyone wants to know what we're doing round the back, we're hiding from some lads who are out to give you a smacking for nicking one of their girls.'

George shrugged.

'If anyone asks, we just tell them to fuck off.'

'And if it's a copper? Do we just tell him to fuck off?'

George thought about it. Jimmy was careful, maybe he was right to be careful.

'You've got a brain as well as talent Jimmy, you're wasted on the buses.'

'Don't get ideas, George, I like the buses. I want to be a bus driver and marry Bernie. This is just so that me and Bernie can get married a bit sooner.'

'Want it nightly instead of weekly?'

George gave a leer, then stopped smiling. He didn't like the way Jimmy was looking at him.

'Want to repeat that, George?' asked Jimmy slowly.

'No, it was a stupid crack, it just came out. I know you and Bernie are…' he looked for the right words, 'sort of special.'

He relaxed as Jimmy relaxed.

'You're alright, George, but you've picked up some nasty ways. I like you but it's you I like, not your language or your friends or what they do.'

'Do you know what they do?'

'No, and I don't want to.'

'So, when shall we go?'

Everything went just as George had said. A few nights later, they broke into the laundrette under the jazz club in the early morning, forced open the drawer and took away the cash box. It was easy.

'He's loopy, the old bloke who runs the place.'

George was excited and cheerful as they walked down the street with the cash box in a carrier bag under some overalls and a full sandwich box. The excitement made him talkative.

'He thinks if he empties the machines on a different night each week, nobody will know when he does it, but it's easy to know, 'cos he always stays twenty minutes longer to count it.'

'Why doesn't he take it to a night safe?'

'Afraid of carrying money at night I suppose. He comes back next day, opens up and gets the money and takes it to the bank then.'

They came to a junction and stopped.

'See you,' said Jimmy turning in the direction of his home.

'Don't you want your split?'

'No, not now. I'll see you tomorrow after work. Bring it to The Hind in a plain envelope. It'll all be coin and I don't want coin. Change it and I'll see you tomorrow, about eight.'

'Okay, Jimmy,' and George and watched him go.

It was typical of Jimmy to trust him. And he was right to trust him, they were mates, he wouldn't gyp Jimmy, it would be 50:50. Well, 60:40, which was almost as good, everything considered.

George liked the overalls and sandwiches. A nice touch, that was. Jimmy was someone to bring on.

About ten past eight the following night Jimmy arrived at The Hind. George was sitting at a table with some of his friends, men Jimmy didn't want to know. They were talking and laughing, George seemed well settled amongst them. Jimmy went to the bar. Mr Lonsdale himself came to serve him. It was the first time he had got such personal attention.

'It's Jimmy isn't it, and you drink mild, yeah?' He was being friendly. 'Have this on me. A good story's always worth a pint. Seven pound fifteen shillings and sixpence, that's good, Jimmy.'

He laughed as he pulled the pint. Then he put the pint

on the bar and laughed again, 'A good story,' and he walked away.

Jimmy felt uncomfortable. He didn't know Jack Lonsdale and he didn't want Jack Lonsdale to know him. He didn't know a funny story and he didn't know where seven pounds, fifteen and six fitted in. He looked across at George. He was talking and the others at the table were laughing. Jimmy's mind turned things over slowly. He stayed at the bar, sipped his mild and began to make connections. After a while, George came over and joined him.

'Here we are then.'

He held out a brown envelope and Jimmy took it and slipped it into his pocket.

'Did I get a hundred quid or seven pounds, fifteen and six?'

George paused.

'How did you know?'

Jimmy remained silent.

'On my oath, Jimmy, there was only just over fifteen quid in the cash box and where the bloody sixpence came from I don't know.'

Jimmy was still looking at him.

'That's it? I get seven pounds fifteen shillings and sixpence?'

'We both do. You can't have what's not there.'

Jimmy looked at the men at George's table. They weren't looking at him but they weren't talking either. Jimmy nodded at them.

'They know about it, about me?'

'Sure, but they're alright, they don't talk to anyone except each other.'

'And Lonsdale, he knows?'

'Well, I had to tell Jack. Look, it's not the money. We'll score some other time, but it's the way we did it, all the touches. They're impressed, Jimmy, they know talent and brains when they see it. We've done okay, seven quid odd each in money but fucking hundreds in respect, a few more like that and we'll have some real dough, and then we'll get taken on board.'

'You gave me to them, George?'

The threat was not in the words but the way they were spoken as Jimmy moved slightly away from the bar. George recognised the threat immediately and also moved slightly away from the bar.

'You were with me on it, Jimmy, so credit where credit's due.'

Suddenly there was a knife in George's hand.

'Easy, Jimmy. I don't face down in here, there's people watching I can't let down.'

'You do what you have to George. So will I.'

Jimmy moved forward watching the blade. George feinted with the knife but it was his boot to Jimmy's leg that was meant to do the damage. Jimmy wasn't expecting that but although the boot took him painfully on the shin, he had stepped close enough to avoid any real damage. His left arm took the blade as it slashed across but his right fist travelled hardly any distance as it hit George on the lip, just under his nose.

George's eyes flickered and he vaguely felt his mouth fill with blood from inside the upper lip split wide against his gums. It stopped him long enough for Jimmy to hit him again in the face and then stand back and hit him hard in the solar plexus, just below the heart. It was all over. George dropped the knife and sagged. Jimmy hit him again on the side of the head and George began to fall. Now it was a formality. Holding George up with a cut arm wasn't easy but Jimmy didn't want him on the floor. He wanted to make a point very clearly to the people quietly watching. Methodically he hit George, no hurry, hard in the gut to fold him over, then his back, break some ribs but avoid any important organ. Hurt him, hurt him badly, but no permanent damage. It was a message. It had to be enough but not too much, George was his friend.

George fell to the floor when Jimmy was finished. Jimmy looked at the left sleeve of his jacket. Blood had begun to run from under the cuff onto his hand and onto the floor now that the arm was hanging at his side. He looked around at the silent faces. At each door were large men. No one had come in, no one had gone out, everyone had sat very still. From George's table a thick-set man of middle height got up and came across. When he reached Jimmy he turned to the room.

'Show's over.'

People looked away and kept their eyes down. The men on the doors went back to their tables. A few people got up and left hurriedly, most returned to their conversations, but quietly and without the laughter. The thick-set man took Jimmy's arm gently, lifted it and looked up the sleeve.

'You'll live, son.'

'I intend to.'

'Good boy. That's the style.'

He turned to the others at his table.

'Harry, Len, take George to Casualty. Tell them he was done over by a gang of Teddy Boys, take his wallet and say it was stolen. Get them to tell the police, make it all natural. Say it all happened in that alley by The King George, that's nice and appropriate.'

He turned back to Jimmy smiling.

'The King George, I like that. Come on, I'll take you to another Casualty. We'll say a couple of razor boys tried to steal your wallet but they didn't get anything.'

'No thanks.'

'Son, you've made your point. Everybody in here except me has forgotten your name and now everyone knows you weren't involved in George's little outing, but you're cut, you're losing blood and you'll need stitching up. I heard you had talent, brains and were careful. Don't make me revise my opinion.'

Jimmy nodded. He was getting light-headed.

'Alright.'

The man turned. 'Get the car, Richie, and give me a bar towel, Jack, a clean one. I like you, Jimmy, but I don't want you all over my upholstery.'

He took the bar towel, wrapped it around Jimmy's arm

and they went outside. They waited a few minutes until a big white Jaguar was driven up and stopped beside them. They got in and the car moved off. The man spoke to Jimmy.

'You're a natural, Jimmy, a mechanic. There's plenty of roughhouse yobs out there who can beat someone up, but they don't have any science and you can't teach them. They get excited and overdo it, or they get some punishment and take fright. You're different. It could be a job for you, a profession. You've got educated hands.'

Jimmy remained silent.

'How much did George say you'd get?'

'Hundred quid.'

The man laughed.

'I like you, sunshine, so I'll tell you what I'm going to do. Keep me company for one night and I'll give you twenty-five quid.'

Jimmy looked at him.

'No, it's not your arse I'm after. I just want to look you over. You may be someone I've been looking for and a pony is nothing to me.'

And, as if to prove a point, he pulled a thick roll of bank notes from his inside jacket pocket. In the half-light of the street lamps as they flashed past he counted out twenty-five pounds and stuffed the money into Jimmy's jacket pocket.

'Just come to The Hind any night in the next two weeks and sit at my table for an evening. That's no problem is it?'

Jimmy didn't reply. He turned and looked out of the car window, but he didn't take the money out of his pocket. The man smiled.

'There you are, not too difficult. By the way my name's Denny, Denny Morris. And Jimmy, when you come, you buy your own drinks. I'm generous but I'm not that generous,' and he laughed and sat back and the Jag purred all the way to the hospital.

George was okay, thought Jimmy. He had really understood just how okay when he had gone to visit him two days after their turn up. Jimmy's arm, with the wound stitched and healing, was still in a sling. George had smiled when he saw him walking down the ward and his first question had been, 'How's the arm coming, was it bad?'

'You should know, George, it's your work.'

'I've never used a knife seriously before, Jimmy, but you've got to carry something. I'm glad it was only your arm. A novice like me might have really hurt you by accident.'

'It's only a few stitches. Losing the jacket was worse, and explaining to Mum.'

'What did you tell her?'

'I said a drunk did it falling into me and breaking a glass into my arm.'

George started to laugh but stopped immediately and grimaced.

'Bugger it, laughing kills you,' and he paused for the pain to ease. 'Even your mum can tell a knife cut from a glass one.'

'Not through a sling and bandages.'

'What about your jacket?'

'I threw it away. I told her it was ruined.'

'That's alright, I'll get you another one. Something a bit flash, maybe a leather jacket, a smart one.'

Jimmy was surprised.

'No need. How are you?'

'I'm alright. Broken ribs and a lot of bruising but only the lip shows, nothing else that anyone except a girlfriend will see and no internal damage to speak of. It was an ace job. I'm only sorry I got it instead of watching it. Denny said you worked me over like a pro even with only one hand operating properly. He was impressed.'

Jimmy sat down on the edge of the bed and looked at his hands. 'I can't say sorry, George, you know I'd do it again if I had to.'

'There's nothing to be sorry about. I knew I'd have to take a smacking one day. That's how it goes. You earn a bit, learn a bit and move up a bit. I'm glad they said we put on such a good show. I don't remember much after my mouth filled with blood. I know it all hurt like fuck but I can't say I really remember it.'

'Why did you give me to them? It wasn't necessary.'

'Not to you, maybe, but it was to me. Any number of cocky young fuckers tell stories about what they're going to do but the likes of Denny Morris judge you by the company you keep and what you do. That little job was just something to do, to talk about. I didn't know how much the old idiot left overnight, but I knew it was there and the way we took it, well, it was done like a real job, properly done. As it happens it was small change, not a couple of hundred, but it might have been. And you, Jimmy, people have noticed you. For me to get you alongside and get you to stick your neck out, well, that was what it was all about, really. I knew how you'd feel when you found out I was putting your name about and the blade made it look right. I wanted you to do a good job,' George smiled, but stopped straight away and held a hand to his lip. 'And now I've got the bruises and cracked ribs to show how well you did it. We've done alright, Jimmy, we get taken a bit more seriously now by the right blokes. We didn't earn much, but we learned a lot and we moved on a lot, don't tell me Denny hasn't spoken to you?'

Jimmy nodded.

'And offered you something?'

He nodded again.

'I think so.'

'Fucking marvellous, on board in one go. You're a natural, Jimmy, I'll do okay in this trade but you could go right on up.'

Jimmy was not getting excited.

'Think about it, think about the money you'll have. You'll never marry that girl of yours with what you get on the buses, and nobody waits for ever.'

Jimmy didn't answer. Bernadette would wait and they'd marry on what they had if they had to. But George was genuinely trying to help, it was clear in his voice and manner. He was being a friend in the only way he knew how.

'Open that drawer will you.' George nodded to a drawer in a small cabinet beside his bed. Jimmy stood up and opened the drawer. 'See the keys, they're the keys to my flat. Why not use it while I'm in here? I don't know how you've managed before but no need to rough it while my place is empty, no need for a double bed to go to waste for no reason.'

George just took it for granted that Jimmy and Bernadette were already having sex. Jimmy pocketed the keys.

'Thanks, George. I'll be going now, take it easy.'

'What else can I fucking well do? But when I get out I'll want my bed back quick, so get cracking, eh.'

Jimmy nodded and left the ward.

Bernadette had listened to his awkward suggestion of using George's flat and surprised him by quietly agreeing. The only thing she had asked was whether he would be able to manage with his arm. Jimmy had given the same story to Bernadette as he had to his mother and she, like his mother, had accepted it.

Jimmy had been pleased and puzzled by the way Bernadette had agreed. He had expected to have to persuade, argue and cajole. It was as if she had been expecting it and already decided to agree. Bernadette was a mystery. A good Catholic herself, she was prepared to commit this grave sin with him, for him, and he guessed that made him a bad Catholic.

Once he had asked and she had agreed he had become aroused and agitated. He had never had sex before and suddenly it had become the most important thing in his life. Now, on a Thursday afternoon like any other, their world was going to change for ever.

Thursday was Jimmy's day off and the day the Post Office closed for the afternoon. Bernadette and Jimmy were walking along the street together. They didn't hold hands as they usually did and there was no conversation. This was a special day for them both.

When they were in George's bedroom and undressing they were both hesitant and awkward. The sight of Bernadette naked had thrilled and excited him as nothing else he could ever remember. His own arousal and nakedness in her presence created sensations of embarrassment and elation which almost made him dizzy. Bernadette had patiently waited for him to lead. At first he was too hurried, he wanted to look at her, touch her, feel her and penetrate her all at once.

'Let's get into bed,' she had said after Jimmy had fumbled, groped and pushed clumsily.

Once in bed after much ineffectual pushing and some pain she helped Jimmy to enter her. The sex lasted hardly any time at all and after it Jimmy had lain heavily upon her, surprised at the suddenness of the climax. He now felt spent.

'Roll over, Jimmy, you're heavy.'

Jimmy had tried to be gentle and romantic but the difficulty at penetration had reduced him to little more than animal effort. Sex, he felt, was marvellous but it wasn't beautiful. They had lain in bed and talked about their future and then come together once more, more easily but no more romantically. Then they dressed and left the flat to walk back to Bernadette's house.

'Will I get pregnant now?' she asked eventually as they walked along.

'I suppose so, we did it twice.'

Both had learned about sex in the school of ignorance and sin. Once was a risk you might get away with, twice made it a certainty.

'Will we get married, Jimmy, before anything shows?'

Bernadette's question was not a demand nor was it in any sense a weak plea. Jimmy understood it for what it was, a powerful statement of what she would do. Bernadette would have her baby, married or not, she would accept the rejection and humiliation that would inevitably be inflicted on her by family and community. She would shoulder the awful responsibilities, financial and social, of an unmarried Catholic mother with an illegitimate child. She would become poor, despised and rejected, she would sacrifice her whole life to that new life inside her, begun because Jimmy needed sex. Her question was more of a statement of what she would do, how she would work out her guilt for the awful sin she had just committed. The question was telling Jimmy all of this, but it also told him that he was free to do as he wished, marry her or not as he chose. The sin was hers, she could have, should have, said 'no'. The woman gave Adam the apple. Jimmy was free to go to Confession and carry on, there was no new life in him. Jimmy was a man, it was different for men.

'Yes, Bernadette, we'll get married, it's all I've ever really wanted. We'll get married soon.'

Bernadette thanked God in her heart. They would marry, the child would have a father, there would be some small disgrace at such a quick marriage but not humiliation and rejection. The sin could be forgiven, life could go on.

Three days later Bernadette's period began, regular as clockwork.

Chapter 6

Paddington, February 1995

EDDY CLARKE WALKED back to Barts with Jimmy and then drove to Paddington Rolfe Street Police Station. He went to Inspector Deal's office and knocked.

'Yeah.'

He went in.

'I've found out who Costello is.'

'And told him he's surplus to requirements?'

'He knows you want him out, boss.'

Deal put down the papers he was reading and gave Clarke his full attention.

'You told him to go or what?'

'I thought you might want to hear what I found out before you turned push into shove.'

'Why, is he armed and dangerous?'

'He's not armed.'

'Alright Sergeant, tell me all about Mr James Costello.' Deal sat back in his chair and listened.

'He was a copper, a DS, worked out of a north London nick. He retired about three years ago and left London, disappeared.'

'So what?'

'Well, his retirement was one step ahead of something, and it was serious. It was connected to the death of a villain, Denny Morris.'

'And?'

'If you ask me, no one wants him back. You'll be in good company, boss, the cream of both sides of the street will want him gone.'

'And if we move him, if I move him...'

'Some very important people would notice.'

'So why shouldn't push become shove? Seems to be the right result for everyone.'

'Well, I don't know any details, of course, but if you're going to get him out you might want to know just what it'll take before you start. Maybe you should talk to someone who knows the whole story.'

Deal considered.

'He doesn't look much to me. But...'

'It might be a story worth knowing, something to show how well you know the town.'

'Alright, Eddy, it might be worth making a phone call to set up a meet. Anybody special I should talk to?'

'I wouldn't know, boss, it was hard enough to get what I got. You know how people clam up when it's something in the family.'

'Eddy, I asked who I should talk to.'

Clarke thought for a moment. Deal could do things with a duty roster that other people did with their boots in a cell.

'Flavin would be your best bet, DI Tommy Flavin. He grew up in the same neighbourhood as Costello, they became coppers round about the same time. He'll know all there is to know. If he doesn't tell you, nobody will.'

'Then I'll talk to Flavin.'

'Don't mention my name, boss. The Internal boys at AIO never got involved on this one but it could still be sensitive in high places.'

'Don't tell me the procedure, Eddy. I know how things work.'

'Sure, boss.'

Clarke left and Deal sat thoughtfully in his chair. It was an expensive chair, it was leather and well padded, it swivelled and rocked, it had little wheels so you could move about in it. He liked his chair. He turned round in it, slowly, until he faced the office window and rocked gently. After a few moments he turned and picked up his phone. A voice answered.

'Sir?'

'Get me DI Thomas Flavin. I don't know which nick he's at.'

'Yes, Sir,' replied the voice.

Deal put the phone down and turned to the window again. Costello wasn't important. He might have been something once, but three years out of it changes a man, after three years you've lost touch. He wouldn't be a problem but was he worth the effort? Who, exactly, would notice if he bounced Costello? The phone rang. Deal spun round and picked it up.

'Thanks, put him on.'

There was a pause.

'Hello, Joe Deal here, Paddington…' He laughed. 'No, not Paddington Green, nothing so grand, the other one…'

He laughed again. It was a good joke, he'd remember it.

'That's right, Rolfe Street, the one with the bike sheds and outside toilets. Listen, a Sergeant here, Eddy Clarke, gave me your name, Tommy. I want to talk about someone who's turned up on my patch. That's right, Costello. You've already heard. No, it's not part of an investigation, it would just be something between you and me. I like to stay in touch with who's who. When? Tomorrow is fine. What about Bertani's? No, it's a bar-bistro. Where then? What time? Good, see you tomorrow, Tommy.'

Flavin put down the phone, waited a moment and then picked it up again and made a short call. After that he got up and left his office and the station. He walked a little way down the street and then waited until he could flag a taxi.

'The Rose and Crown, Thorpe Street.'

Sitting in the back of the taxi as it pulled out into the traffic he thought about things. Jimmy was back and now Deal was sniffing. He didn't like Deal. Everybody knew about him and nobody liked him, nobody who was an old-fashioned copper. He was a smart-arse and a bum-licker, but give him his due, he knew how to get close to people who mattered and he was moving up fast. Now some stupid nothing of a stabbing had put him beside Jimmy Costello and he was asking questions. Well, someone would know what to do about it, if anything needed to be done.

At The Rose and Crown, Flavin went to the bar.

'Back room free, Ken?'

'Yes, Mr Flavin. Anything to drink?'

'Coffee, and today's paper.'

'It's the *Telegraph*,' said Ken apologetically, taking a paper from under the bar.

Flavin looked at the broadsheet in the barman's hand.

'No thanks, just coffee.' As he walked away he added, 'Mr Forester will be coming. See to it we're not bothered.'

'No calls?'

'No calls, and Ken...'

'Yes, Mr Flavin?'

'Pop out and get me a *Daily Mirror* will you?'

About half an hour later a man walked into The Rose and Crown. He nodded to the barman.

'Want anything, Mr Forester?'

He ignored the barman's question and went into the back room. Flavin looked up from his copy of the *Mirror*.

'Hello, Norman.'

'Hello, Tommy.'

'I've had that prick Deal from Paddington on the phone, wants to talk about Jimmy Costello. What's the starting price on all this now?'

'Nothing much. Deal's got a murder investigation on, Costello's involved but there's no problem there. It's a nothing.'

'That's what I thought, but Deal says it's not to do with the investigation, just him and me he said.'

Forester looked puzzled.

'He doesn't know about Costello, he wasn't even in this

division then. Who gave him your name?'

'Eddy Clarke, a Sergeant at Deal's nick.'

'Know anything about him?'

'He knew Costello. He knew what happened.'

'So did a lot of people but nobody's ever said anything. Why is Clarke talking now?'

'I don't know. That's why I phoned you, this is a bit rich for my level.'

'Yes, you're right. Leave it to me.'

'What shall I say to Deal?'

'Tell him what he wants to know, but leave out the bits that want keeping quiet. Tell him what he could find out somewhere else if he tried hard enough.'

'What about Clarke? Shall I have a word with him?'

'No, leave Clarke alone.'

'Just as you say. Is there going to be any trouble?'

'No, Tommy, we don't have trouble any more, not from the likes of Costello anyway. I don't know why he's back, but there's bugger all he can do.'

'What about Deal?'

'Deal couldn't crap in a bucket even if he was sitting on it. He thinks he's going right to the top, but he's going nowhere. He's only made DI because he's shit hot at paperwork. Did you know he helps the old man with his speeches?'

'No.'

'The old man showed me a bit of his stuff the other day, "The role of senior management is to create the strategic envelope which ensures the accurate and efficient delivery of the core message". He liked it, he'll use it at our next briefing.'

Tommy grinned.

'Does it mean anything?'

'It's just a way of saying top brass don't go near the sharp end. The only job for senior management, Tommy, is the delegation of blame.'

'Too true, too fucking true. Do you know what the bobbies at the nick call him?'

The man shook his head.

'Boy.'

'Boy?'

'For Boy Wonder. He's never grown up and it's a wonder how he got where he is and a bigger wonder how he stays there.' They both laughed. 'Do you know what he makes the DS's he works with call him?'

Forester shook his head again.

'Boss.'

'I don't believe it.'

'It's the truth, so help me.' They both laughed again.

Forester got up.

'Well, Tommy, I'll be seeing you. Give my regards to Alice.'

'I will, Norman.'

Forester left the room and walked out of the pub. Flavin left the room five minutes later. He put his empty cup on the bar. The barman came up.

'Everything alright, Mr Flavin?'

'Fine, Ken, fine. I'll have a whisky before I go. It's damp outside.'

The barman turned to the optics, drew a double Glenmorangie and put it on the bar. Flavin opened his newspaper and turned the pages slowly, looking at the pictures and some of the headlines as he drank his whisky. It took him about three or four minutes.

'I've finished with my paper, Ken, you can have it if you like,' he said as he left the bar.

'Thank you, Mr Flavin,' said Ken and, after the policeman had passed through the door, added loudly, 'very fucking generous, I'm sure.'

Flavin walked along the street until he came to a phone box. He put his money in and dialled.

'This is Tommy Flavin, let me speak to Nat. Hello, Nat. You know Costello is back? Yes, I know it's old news, but there's this Inspector called Deal in Paddington, you know who I mean? Yes, that's him. He's asking about Costello, about what happened. He's got a DS called Eddy Clarke who pointed him at me. Clarke knows a lot, he can tell Deal most of it. Do you want things raked over, Nat? No, I didn't think so. You will. Alright, if you say so. See you, Nat. Take care. I know you do.'

He left the phone box and walked along the street. He wondered on the wisdom of not moving Costello straight away. He wondered about Nat's judgement. Then he thought of Norman Forester, 'we don't have trouble any more'. They knew best, they kept the lid on things, there wasn't any trouble any more. And he added to himself as he hailed a taxi, 'certainly not from the likes of Costello,' and then he smiled, 'or Deal. A has-been and a never-was.'

Kilburn, January 1963

Jimmy walked into The Hind, went to the bar, bought his usual pint of mild and took it to the table where Denny Morris sat with his friends.

'Hello. Come to join us for the evening?'

Jimmy nodded.

'Good. Get a chair for Jimmy, make room.'

A chair was brought, room was made, Jimmy sat down. It turned out not to be a good night for him. He didn't like the talk, the dirty jokes, the football, then more dirty stories, shagging this one this way, shagging that one that way. Football. 'Did you see that story in the *Mirror*?' It was not a good night. Jimmy drank slowly and said very little, he listened to the talk around the table. It was mindless, it filled the space where otherwise there would have been silence and thoughts, and these men didn't come to the pub to think. The pub or the club was their church, this talk was their prayer, this was where they celebrated their faith of violence, sex, money and power.

By eleven-thirty he was only on his third pint. Two men at the table were very drunk and one had left, but Denny Morris and another man were stone cold sober. Jimmy couldn't remember if they had been drinking much but they were clearly still fully in control.

Denny Morris stood up.

'Good night, lads.'

The drunks looked up unsteadily and slurred their farewells. The other sober man also stood.

Denny looked at Jimmy.

'Come on, I'll give you a lift.'

'No thanks.'

'It wasn't a question, Jimmy. I'm giving you a lift.'

Denny's Jag was outside with a driver at the wheel and the engine running. They all got in. Denny sat in the front, Jimmy and the other man in the back. Denny nodded and the car pulled away. No one talked as they travelled out of Kilburn and on towards Highbury.

Soon after passing the Arsenal football ground the driver turned into a side street and pulled into a service area behind the shops on the main road. Denny opened the glove compartment and handed a torch to the man in the back seat. The man took the torch and got out of the car. Jimmy noticed he was now wearing gloves.

'Keep him company, Jimmy, this can be a rough neighbourhood at night. See he picks up my parcel and gets it to me okay will you?'

It was dark out of the torchlight. They walked over to the shop backs and stopped outside one which had bars across the windows and a strong door. The man flashed the light onto the handle. The lock had already been neatly forced. He opened the door and they walked in. They were in a small office with a safe on the floor.

'Hold this,' the man handed Jimmy the torch, 'on here.' He crouched by the safe door.

Jimmy shone the light on the safe. The man held a piece of paper in the light and, from the paper, dialled the combination for the safe. The door swung open and the man rummaged around amongst the papers and other items and took out two packages, one quite small and one larger. Then stood up and took the torch from Jimmy.

'It wouldn't have taken much longer without the combination,' he said scornfully. 'Keeping stuff in a thing like that, he deserves being knocked over. Let's go.'

They returned to the car and got in. The man handed over the smaller package to Denny and kept the larger one himself. The car reversed out then pulled away. The driver didn't hurry. As they pulled out on to the main road Denny turned round.

'Simple, eh? You and George break in and get eight quid each, Harry and you walk in and get about four grand. Keep it simple, Jimmy, and get an inside mug to do the hard work and take the risks. That's right isn't it, Harry?'

'That's right, Denny.'

Denny faced forward but carried on speaking.

'The prat who works in that jewellers thinks his girl's going to meet him tomorrow night with four grand's worth of kit. Well, he's got a long wait coming. She's back at work and if he wants to get into her knickers again he'll have to pay for it like her other customers. This lot,' and he held up the little parcel, 'the good stuff, I keep. That lot, Harry knocks out for what he can get, that's his end. Is Jimmy in for any of your end, Harry? He kept you company, brought you safely back, didn't he?'

They all laughed except Jimmy. He could see Harry smiling in the light of the street lamps. It was not a pretty sight.

'Yeah, Denny, why not? Everybody's got to start somewhere. Ten per cent.'

'There you are, my son, five minutes of the easiest work you'll ever do for round about a ton. It should fetch a grand, maybe more. You're a lucky lad. If I hadn't given you a lift you'd have missed all this.'

The car went on until they reached the edge of fashionable shopping London. The car pulled up outside a small jewellery store. The sign over the display window announced 'Setter's Jewellery' and below it, 'The High Street Store with Wholesale Prices'. Denny got out and went to the shop door, took out a key, unlocked the door and went in. He came out after about five minutes and got into the car.

'That's the way to do it, Jimmy. Those pieces will be knocked out at twenty per cent lower than they would fetch in any other jewellery store.' The car moved off. 'And when anyone asks how we do it, we tell them the truth. We keep down overheads by cutting out any middleman.'

The driver laughed.

'That's right, Denny, everybody gets good value.'

'We do it right. The bloke we took the stuff from is insured and our customers get bargains, not even that prat who set it up loses. He got laid a couple of times without paying, so everyone's a winner. Even you.'

The car eventually stopped at the end of the street where Jimmy lived. He got out.

'Harry'll have your end by Friday, that right Harry?' Harry nodded. 'Collect it from him any time you're in The Hind.'

The car pulled away. Jimmy stood for a moment then walked home. He would have to be quiet. He looked at his watch. It was nearly two o'clock and he had to be up at half past five. He needed to think but he wanted to sleep. He let himself into the house and went upstairs. He was soon in bed and was vaguely surprised at how easy it was to clear his mind and get ready to sleep.

Jimmy sat at the back of church. It was nine o'clock on Saturday morning. He had made sure that it would be Father Liam who was hearing morning confessions and he waited patiently for those others who had come to finish and leave. Finally the last one went to kneel in front of the statue of Our Lady on the far side of the church to say his penance.

What sins has an old man like that to confess, Jimmy wondered as he walked down the aisle towards the half open door of the confessional. He went in, closed the door and knelt before the small grille in the wall.

'Bless me Father for I have sinned. It is…' he paused, 'a very long time since my last confession.' There was silence from behind the grille. Jimmy fell back on the safe litany of his childhood sin-list.

'I have told lies. I have had impure thoughts. I have missed my morning and night prayers.'

Was there ever a time, or a world even, where such things mattered, where such things were sinful, needing forgiveness and penance?

He tried again.

'I have used bad language.'

His memory was failing him and it was all beginning to become ridiculous. How had he ever taken this seriously? How could this have ever been a part of his life? He knew what sin was now, and equally he knew he couldn't bring it into this stupid little room, he couldn't even bring it into church. It was real but you couldn't uproot it and bring it into the confessional box and say, 'Look Father, here is theft, violence, corruption, and pleasure taken in all of them, real people hurt, money made and the firm intention to carry on.'

You had to be in it, part of it, to see what it was.

'Anything else?'

'No, Father, nothing else.'

'Ask Our Lady's prayers to help you with your impure thoughts. For your penance say two Hail Marys and a Glory Be.'

'Now say an Act of Contrition.'

Jimmy began, 'Oh my God, because... because...'

The words that had once been automatic were gone.

'I'm sorry Father. I can't remember...'

'It's on the card in front of you.'

Jimmy looked at the small piece of card below the grille. The priest was right, memory was as little required as anything else. He read the words from the card. The priest began to intone the Latin words of forgiveness, of absolution. At the words of the blessing, Jimmy automatically crossed himself and got up.

'I'm the last one, Father.'

'Thank you.'

Jimmy opened the confessional door and stepped out. He went to the nearest bench and sat down.

Ask for Our Lady's help with your impure thoughts. What the hell did that mean? He sat and waited.

The priest in the confessional was sitting still reading the book on his lap. It was a Raymond Chandler thriller. He always took a good read into the confessional. He sat reading long enough for the last penitent to leave the church. After a while he looked up from his book.

'Was it a man or a woman?' he thought.

He tried to remember.

If it was a woman, an old woman, he would have to give her ten minutes at least. No, it was a man, it was a young man. He would be out of the church quickly.

The priest closed his book and put it in his jacket pocket. He took off the small sacred stole that he wore in the confessional, put it to his lips, folded it and put it in his other jacket pocket. Then he stood up and came out of the confessional. As he turned from closing the door he saw Jimmy but ignored him. He wasn't being rude, just observing the unwritten rules. If Jimmy had been the last penitent the priest must maintain the fiction of anonymity. The sins recently confessed must be kept quite separate from the ex-sinner outside the confessional.

'Good morning, Father.'

'Good morning, Jimmy.'

If he wanted to be noticed, that was okay. Jimmy had made the first move.

'Did you want something?'

'Yes, Father, could I talk with you?'

'Of course, what about?'

What about indeed? My immortal soul? Jimmy wondered.

'A couple of things, Father, about me and Bernadette.'

The priest readied himself. Was Bernadette in trouble, or was it good news?

'If we wanted to get married, how long before the wedding would we have to see you to sort things out?'

Alright so far. If Bernadette was in trouble at least Jimmy was doing the decent thing.

'It's really Father McGinty you should see, he's the parish priest.'

'We'd both want you to do the wedding, Father, would that be alright?'

'Yes, if that's what you and Bernadette want. When were you thinking of?'

The priest pulled out his pocket diary.

'We thought March, Father.'

So it was bad news.

'That's very short notice, Jimmy. We'd need a very good reason to get things done that quickly.'

He wasn't going to make it easy. He may be doing the decent thing, but he'd had his fun, now he must pay the price.

'Next March, Father, not this one. We wouldn't want to get married till we could afford a place of our own.'

The priest smiled. It was good news after all.

'Oh, that's fine. Have you chosen a date?'

'No, Father, but we'd like March.'

'Well see me again about six months before, no, make it eight months. That way you should get the day you want.'

'Thank you, Father.'

Jimmy stood still.

'Is that it?'

'There's something else, but if you're busy...'

Jimmy made to leave.

'No, not if it's important. Is it important?'

Fr Liam asked but he already knew the answer. Of course it was important. When someone who obviously didn't want to talk to a priest asked a priest if they could talk to him, it was always important and always serious.

'You could say that.'

'Will we talk in here or would you rather talk somewhere else?'

Jimmy looked around the familiar church.

'Is there somewhere else?'

The priest dismissed the presbytery straight away. Father

McGinty had no idea of anyone's privacy except his own, and Mrs Walker the housekeeper listened at doors to gather in the gossip that was her currency of exchange amongst the group of parishioners of which she was the leading light.

'How long will it take? I need to be here for someone at one.'

'I don't know, not long.'

'Right then. Come with me.'

The priest set off down the aisle, blessed himself at the holy water by the main door and led the way out into the street. Jimmy followed him.

'We'll catch a bus.' The priest walked to a nearby bus stop. They stood together.

'Where are we going?'

'Wherever the first bus is going. Don't worry, I know what I'm doing. Just now buses going in are busy and those coming out quiet. We can sit upstairs and I can smoke.'

A bus pulled up, Father Liam got on and went upstairs, Jimmy followed. They sat on the back seat. It was as Father Liam had said. There was only one other person upstairs. By talking quietly they had as much privacy as they needed. Jimmy liked the idea. It wasn't The Hind but it was somewhere real enough so that he could think straight and talk about what he wanted to talk about. Father Liam lit a cigarette and waited. If it was serious, and it wasn't Bernadette, he couldn't guess. So he didn't try. The clippy came upstairs for their fares. She smiled and nodded to Jimmy who nodded back. Father Liam got two tickets to the terminus and the clippy went back down to the lower deck.

'What's a mortal sin, Father?' asked Jimmy eventually.

'Were you never told?'

'Yes, I was told. Something that turned your back on God.'

'Well?'

'But, can you give me an example?'

'Well, murder and the like.'

'That's what I thought but at school when I was a nipper

they said missing Mass on Sunday as well and swearing and small stuff, stuff that isn't even important.'

'Missing Mass is always important.'

'Okay, I know it's important, but how can you put all that small stuff beside something like murder? If missing Mass sends you to Hell for ever, well, most of everything else people do is worse. That means we'll all go to Hell unless we spend the second half of each day confessing what we did in the first half.'

It wasn't what he wanted to say or had intended but it was what came out.

'You give me an example, Jimmy. Let's start there.'

'Stealing. Is stealing a mortal sin?'

'It depends on what is stolen and why. Do you want to put in some details so I can think about your example?'

'Breaking and entering. Stealing from a jewellers.'

Fr Liam spoke slowly with an exaggerated thoughtfulness as he drew on his cigarette.

'Alright, breaking and entering, stealing from a jeweller's. That's a good enough example.'

The priest was accepting the fiction of an example. Jimmy knew he could stop at any time and, knowing he could stop, told the priest everything.

They eventually got off the bus half an hour later. The priest looked at his watch.

'I'll get the Tube back, I have no idea how often that bus runs. What about you?'

There was a pub across the road.

'No, I'll stay here for a bit. Thank you, Father.'

'Do you want absolution, Jimmy?' said the priest quietly.

'I don't understand, Father. We've just been talking, it wasn't a confession.'

'It could be if you want it to. All it needs is for you to say you're sorry and ask God's forgiveness. Are you sorry, Jimmy?'

Jimmy thought, then nodded, and the priest said the words of absolution so quietly not even Jimmy, standing next to him, could hear.

'I'm off now. Say an Act of Contrition whenever you can,' Father Liam said, then he smiled. 'And for your penance say as many Glory Be's as you can before you get inside that pub. After that it's all up to you.'

Jimmy smiled back and they shook hands.

'Thank you, Father. See you.'

The priest turned and set off to find the nearest Tube station. Jimmy watched him go.

'Glory be to the Father...' he said silently to himself and God, and crossed the road.

Inside the pub he bought a pint and went to an empty table. Confession on a bus, forgiveness in the street, it wasn't what he had been taught and it wasn't what he was used to.

'I suppose you have to grow up in everything,' he thought. 'I was still a kid in the confessional, but I grew up on the bus.'

He began to think about the eighty pounds in his wallet that he had collected from The Hind the previous evening. He thought about how Father Liam had told him that knowing something was wrong was not enough, there had to be restitution, if possible, and a real desire to change. And Jimmy didn't want to change. Anyway, there was no way of giving the eighty quid back. Who would he give it to, Harry? The jeweller? He knew he was good at what he could do. If he did it for Denny Morris, he and Bernadette could marry whenever they wanted. They could get somewhere nice to live, not some cramped little flat. And he wanted to be married as soon as possible. He and Bernadette had not had sex again. Jimmy had understood what she had risked for him and he wouldn't ask her to take that risk again. If Bernadette wanted to have a proper wedding with a proper wait, then he would wait.

How could he be expected not to change but still marry Bernadette? They would never marry on a conductor's pay. Even on a driver's pay, if he ever became a driver, there wouldn't be enough for anywhere decent to live and have kids. They would get some crummy room and have about twenty years to wait on the council housing list. Jimmy knew he would need money and the only thing he was really good at, the only thing he could do to could get enough money, meant mixing with Denny Morris, Harry, George and the rest.

He took another pull at his pint.

Who was he kidding? It wasn't the money and it wasn't about marrying Bernie. Their world was his world, he fitted in, he belonged. In that world he could be somebody. What was it the Bible said? If you've got a talent and you don't use it, you're in deep shit. But the talent God had given him got you into trouble if you used it outside a boxing ring, and it was too late to go down that road. The bloody Church, they got you coming and they got you going.

Jimmy finished his pint and sat for a time looking at his glass. He knew he couldn't change the way he was, he knew where he fitted in, and he still needed the money.

He turned it all over slowly in his mind. Then he looked up. He had made a decision.

It was his world, he would stay part of it and he would get the money that he and Bernie needed. He stood up and took the empty glass to the bar.

'Another?' asked the barman.

'No,' said Jimmy, 'no thanks, I've got to get going.'

Two weeks later George went into The Hind and walked over to the table where Denny Morris was sitting. He was alone for once.

'Mind if I join you, Mr Morris?'

'I mind. Fuck off.'

But George persisted.

'It's just there's something I thought you'd want to know.'

Denny looked at him nastily but nodded to a chair.

'Well?'

Denny was in a dangerous mood. Something had upset him and he was looking for a way to express himself. George was a good guesser, he hoped to God he had guessed right this time.

'It's Jimmy Costello, Mr Morris.'

'What about him. I haven't seen him for a bit. Something horrible happened to him has it?'

'Sort of, Mr Morris. He's gone off to be a copper.'

George waited. Suddenly Denny slapped the table and laughed loudly. George breathed freely, he was still a good guesser.

'Has he, the fucker? Well, good for him, I knew he had something about him.'

'It's alright then is it, Mr Morris? Jimmy being a copper after working for you. Is that okay?'

'Course, George. Jimmy's worked for me once and when he makes his way up, he'll work for me again. Course it's okay. It's the best news I've had this week.'

He was cheerful now. He took out his wallet and pulled out two five pound notes and threw them on the table.

'Here, George, buy yourself something nice.'

George took the money and stood up.

'Thank you, Mr Morris.'

'Oh, and George, as you've cheered me up I'll give you some free advice. Don't ever bring me any bad news, unless, of course, you have no further use for your dick.'

Then he laughed loudly. George laughed as well, but not so loudly, and left.

Chapter 7

King's Cross, February 1995

INSPECTOR JOE DEAL did not drink and didn't like pubs, especially pubs like the one in which he found himself waiting for Tommy Flavin. He had asked for coffee. That exotic drink not being available, he had settled, after some discussion with the barmaid, for bottled water. It was a brand he had never heard of.

He felt and looked out of place. The pub was in a back street in a part of London he didn't know and didn't want to know. There was no food, it smelled of stale cigarette smoke and it was dirty. All the tables had ashtrays and they were all full. He assumed they paid someone to fill them before the pub opened because it was only mid-day and there were only himself and two other men in the bar.

He sipped his water. The two men smoked and shared a table in silence, except for the occasional hacking cough. Each had a pint glass on the table which they occasionally noticed, considered, and took a drink from. The barmaid stood wiping a glass with a grimy cloth. She managed to cough occasionally without losing control of the fag that hung from her mouth. She had certainly not been employed for her looks, conversation, social skills or hygiene. Her talents, whatever they were, remained a mystery to Joe Deal.

He looked at his watch. Flavin had said twelve. He would wait until twelve-twenty and then leave.

He would not have another drink.

About five minutes later the door opened and Tommy Flavin walked in, came to the table and sat down. Clearly he was not going to be the one to supply the drinks.

'What'll you have, Tommy?'

'A pint. No good coming here if you don't have a pint. The beer's the only good thing about this dump. Best pint in London, some say, and I don't say they're wrong.'

'It's a bit early for me.'

'It's only beer, Joe, not real alcohol, it won't slur your handwriting. Let's make it pints, eh?' and he looked significantly at Deal.

Deal went to the bar. There were two handles and three automatic taps.

'Which is it, Tommy?'

'Stanley's, the rest are rubbish.'

Deal turned back to the bar. The barmaid continued wiping the glass, ignoring him and everything else. Deal tapped on the counter with a coin. She put down the glass and cloth and came and stood before him, silent.

'Two pints of Stanley's.'

She moved down the bar and began pulling the pints. This pub might be worth mentioning, Deal thought, *a dump, of course, where you need breathing apparatus and maybe a tetanus, but worth it for the Stanley's*. He must write the name of the beer down. *Some say it's the best in London, I wouldn't disagree.*

Two pints of murky liquid each with a thin foam on top were placed in front of him.

Back at the table, he took a sip. It was revolting, worse even than it looked. He concealed his reaction as best he could.

'Thanks for coming, Tommy. Jimmy Costello, you know him?'

Flavin nodded. 'This isn't part of your murder, then?'

'No. What I want is just for my own personal use.'

'Off the record?'

Deal nodded. He decided not to try any more beer. Even

that water had tasted odd.

'Alright, you just drink your pint and I'll tell you all about Jimmy Costello.'

And he waited.

Deal slowly picked up his glass.

Flavin waited.

Deal realised he was going to have to drink the foul stuff and seem to be enjoying it if he was to get the story out of Flavin. With a weak smile on his face he raised his glass.

'Cheers.'

He consigned his soul to God and took a long drink.

Tommy began his story.

'Jimmy was as Irish as it gets in Kilburn. Born there, grew up there. Dad from Mayo, mother from Cork City. I was from round that part of London as well and I remember his mum, Betty. Her accent was so thick, some stranger once asked me if she was Polish. Jimmy was never in trouble as a lad, boxed at a Catholic club, very useful I heard but it never went anywhere. He was an altar boy. No Holy Joe you understand, it was just something he did. When he left school he joined his dad and worked on the buses for a few years, then went off to be a copper. He made good progress and joined the CID. He married a local girl, Bernadette Callaghan, nice girl, very quiet, very devout. He met her through church, something like that. Anyway, Jimmy got to be a Detective Sergeant. He was steady more than clever, but he could have gone further up. As it was, he stayed a Sergeant and stayed local. He made quite a name for himself, he was respected. He took money but no one ever felt they'd bought him and he never took money for something he didn't want on his patch. Ordinary villains knew just where they stood. If it was yes you were told the price, paid, and got on with it. If it was no, it was no. Further enquiries were not encouraged.'

'How did he get away with it? How come no one pushed past him? There must have been plenty about who wouldn't take no from a DS.'

'Depends on the DS, and it depends on how far he'll go.

Jimmy went all the way. One time he was in a club with two other coppers. They were drinking and playing cards, just beer and gin rummy, nothing serious. Anyway, they're sitting there and in walks this girl, a knockout, about sixteen or seventeen. She walks over to their table and leans on it and lets her coat fall open and underneath she's stark, bollock naked. She asks which one's Costello. They tell her and she says to him, "I'm a little present for you, want to take me somewhere to unwrap me?" Well, as I say, she was something but Jimmy just says, "I don't take presents, just money, tell your pimp." She looked at him, closed her coat and left. Next minute in walks this big bloke, very expensive. He comes to the table, takes out a bundle of notes and drops them in front of Jimmy. He leans down, puts his hands on the table so his face is close to Jimmy's and says, "There's a grand – cash. I'll have my girls on the street tonight and I don't want to hear from you again, ever. That's all you get." Next thing Jimmy puts his pint glass straight through the bloke's face. What a mess, a total mess, blood everywhere. Up gets Jimmy, grabs the bloke, slams him face down on the table, cuffs him, and says, "this is what happened, he came in drunk and wild, went for me and his head got pushed onto a beer glass on the table while we tried to restrain him." Calm as you like, as if he had the story ready. Then he counts out five hundred quid, pockets it, pushes the rest into the bloke's pocket, then holds him up and says to him, "when you get out you can have two girls on each of the streets I tell you and I want a steady hundred a week from you." Then they take him off and bang him up. We told the story like Jimmy says and the bloke went down for six months for assaulting an officer.'

'So Costello didn't like girls and was violent with villains. Nothing special there.'

'That's one way of looking at it.'

'Is there another?'

'Yes.'

'What is it?'

'Jimmy Costello was mad.'

'What? You mean a psycho?'

'I mean mad. He was married with two kids and he went to Mass with his family every Sunday regular as clockwork. He never looked at another woman and at home he was the best dad a kid could have. But on the street, he'd do you in without a second thought if you worried him.'

'How do you mean, worried him?'

'There was a bloke called Zylinski turned up. He was violent, dangerous, definitely on the way up and quickly, but he had a slack mouth. He was talking in a pub about how he was moving in and how he knew Jimmy didn't take gifts, just money. He said that Jimmy wasn't getting any money but if he got in his way he'd get a present, one of his kids' heads in a box. Jimmy's kids, Michael and Eileen, were only nippers then, about seven or eight.'

'So?'

'Two nights later they fished Zylinski out of the Thames. He had half a bottle of vodka inside him and a bang on the head commensurate with a fall. The bottle was still in his pocket.'

'A nicely organised accident.'

'All the best accidents are, Joe, you know that. But the point is nobody felt like going for Jimmy's family after that.'

'So he's a killer.'

'It was an accident. It wasn't even investigated.'

'So Costello never had a mark against him?'

'Oh yes. AIO looked closely at Jimmy at least three times but nothing got proved. The first time he got pulled I was making my first try for Inspector. Some copper had said something to AIO. I don't know why or who but I heard Jimmy knew so I went to see him. Nobody wanted a copper's body fished out of the bloody river. But I needn't have worried. I remember exactly what he said: "It's alright, Tommy, I don't mind standing up for a look over by the Internals. I've been careful, you don't need to be violent if you're careful." And he was right, they never had anything on him. When he went it was with a clean record.'

'So he was on the take, killed at least one person and fronted like a good family man.'

'You're missing the point. He only took what was coming to him, he protected his wife and kids. He really was a good family man and he really took Mass and all that crap seriously.'

'You can't have it both ways.'

'You can if you're mad. The Krays were like that, Denny Morris was like that, Lenny Monk was, before he let things slip. They were all mad. I've seen Jimmy go up against a professional and the professional back off because something had been switched off in Jimmy. He knew that he would go down but he let you know he'd hurt you before you could put him down, hurt you enough to make it matter. You had to be prepared to go all the way with Jimmy or leave it alone. Mind you, he wasn't violent normally, usually he was a quiet bloke. I asked him once, after we'd done a nasty lift, if he was ever frightened. He said he was frightened most of the time, but his mum had told him, "You'll often be frightened son, but don't let it interfere, just do what has to be done and leave the rest in God's hands." And that's what he did, although I don't think God had ever shaken hands on the deal. And Jimmy was a good copper.'

'A good copper?'

'A good detective. His arrest rate was something special. But more than that, he got a result in court more often than most. If he was on the case and someone got nicked you had a very fair chance of getting the verdict. And he didn't fiddle the evidence, he did it all by hard graft. When I went back to his nick as an Inspector I always saw to it that the roster got me Jimmy as my Sergeant for the times you needed a good detective.'

'So why did he leave?'

Tommy looked at Deal.

'He took early retirement.'

'He wasn't pushed?'

'I'll tell you, Joe, because you're a good copper and you'd

find out anyway.'

Deal smiled. He thought he was a good copper too, but he liked to be told. It almost compensated for the beer. He forced another sip.

'Jimmy's kids left home. Michael became a priest, some sort of missionary I think. Jimmy was dead proud of that. Eileen got married and went to live in Australia. Then we hear Bernie's got cancer. Next thing she's in hospital and then she's dead, quick as that. We all go to the Requiem Mass and back to Jimmy's house. He seemed alright. That night Jimmy goes out. There's a tearaway who specialises in burgling old ladies and beating them up but he's clever and no one can touch him. Jimmy goes round to his flat and beats the living shit out of him. Next he picks up Denny Morris, he just asks him, very polite, to come along. No problem, Denny knows he's fireproof and he knows Jimmy, so he goes. Nobody stops Jimmy because Denny's an untouchable, nothing can happen. He's got everyone who matters in his pocket or on his payroll. What Denny doesn't run himself, he lets others run and takes his share. He's got an outfit that could chew you up and spit you out whoever you are. When Jimmy got Morris out of the pub he took him to a building site and broke both his legs with a pick-axe handle and then kicked the shit out of him as well. How he managed it nobody found out. Denny was a hard bastard, nobody thought Jimmy could take him but he nearly killed him, would have killed him if he hadn't phoned the nick. They got Denny to hospital and he lived.'

'What was it all about?'

'I don't know. Denny was a dirty piece of work and Jimmy had tried for him once but you couldn't touch Denny.'

'So Costello scarpered?'

'No, he just went home as if nothing had happened. He didn't do anything, just stayed at home, did his shopping and went to Mass on Sunday.'

'Nobody went after him?'

'No, they kept an eye on Jimmy in case he ran and waited for Denny to say what he wanted. Jimmy wasn't just going to die, Denny wouldn't let him off that easily.'

'So what happened?'

'Morris didn't die and soon the word came out that ten thousand was waiting for anyone who brought Jimmy's eyes, thumbs and bollocks to him in a bottle, with Jimmy along in enough of a state so he could apologise before Morris took out his tongue himself. That's what Denny said he wanted.'

For a moment both men were silent.

'Who saved Costello? Not the police?'

'No, not the police. They were running round shitless wondering what to do, run Jimmy in or protect him from being butchered.'

'So what happened?'

'There was a takeover bid.'

'What?'

'One morning they found Denny's wheelchair by his Jag on a building site and nobody ever saw him again. Nat took over. He was Denny's right-hand man.'

'Why didn't he do Costello?'

'What for? If anything, Jimmy had done him a favour. Nat was good but he needed Denny down before he could put him out, and he wouldn't pay ten quid for any part of Jimmy, head, bollocks, feet or fart.'

'So Jimmy got off?'

'Yeah, but he couldn't stay. The tearaway business got sorted, the lad was told there'd be more of the same if he didn't keep his trap shut and give up his hobby. But like I say, Jimmy was mad, you couldn't have someone like him on the street. So he got early retirement on the grounds of ill health, brought on by stress. He got his pension and, of course, he had what he'd put away. He left, went to Ireland, I think, his house got sold and that was the last we heard of him.'

'So why's he back now?'

'Good question, Joe,' said Flavin, standing, 'a very good question, and a good copper like you should be able to find that out. When you do let me know.'

Deal liked that, a good copper. He finished the last of the

sewage water and stood up.

'I will, and thanks.'

They shook hands and Flavin left. Deal had finished his own pint but Flavin hadn't even touched his glass.

When Deal got back to the station, Eddy Clarke was out somewhere so he left a message with the desk Sergeant for him to come to his office as soon as he came in. In his office he took a tablet to settle his stomach and then dealt with paperwork until Clarke arrived.

'How's the Amhurst case going, anything new?'

'Not that I can see.'

'I've gone over all the reports, there's nothing there either. I think we should clear it up.'

'Okay boss, if you think so.'

'Have you got anyone to suggest?'

'You've got quite a choice. You always have if you want to take something nasty off the street. There's plenty out there.'

'Right. Put this killing alongside something we definitely know is down to our patsy and make it all watertight: evidence, witnesses, forensic. I want a guilty plea for this one. And make it someone white, will you? It might be worth a slot somewhere for me to say how we're not as driven by racial stereotyping as the media try to say we are. We have open minds on all our cases.'

'I don't know the choice is that wide boss, not if you want all that.'

'I'm sure you'll find who we're looking for.'

Clarke left and Deal looked out of his office window. Now that the Amhurst case was closed, should he wrap it all up by getting rid of Costello? Maybe, maybe not. It wasn't clear what would do the most good. One thing he could do. He switched on his computer and began to prepare a report for AIO, naming Inspector Thomas Flavin as his source. You never knew when a good report might come in useful.

Kilburn, September 1975

'Evening, Mr Costello.'

The Glasgow accent was not so out of place in the parish club, the black leather jacket was, but not the accent. If Jimmy had been in Glasgow, alone, he would probably have gone to just such a parish club for a drink rather than chance his arm amongst strangers in some pub or suffer the frigid safety of a hotel bar.

The man walked on and took his pint to an empty table. Jimmy had not acknowledged the greeting. He didn't think he knew him.

He returned his attention to his pint of bitter. It wasn't bad beer but he missed the mild. The club steward had taken if off because there was no real demand any more. Jimmy didn't mind that it had gone, you couldn't expect the club to keep mild on for one member, some things were just too much to ask.

Jimmy liked being a detective. He had been one for two years now. He had liked being a beat bobby but being a detective was better. He had never liked wearing a uniform, he would have been happy to stay a beat copper if it hadn't been for the uniform. He didn't like to stand out. He hated being noticed and beat bobbies got noticed, it was part of the job. Another thing he liked about being a detective was that he was good at it, he enjoyed his work.

It was early and the club was quiet. Later it would fill and he wouldn't be able to sit like this, by himself, and just think. The one thing he didn't like about his work was that anyone who knew you were a detective could never tell if you were on or off duty. That had been the good thing about a uniform. In the parish club if things got lively, which very occasionally they did, no one expected him to do any more than anyone else. But being a detective, and everyone in the club knowing it, he felt happier having an early couple of pints after work and leaving before it began to get busier. When Michael and Eileen were younger and more of a handful he had tried to get home in time to give Bernadette a rest. Now they were older there wasn't any hurry. Jimmy thought about Bernadette and the kids, their life together now and as it had been when they married. He was happy. He finished his pint and left his empty glass on the bar.

'Night, Mr Costello,' said the barman as he left.

Jimmy walked down the High Road. He and Bernadette had a comfortable two-bedroomed house in the parish. When Bernie had found it shortly after they were married he had not been keen. Why live in the same place you've always lived? Why not have a change? But, as always, she had been right. Being a copper was enough change. The same people, the same church, the same club to drink in, knowing and being known, that was good. Eileen and Michael went to the same primary school that he and Bernie had gone to, he liked that. It gave him a sense of belonging.

'Excuse me. Could you tell me the way to...'

The question from the man in the car didn't finish. It had stopped Jimmy long enough so he could see that the driver, who was leaning across the front seat, was aiming a gun at his stomach through the open window. The back door of the car was opened by a man in a black leather jacket who had come from behind him.

'Get in.'

Jimmy got in and the man shut the door and got in front beside the driver, took the gun and sat, half turned, watching him with the gun out of sight. Jimmy recognised him as the man with the Glaswegian accent from the club. There was another person in the back seat, a blonde, middle-aged woman wearing a fur coat and a skirt too short for a woman of her age and with her sort of legs.

The car moved off.

'Hello, Jimmy.'

Another Glaswegian.

'Do I know any of you?'

'You don't have to. I know you.'

Jimmy indicated the man in the front seat.

'Does he know that carrying that firearm is a serious criminal offence, if he hasn't got a licence for it, of course?'

'No, he doesn't. You see we're used to Scottish Law, guns are compulsory where we come from.'

Jimmy sat back and looked ahead as the car drove down the High Road and passed the end of the road where Bernadette was waiting for him. They drove in silence for several minutes, then the blonde spoke.

'I like you, Jimmy, you're not a gabbler, you wait and see. Jackie, give the packet over.'

The passenger in the front put his hand inside his leather jacket and pulled out a thick brown envelope which he threw onto the back seat between Jimmy and the blonde. She nodded down to it.

'Take a look. It's yours, you're going to earn it.'

'It's a serious criminal offence to offer…'

'Fucking hell,' laughed the blonde, 'is everything down here a serious criminal offence, and if it is how do you propagate the fucking human race in this town then?'

Jimmy took the package and tore open one end. It was a lot of money, enough to make whatever it was serious, dangerous and best avoided. Jimmy wanted to get rich but there were other things he wanted besides being rich, staying alive and out of prison being very high on the list. He put the packet back on the seat.

Blondie laughed again.

'Good man, no questions. It's my party, so I entertain. Alright, it's a simple job. Let's talk about Lenny Monk. You know who Lenny Monk is?'

Fuck, thought Jimmy. Lenny Monk ran most of North London.

'I know who Lenny Monk is.'

'Thought you might. Well Lenny sent a man to Glasgow to talk but he sent the man to talk to the wrong people. I know Lenny's getting old but he shouldn't get stupid. I don't want him in Glasgow so I sent my youngest son down here to let Lenny know. I was friendly, Jimmy, I didn't send Lenny's wee man back in bits. I just put him on a train in a box, and I sent my son, Jamie. Not a crew, no violence see, real diplomacy. It was like in the Bible, I sent him my own son.'

Jimmy waited.

'I want you to find Jamie.'

Blondie wasn't laughing any more.

'How long has he been down here?'

Blondie was silent for a minute.

'Three weeks.'

Jimmy pushed the packet across the seat to her.

'Sorry girlie, I can't help. He's dead.'

Blondie was staring down at the rings on her puffy white hands, which lay on her short, black skirt. The nails were a vivid red. After a minute she looked at him and for the first time he saw her eyes clearly. They scared the shit out him.

'I know that fucking well enough, and it's Bridie, not girlie,' she paused. 'Find my son, I want him home for a proper burial.'

So that was it, find a body. That was it, but was that all of it?

Lenny Monk was a top villain, Denny Morris's boss. If he was involved it was very serious, and if Lenny was trying to make connections in Glasgow, bits of people were going to be flying around. He didn't want any part of it.

'Find Jamie? That's all?'

'That's all.' She nodded to the packet. 'That's a lot of money, plenty just to find a dead body.'

'It is, but if I could find him I would probably find out a lot of other things you might want me to tell you, things other people wouldn't want you to know. A lot of money's no good to somebody who's dead.'

'Listen, I know Monk did it or had it done and I know why he did it, there's nothing else to know. I'll deal with him in my own time and my own way. And if it wasn't Monk who did it himself I'll find the trigger and deal with him as well. I don't need any information or help from you. All I want is to bury my boy properly, have his Requiem said and have him in a cemetery near me. Find him so I can take him home.'

She pushed the money towards him. Jimmy pushed the packet back.

'Alright, Bridie, I'll do what I can, which might be nothing at all. If I find anything I'll let you know and then I'll tell you how much it will cost you.'

Bridie smiled.

'I was told you were a good detective, Jimmy.' Then she stopped smiling. 'You find my son or I'll find yours.' Her eyes delivered the message.

Jimmy knew that if Bridie so much as sniffed fear from him now, he would never see his family again.

'Don't threaten me, Bridie. I haven't taken your money yet and when I do, if I do, it'll be payment for services rendered. And don't ever try to use my family.'

'Or what?'

'Or no business will get done.'

She thought about it.

'You know The Albion on Walker Street?'

He nodded.

'The barman there will get a message to me. Where can I drop you?'

He looked out of the window.

'Two streets down and turn left.' The car went two streets down and turned.

'First right.' The car turned right. 'This'll do.'

The car stopped. Across the street was a wide doorway with a blue police sign above it.

'You're not thinking of doing anything silly?'

'No, Bridie, nothing silly.'

Jimmy got out and stood on the pavement as the car pulled away, then he crossed the road towards the police station. What he needed most at this moment was a dry pair of trousers.

The two big saloon cars were parked at either end of the quiet suburban street. The fact that they each had two men in them and that their engines were ticking over was not noticed by the very few people who passed them. When the security van which collected the cash from the bank's branches in that district turned into the street and was between them they both moved, forcing the van to skid to a halt and preventing it from reversing. The men were out of the cars quickly and the security guards were almost as quick to open the van's doors. The sawn-offs encouraged a willing co-operation.

The sacks of money were out of the van and into one of the cars along with the four men in under three minutes. The car behind the security van with the men and money in it headed back along the street at speed but, turning right at the first junction braked hard and skidded to a halt, slewed sideways across the quiet road. The road was blocked by police cars backed up with armed police. Two other police cars came up behind, squealed to a halt and blocked any exit.

No one panicked, no one shouted. The police were armed and would shoot. Sawn-offs frightened people, killed people if necessary, but only at close range. They were of no use here and were thrown out of the cars as the blaggers came out of the car quietly, showing it was all over.

Everyone was very professional.

'Against the cars, boys, let's not have any fuss, eh?' a police voice shouted.

The four men turned and stood facing their car with their hands on it in clear view as the police slowly walked towards them. They were given the once-over, handcuffed and lined up. The Chief Inspector leading the operation walked along the line then went back towards the first blocking police car and spoke to the man in the back seat.

'Not there.'

Jimmy looked at the men by the car. Tommy wasn't often wrong, hardly ever. His information was usually good and this time Tommy had said it was Gospel.

'They're all Denny's lads, Jimmy, but no Denny.' The CI turned and looked at the men. 'Except that big black bloke at the far end. I don't know him.'

Jimmy looked.

'He's one of Denny's. Been with him about three months, clever lad, keeps himself quiet but he's useful.'

'Denny must have got a tip then.'

Jimmy shrugged. He wasn't getting into this any deeper.

'It was your information, Jimmy. Who else knew?'

Jimmy shrugged again. He would have to talk to Tommy about this. It didn't smell good.

'The chief, maybe a couple of people he had to tell, and Tommy Flavin. It originally came from Tommy. We tried to keep this tight, we really wanted Denny.'

'Well we fucking well didn't get him, did we? Alright, Costello, wrap it up and see what you can get.'

The Chief Inspector went to his car and left. Jimmy watched him go.

Keep it tight. What a joke when everything was for sale, almost everyone in his station knew about it and it wasn't even his nick's work. Jimmy and the rest of the team had been specially pulled for it. Tommy Flavin could be a devious bastard. Was it him that had put in the fix? But if it was, why pass on the tip in the first place? It had to be some kind of set-up, but what kind? What the hell. Mark it down as just another balls up. The way the lift was organised might have been made more public, but only if they had taken a lot of television time. It could have been anybody. A Sergeant came up to him.

'Denny's got important friends, this sort of thing happens. You did everything you could. What does the CI want doing with these blokes?'

Jimmy opened the car door and got out. He and the other Sergeant walked towards the handcuffed men who were standing by their car looking sullenly at nothing in particular.

'The usual. See what we can get and then tag on whatever they'll stand for from the backlog.'

'Which nick?'

'Suit yourself.' Then he changed his mind. 'Make it mine.'

Jimmy walked to the line of men. He knew them all and they all knew him. They looked at him when he came up.

'Okay lads, decide how much you'll cough to and we'll see what we can work out.'

Officers took the men to the police cars, a DC came up to Jimmy.

'Why your nick? It's a bit far, isn't it?'

'Not for me,' and he rejoined the Sergeant. They went back to the car and drove off.

The police cars left and the street returned to suburban peace. Only one uniformed officer remained. He stood by the get-away car to keep it company until the recovery vehicle came to collect it. A few lace curtains continued to twitch but the show was over, the circus had left town.

Jimmy and the other Sergeant went for a couple of pints before Jimmy was dropped off at his nick. When he went in, the duty Sergeant called him over.

'I've been waiting for you. That big spade they brought in with Denny's lot says he wants to talk to you particular. Said keep it quiet but make it quick.'

'What did you say?'

'Nothing, I kept quiet and made sure I was around when you came in, that's all.'

'No one knows he's asked for me?'

'No one.'

'Thanks, Arthur.'

Arthur was scared, that was good. If Arthur was scared it meant that he might have kept quiet. It also meant that the black bloke was serious. You had to be very serious to really scare a bloke like Arthur if all you used were words. He set off to an interview room.

'I'll take them one at a time, Arthur,' he said loudly, 'start with Harry.'

He was sitting at a table in the interview room when Harry came in. There was a DC standing by the wall.

'Hello, Harry.'

Harry sat down.

'Hello, Jimmy.'

'I'll do all this by myself, Eddy. I have some negotiating to do. Alright?'

Clarke nodded. It wasn't procedure, but if that's how Jimmy wanted it he wasn't going to argue.

'Anything for me, anything you think I should know?'

Harry shook his head.

'Anything you want, a brief or something?'

'A girl, a bottle of whisky and the fucker who gave us to you.'

'In that order?'

'Just as they come to hand, Jimmy.'

'What'll you stand for?'

Harry shrugged.

'Anything that doesn't add time, bits and pieces. The usual.'

'You're getting too old for this kind of stuff, Harry. Maybe you should learn book-keeping when you go down this time. Come out and be a book-keeper. Accountants are the ones who steal the real money.'

'You know how it is, you stick to what you know.'

Jimmy nodded.

'Okay, Harry, off you go. You know the way, tell them to send another one up.'

'Anyone special?'

'No, just as they come to hand.'

Harry got up and left the interview room. Jimmy sat and waited. After a few minutes another man walked in, he wasn't black. Jimmy said the same sort of stuff to him and they chatted for a while before he sent him off. The next man was black. He came in and sat down.

'The duty Sergeant said you wanted to see me. That right?'

The man sat and looked at Jimmy.

'This normal?'

'What?'

'Walking about. No copper with us when we come up here, just come here to you like homing pigeons. What's to stop any of us just walking out?'

'Walk out if you want to, sunshine, but when we pick you up we'll kick the shit out of you for fucking us about and charge you with all we've got on the books.'

'What if you don't pick me up?'

'Then Denny'll pick you up, but he won't just kick the shit out of you for fucking us about. He'll cut your balls off. Look, none of us are tearaways or stupid Jack-the-Lads, we all know the score. If Denny can get you off he will. If he can't, well, he can't, and you sit still and take the best he can get for you. It won't be much so why piss about? Denny doesn't want any of his operations screwed up by a lot of coppers charging about looking for some prat who's done a runner and we want a nice clean result with a bit of the backlog off the books, so we all go through the motions. Nobody rocks the boat.'

The man thought about it.

'Okay.'

Now, what did you want to say to me?'

'Nothing. I've changed my mind.'

'What's your name?'

'Nat.'

Jimmy grinned.

'Short for Nat King Cole?'

The man didn't seem to see the joke, or maybe he'd heard it before.

'You got form, Nat?'

Nat shook his head.

'Not done time?'

Nat shook his head again.

'You'll have both soon.'

'You think so?'

Jimmy nodded. He stood up and walked to the side of the room and looked at the man sitting at the interview table. Then he came back and stood beside him.

'You're new on this patch, so I'll break a rule and give you some advice. Denny won't get you off this.'

'No?' Nat didn't agree. 'If you think that, you don't know Denny.'

'Yes I do, I know Denny very well and I'll tell you something else I know, this was a set-up and it was an important set-up.' He paused for a second. 'Denny was supposed to be in on this one, wasn't he?'

Nat was taken by surprise and had confirmed the answer by his hesitation before he had time to think.

'That was the whole deal. Denny was the target, see? But he got wind of it somehow and somebody got put in for him at the last minute. Am I right?'

'I'm listening.'

'So now you'll all have to go down, and you'll all have to go down heavy so that someone high up on our side can show Denny that it wasn't a set-up. If we let you walk away, Denny will know for certain we weren't really interested in what we got. Don't take my word for it though, ask Harry or Reg.'

Nat was thinking again.

'Still don't want to talk to me?'

Nat thought some more.

'Suit yourself, there's not much anyone can do on this one anyway.'

'If something could be done, how much would it cost?' Nat asked.

Jimmy was fishing. That's what he had been doing, a little careful fishing, and now he knew he had the beginnings of a bite.

'I dunno. But it would probably have to be more than money.' Keep it sounding real, Jimmy, don't lose the fish. He grinned again. 'Although money would be nice.'

And he waited.

The float went under.

'If I had something to use, how do I know I get to walk?'

'You don't get it, do you? You just don't get how hard it is to fix. If you walk then you all have to walk. If it's just you that walks you'll be dead meat, because whatever you give me I'll use and when I use it somebody will make the connection and then everyone will know it came from you.'

'Why so sure?'

'Because if it's any good, if it's going to make me run for you, it's got to be something bloody good and something I can't get anywhere else. It has to be something only you can give me, or why do you the favour? See it now? Remember, none of your mates out there need proof. They're judge, jury and hangman on their own. If you have something worth getting me on board, great, I'll try to save your black arse. But when I use it, if they think they've made a connection, that's it, you're dead.'

Nat thought about it. He took his time. Jimmy liked that. He liked working with people who took their time, clever people.

'And can you do it so we all walk? So no one makes any connection.'

'I don't know, maybe. It's a big ask.'

Now Jimmy took his time. He wanted to wrap it up, he could feel in his stomach he was close to something good. But he had to wait, it had to look right.

He took a turn around the room. He could feel Nat's eyes watching him. Then he went back to the table and sat down.

'If I did sort it, the price has to be right. It's got to be something really special. It's got to be someone from the top, someone like Denny Morris.'

'That's special, okay.'

Jimmy was nearly wetting himself in anticipation. Please, God, make it good, make the name a top fucker.

'So? What can you give me?'

'I can give you Denny Morris, and I can give him you for life.'

Jimmy nearly jumped from his chair punching the air.

The jackpot, only the fucking jackpot.

He wanted to run around the room shouting.

What he actually did was try to make his face look as if nothing had happened, as if he was thinking it over, but it didn't need to take very long, this boy was no mug, he wasn't farting about. He could deliver, for Christ's sake, he could deliver Denny Morris.

'Go on then, give me Denny for a cast-iron life stretch. I want him served up on a plate with watercress round him and no chance of a slip up. Go on, Nat, Denny on a plate.'

Nat looked at him. Then he began to tell him his story, and Jimmy listened very carefully. At the end he nodded appreciatively. It was all there, dates, times, names. Jimmy knew where the body was buried now. He had Denny on a plate, just where he wanted him. One day he would use his information, a day when using it would finish Denny, permanently.

'Okay, Nat, I'll take it, and if I can swing it, everyone walks. That's Gospel from me to you.'

Nat got up.

'It had better be, sunshine, I'm not a forgiving person.'

Jimmy smiled at him.

'Don't threaten me. Just now I'm the only friend you've got.'

Nat left.

Jimmy saw the last one and then left the interview room. He found Eddy Clarke.

'Finish them off Eddy, what they want and what they'll take. I've got to go and talk to a man about a dog.'

'Okay, Jimmy.'

Jimmy went to a phone and dialled.

'Hello, Tommy, I need to see you. No, now.' His voice hardened. 'Now, Tommy, it's important and I'm not talking about it on the bloody phone, or maybe you want me to take what I've got to someone else? Okay, in twenty minutes.'

Jimmy went to the nearest Tube station. Twenty-five minutes later he walked into The Rose and Crown. He went past the bar into a small back room where Tommy was waiting with a large whisky on the table. He was trying to look as if nothing was bothering him, but he wasn't fooling himself or anyone else.

'Nothing to drink, Jimmy?'

'No.'

He sat down.

'Alright, what's so fucking urgent?'

'We were supposed to get Denny Morris, weren't we?' Flavin didn't answer. 'It's okay, I can work it out. Denny's on the up and Monk's losing his touch. Who would anyone back?'

'I don't bet. Just tell me what you've got.'

'Monk tried to give us Denny, but Denny's too smart and he screwed it. For God's sake if this sort of thing keeps happening we'll have a fucking war. Monk's making mistakes and that means everyone has to be careful, very careful.'

'You're not giving me anything, Jimmy.'

'Okay, smart-arse, I'll give you something. I'll give you a big, flashy old girl called Bridie. She dresses like a tart and gets driven around in a big Merc by clever boys who know what they're doing and she comes from Glasgow. Is that anything, Tommy?'

Flavin got up, left the room and came back with another stiff short which he added to the drink in his glass.

'Fuck me,' he finally said when he'd had a strong pull at his drink and settled. 'That's Bridie McDonald you're talking about? Where does she fit into all this?'

'No, Tommy, not yet. I've told you something, now you tell me something. That's how this is going to work.'

Tommy finished the rest of his drink in one go.

'Okay, Jimmy. This is what I've got. Denny starts pushing Monk so Monk arranges for Denny to be picked up. I'm given the tip and told not to use it myself but pass it on. I pass it on to you because if it's Denny in the frame I know you'll get it organised. But like you say, there's two sides to this question and I'm told to make sure Denny can get wind of it and then we wait and see who comes out on top. For Christ's sake, this is all being dealt with from way up. You and me, we're just foot soldiers, we don't count for shit in this.'

'Look, Tommy, I don't know who's running this comic strip but it's all gone arse up. Now Denny knows he's been targeted we'll have a war on. Monk's still good but he's slipping, it all needs managing. He needs easing out and Denny needs easing in. We can't just sit about and see who comes out on top, too much blood will get spilt.'

Flavin wanted another drink. This was too rich, and far too fucking dangerous.

'Why don't you look for promotion? I tell you what, why not miss out all the in-between bits and go straight for Chief Superintendent? It's easy to say what needs doing, but it's not so fucking easy to get it done.'

'Listen, you've got a pipeline to the man upstairs who set this up and whoever he is he needs telling that you don't fuel a war.'

Flavin thought about it. He didn't want to get into this deeper than he had to, but what Jimmy was saying made sense. Maybe saying it to the man upstairs would do him a bit of good.

'Tommy, don't be on the wrong side when the last man's standing. He'll pay off debts.'

Flavin stopped thinking. It was hurting his head and Jimmy had always been better at it than him.

'So, what do you suggest?'

'Throw the book at the lads we picked up, go for it big-time. But square the briefs so that the defence can get a result on entrapment.' He paused and then made his big throw. 'And give the Internal boys your man upstairs as the one who set it up. If he's backing Monk he's on a loser and if he makes another balls up like this we're all in the shit. AIO will eat it up, that way it's a big score for Internal. The lads get off on a technicality and everything looks kosher, everything can be squared. Lenny can get early retirement and go and live in the Costa del Crime and Denny goes to the top of the class and stops being pissed off and looking to chew people's legs off.'

Tommy liked it. It might work.

It might work all round. Jimmy was a clever bastard alright. Maybe too clever.

Giving AIO the man upstairs was risky.

It was a nice touch, but it was risky.

'I'll see. It's over my head but I'll see. I don't say you're wrong and I don't say it doesn't sounds good to me, but I'm just a poor fucking DI and there's a limit to what I can do.'

'I know, Tommy, life's fucking hard.'

Flavin looked at Jimmy.

He was known for not swearing as much as everyone else, he was fucking odd about it. If Jimmy was using strong language, well... Why worry. Jimmy's problems were his own. He's a good copper, though, thought Flavin. Why the hell was he still only a fucking Sergeant?

'Look, Jimmy, seriously, why don't you go for promotion, you've got the brains, if it's just the exams...?'

'It's not the exams. I'm okay as a DS, and I don't want to get out of my depth.'

Flavin looked at Jimmy the way Jimmy was looking at him.

'You mean like me?'

'Just like you.'

Flavin's head dropped and he stared at the empty glass on the table. Eventually he spoke, and when he did it was with an honesty he hadn't used for a very long time.

'Fucking hell, where did it all go wrong, Jimmy?'

Jimmy sat and thought for a moment.

'A long time ago, Tommy, a long fucking time ago.'

Chapter 8

Paddington, February 1995

PHILOMENA FOUND JIMMY cleaning the kitchen floor.

'Jimmy, that Sergeant who came and interviewed us with the Inspector called on the phone and told me they have arrested someone for Mrs Amhurst's murder.'

'That's good.'

'I think so. Apparently he's an addict and a dealer. It's good that he'll be off the streets. If he's found guilty, maybe they can help him in prison.'

'It's possible.'

Philomena seemed vaguely dissatisfied about something.

'It didn't take them that long to find him.'

'Well, they know where to look don't they, and they know who to talk to.'

'I suppose they do.' She looked around. 'Have you finished everything?'

'Everything, even the toilets. I would use them myself now if they had doors on.'

'Have you seen Janine? She should be back by now.'

'No. Where is she?'

'Visiting. She went out earlier this morning. She goes out to see some of the clients who don't have anyone to talk to, she pops in when she can. She's a good girl. I should go as well, but I never seem to have the time.'

'You do enough, Sister.'

'Oh well, she'll be back when she's back I suppose. I have a heap of papers in the office. Jimmy, will you stay out here, please, and keep an eye on things?'

'Sure.'

Philomena left the kitchen and Jimmy went into the dining room and stood on his own behind the counter beside the steaming urn. The rubbernecks had faded away and the day shift had thinned back to regulars. Only three or four remained, preferring the loneliness of the silent dining room to the loneliness of whatever they called home. He went round with a tray collecting cups, went into the kitchen and began washing them.

Philomena came up behind him quietly.

'Jimmy.'

He started and dropped a cup into the sink.

'Grief, Sister, you gave me a fright. I didn't know you were there.'

'Janine is in hospital.'

Jimmy wiped his wet hands, put an arm around her, took her to a chair and sat her down. She was in a bad way, he could see that.

'Take it easy, Philomena.'

'I think she's alright. She phoned and said not to worry. She's in the Accident and Emergency. She wouldn't phone herself if it was serious, would she?'

'Of course not.'

Philomena worked too hard and worried too much and now this on top of everything else. Jimmy didn't know much about these things but he guessed that when someone like Philomena folded, they folded right over. He looked at her. She seemed very fragile and far away, like a weak candle flame before it flickers out. Then she seemed to give herself a little shake and she was Sister Philomena again, small but tough as boots. She sat up straight.

'Well, you'll have to go. I can't.'

'Why not close up and we'll both go?'

'Jimmy, I work all the hours God sends to keep this place

open. Shall I close it now to suit myself? You go, bring Janine home if she's fit. See what she needs if she has to stay.'

'You could go and I could stay.'

'This afternoon I have to phone the diocese and my Superior. The bank manager is phoning me and I have to arrange for the Health and Safety Officer to come. There are letters on my desk that should have been answered weeks ago...'

'Enough, I'm on my way.' And he was gone.

Left on her own Philomena sagged in the chair, tears forming in her eyes. Then she stood up, wiped her eyes, blew her nose loud and long, and went into the dining room.

'Everyone alright?' she asked brightly.

'Yes thank you, Sister.'

'I'm in my office, knock if you need me.'

Jimmy took the nearest Tube to the hospital, went into Accident and Emergency department and asked for Janine at the reception desk. He was sent to a nurse, who disappeared for some minutes and then returned to tell him that Janine had gone. He made his way to the coffee shop and snack bar run by the Friends of the Hospital. He knew the place. This was the hospital in which Bernadette had spent the last days of her life.

Janine was sitting at a table with a cup of coffee. She saw Jimmy as he came in. He went over and sat down.

'You okay, Janine?'

'I think so, but still a bit shaken. Jimmy, something dreadful has happened, I didn't want to tell Sister over the phone. Poor Mrs Lally is dead. She's been killed.'

'Killed. How do you mean killed?'

'By someone, in her room.'

'You mean murdered?'

Janine nodded, put her hands over her face and began to sob.

Jimmy moved round the table to sit beside her. One or two people looked at them, but one more crying person and one more comforter were not at all unusual in this place. There was no curiosity.

'We were worried about you,' said Jimmy when the sobs grew calmer. Janine wiped her eyes with her handkerchief.

'I got knocked down, not even that really. Someone pushed into me at the bottom of the stairs that go up to Mrs Lally's room. The police brought me here just in case. They made me come, I didn't want to, I wanted to go back to Bart's. They said I needed to see a doctor.'

'They were right, Janine. Didn't anyone stay with you?'

'Yes, a woman police officer stayed with me but when the doctor said I was alright I told her I'd phone Bart's and someone would collect me. I just wanted to be on my own until I could get home.'

The tears began to run down her face again. Jimmy kept his arm round her and they sat in silence.

Jimmy turned it over in his mind. What did it mean? An old lady, a complete nobody, was dead, and she was connected to Bart's. Two killings, both connected to Bart's. He gave Janine his handkerchief. It was clean and dry.

'Another coffee, Janine, or shall we go?'

They travelled back to Bart's in silence. Janine didn't want to talk in the busy Tube and Jimmy wanted to think. He thought about Nat and Mrs Amhurst, about Bart's and Mrs Lally, but he couldn't see the connections. A casual killing was one thing, but two killings… if it really was like Nat said and he had killed Mrs Amhurst, he had killed Mrs Lally as well. But why? There had to be a reason, and it had to be a good reason. It had to be worth a lot to somebody. Could the killings possibly be unconnected? Was Nat involved?

Or perhaps it was something else? He thought about it.

He really hoped that it wasn't something else.

When they reached Bart's, Janine told Philomena what had happened. She listened calmly and took Janine straight upstairs and put her to bed then came down.

'We'll close this evening. Lock up soon, will you, Jimmy?'

'I thought you said…'

'I've no choice. Janine needs to sleep, I've given her

something. You and I might cope but we very well might not. We'll try to come to terms with this, and then we'll open again tomorrow.'

Jimmy went to lock up. When he came back, Philomena was in the kitchen with a cup of tea. He joined her.

'What's going on, Jimmy?'

'You tell me.'

'Two killings can't be coincidence, can they?'

'It doesn't seem likely, but who kills two people like Mrs Amhurst and Mrs Lally? Mrs Amhurst had a handbag with nothing of value in it. What about Mrs Lally?'

'I'm sure she had absolutely nothing, poor soul. I don't know much about her. She lived on her own in one room somewhere near and she drank a bit. I let her do odd jobs sometimes and gave her a little money to help her out.'

'Well, someone thought there was something worth killing her for. Maybe it was just a break-in that turned nasty. How's Janine, did she say anything?'

'Not good. All this is too much for her. She went to visit Mrs Lally, and was about to go up the stairs when somebody ran down and pushed her over. She wasn't hurt, just a bit frightened. She went up and the door was open. Mrs Lally was on the floor. Janine thought she had fallen, then she saw the blood. She called an ambulance and the police.'

'Have they questioned her?'

'Yes. They'll come tomorrow morning to take a statement.'

Jimmy and Philomena sat in silence, each with their own thoughts. Eventually Philomena spoke.

'It's got to be a coincidence...' she paused, 'unless it's something to do with you, Jimmy. Are you involved in any of this?'

Jimmy didn't mind the question. He was glad she had asked, it showed she still trusted him.

'No, Sister, these killings are nothing to do with me.'

'What about that man who came to see you?'

'Yes, he could have people killed. But why would he kill

Mrs Amhurst and the Lally woman?'

'That's what I thought you might tell me.'

Jimmy shook his head.

'Nat runs things in this part of town. But he had no reason to do any of this, I've thought about it and I'm sure.'

'So he's a gangster?'

'Only in a manner of speaking. He thinks of himself as a service provider with muscle.'

'And you? Where do you fit in to all that?'

'We knew each other professionally. He just came round to tell me I wasn't wanted, that I should leave.'

'But you didn't?'

'I was going to. I didn't think I needed to hurry that's all. I was going to leave soon.'

'So you're sure this Nat has nothing to do with what happened to Mrs Amhurst and Mrs Lally?'

'Can't see it. There's nothing in it for him.'

'When you say you knew him professionally, do you mean you worked for him, that you were...?'

He smiled.

'A gangster? No, I was a policeman.'

Philomena's surprise showed.

'A policeman! But if you were a policeman, surely you could help.'

'I can't help, I'm not a policeman any more.'

'But Jimmy...'

'Look, Sister, I don't want to get involved. What's done is done. We can't bring anybody back, whatever we do. Leave it to the real police, they've got someone for the Amhurst killing, they'll get someone for the other one. Don't go looking for trouble, because you'll find it. I don't know who's involved in this and I don't want to. If it's some crazy thief or addict then I can't help. If it's more than that it's too risky to try. You don't want anything else to happen, do you? Remember what you said, no trouble here?'

'I shouldn't have asked. You're right, we must leave it to the police.'

They sat in silence again.

'Sister, who owns this place, really owns it, the lease and everything?'

'Trustees, on behalf of the order.'

'So if you got closed down and it was empty, the trustees could sell it?'

'I suppose so.'

Jimmy worked the idea through out loud.

'A religious order may have bent trustees who fiddle books, but they don't kill people, at least not usually.'

'No, not usually.'

'What about Janine?'

'She's been here about a year. Before that, she went to India looking for enlightenment and when she was in Goa she became a Catholic. She felt they had found God in the Third World but the First World had lost Him. She actually came here as a sort of missionary. She had a fine letter of introduction from one of our Superiors out there.'

'Could it have been forged?'

'I checked. They knew her and the introduction was genuine. I don't take those sort of chances, Jimmy. If Father Lynch hadn't spoken for you, then you wouldn't be here.'

'Does Janine have any money?'

'She seems to be able to manage. I offered her pocket money when she started but she said she didn't need it.'

'Alright, could Mrs Amhurst and Mrs Lally have had some connection we don't know about?'

'Not that I know of.'

'Well, it looks like we'll just have to leave this to the police.'

'Do you still plan to leave, Jimmy?'

'Yes, Sister. As soon as I can.'

'You know, I really feel as if I can't keep Bart's open after all this happening. I'll try to see it positively. The survival rate of projects like Bart's isn't high and I suppose we've done well to last as long as we have.'

Philomena took the empty cups to the sink, washed them

and then went out of the kitchen, leaving Jimmy with his private thoughts.

Jimmy thought about Father Lynch's words: 'It'll be easy work but I'm sure you will be a big help. With your background, I can't see there being any problems.'

Two murders and Nat wanting a hundred grand, or else.

No, Father, no problems at all.

Southwark, October 1975

The Albion was in a run-down back-street just over London Bridge off the Borough in Southwark. It wasn't much and the barman was less. As a detective Jimmy often had to go to places like this, places he would never choose to go into as a customer.

'A pint of...' Jimmy looked at the taps, 'bitter'.

The barman drew a pint. It looked bad and Jimmy knew it would taste worse. It did.

He paid and went and sat down. The pub wasn't warm, welcoming or clean and it wasn't in a good location. An old derelict sat at the next table mumbling to himself. There was an empty glass on the table in front of him.

Jimmy waited and thought. After about fifteen minutes he went back to the bar and put his almost full glass on it. The barman came and stood in front of him.

'Another?'

'No.'

'A short?'

Jimmy shook his head.

'A fucking signed photograph?'

Aggression was obviously the barman's default position.

'Bridie McDonald said I could get a message to her through you.'

The barman did not respond.

'Tell her Jimmy wants to see her.'

The barman remained silent. Jimmy turned to leave, then turned back, picked up the almost full pint and took it over to the derelict and put it in front of him. The derelict continued to mumble.

Jimmy left.

Outside, he looked at his watch and walked off to the nearest Tube station across London Bridge and from there made the journey to his next meeting.

'Mr Flavin here yet?' he asked the barman at The Rose and Crown.

The barman shook his head.

'Got a paper?'

'Only the *Telegraph*. Or there's a copy of the *Spectator.*'

'No thanks.'

Jimmy went into the back room and sat down and stared at the wall opposite. About ten minutes later Tommy Flavin came in with a pint and sat down.

'How's it going, Tommy?'

'Okay, Jimmy. It looks like things are pretty much okay.'

'So it's going to be entrapment?'

Tommy nodded.

'A good idea of yours, Tommy, that entrapment. I bet they liked you for thinking of it.'

Tommy smiled and took a deep drink.

'You didn't want to get involved. And it had to be somebody's idea.'

'That's right, but it deserves a favour.'

'Of course, but not a big favour. It's only my idea while it's at the bottom. When it gets to the top, where it matters, it'll have become somebody else's idea.'

'I know. I just want a bit of information. What do you know about Bridie McDonald?'

'Fucking hell, you're not still nosing into that. What are you up to? We don't want anything to do with Bridie McDonald.'

'Just background, Tommy, just background.'

Tommy was uncomfortable, but a bit of information, what harm could that do?

'She's a heavyweight, got three sons and between them they run most of Glasgow and she runs them. She's hard, clever and never forgets or forgives. She's never said thanks or sorry and she's never not paid back anybody who crossed her, with plenty of interest. She'd cut you in half just 'cos it's fucking Tuesday.'

'Is she solid? There's got to be others in that town.'

'She's solid, alright. There's others, plenty of them, but they don't matter where it counts.'

'What if I told you Lenny was trying to team up with one of them against her?'

'I hope you didn't pay for that information, 'cos it's got to be so duff it isn't worth the breath it took to tell.'

'Want to know where it came from?'

'Jimmy, my son, the snout who gave you that is a liability. Drop him. He couldn't tell you the time, the day, what the year is or even his own right name. That sort of information comes out of a needle or a bottle or both.'

'Bridie McDonald told me.'

Tommy stopped smiling. Then said slowly and very seriously, 'If that's true, if you're getting inside info from the likes of Bridie McDonald you're running on very high octane for a DS.'

There was a silence. They were both thinking and Tommy was thinking very hard, he was trying to sort things out. Jimmy didn't put on a front, he didn't drop names or try to impress. If he said he got it from Bridie McDonald, he probably did.

'How did you get close to Bridie McDonald?' He was all DI now and Jimmy was just a DS. Tommy scented something. There was real money here or something for the Internals, something anyway, and he wanted to be in on it. He was going to score or he was going to be a good copper. Either way, Detective Sergeants didn't deal with the Bridie McDonalds of this world. This had to go higher than Jimmy Costello and he wanted to be the messenger. He wanted to be the one who would take the information to where it would do the most good. He wanted to get the thanks, or the reward, or both.

'There's nothing in this for you, Tommy, and nothing for anybody else either.'

'Don't fuck with me, Sergeant...'

But Jimmy cut across his words.

'Don't threaten me. I'm calling in the favour you owe me. If you don't like it, go straight for once and arrest me or something, but don't fucking welch.'

Nobody was smiling now. Then suddenly they both relaxed.

'Look, Jimmy, it's not on. If Bridie's getting involved it's something important and it's big, and you're not big enough to be in at any level, not even at the bottom, you know that.'

'I know, but this is different.'

'Have you been up to see her?'

'No, she's been down here.'

'Then it's not different. Just having her down here on the patch is way above my level. Does Lenny know?'

Jimmy shrugged.

'I'm alive so I suppose not. Bridie isn't easy to hide so she must be clever.'

'Okay, Jimmy, but if it's you on your own, count me out.'

He got up.

'Flowers or donations?'

Jimmy smiled.

'Just what comes to hand, Tommy.' And as Flavin got to the door he added, 'If you're out, does that mean you're going to be a good copper?'

Flavin paused. 'I suppose so, Jimmy. If anything happens, well, I'll have to cover myself.'

'That's okay, AIO aren't what's worrying me just now. I just wanted to know.'

Flavin opened the door and left to resume the fight against crime. Jimmy sat for a few minutes then the door opened and Denny Morris walked in.

'Hello, Jimmy. I waited for Tommy to go. I thought we should have a chat.'

'Sure, Denny, just don't make it a long one.'

'Don't hurry me, Jimmy. You might not have anywhere to go.'

He sat down.

'I'm going to do you a favour, then you're going to do one for me. I'm going to forget all about a young lad who became copper and is now a DS, who once helped knock over a jeweller's in Highbury, and I'm going to try and persuade Harry not to use that job to deal with the charge he's up for. I don't promise anything though. How much Harry says depends on a lot of different things. If it looks like Harry and the others have to go down, then he'll use it. Helping with the clear-up rate always counts as a favour and, as we both know, in the jewellery store job Harry really did it, so all the details will hold up, including who he had with him.'

'All of them, Denny?'

'I don't get your drift.'

'Will he be including you? Because I won't forget to mention it, even if Harry does.'

'Me? I'm pretty sure that I was in Marbella when Harry pulled that job. Yes I'm sure I was in Marbella, with about thirty other people who will swear to it if called on.'

Jimmy shrugged. It hadn't been much of a threat, and now he also felt sure Denny had been in Marbella at the time.

'What do you want, Denny?'

'A name, just a name.'

'Whose name?'

'The name of the copper who organised the outing that Lenny wanted. The one where I was supposed to get picked up.'

Jimmy thought for a moment. Was Denny trying to get a cheap confirmation out of him, or did he really not know? Then he decided he didn't give a toss one way or the other. Being clever just wasn't worth it.

'It's too high up for me. Ask Tommy Flavin.'

Denny smiled and shook his head.

'No, if I ask Tommy he'll run straight upstairs and then Lenny gets told and we have to do it the hard way.'

'Ask Tommy and then break his legs after he's told you. He'll travel slower in a wheelchair.'

Denny laughed.

'I knew I was right to come to you, Jimmy. But no, that's no good either. Tommy dead or mangled points Lenny straight to me and there we are again. No, you see, I don't want to hurt anybody, not this time. I just want to give someone a piece of information. I want the top men to know that it's no good working with Lenny any more. Soon, very soon, they'll have to work with me, so why not ease Lenny out and ease me in? It makes good business for everyone.'

'Especially you, Denny. What if Lenny doesn't agree to be eased out?'

Suddenly Denny's voice was full of compassion, a caring voice. 'Lenny's a sick man, Jimmy, a very sick man.' Then he grinned and his voice was normal. 'He's only got a year at most.'

'Why give him a year, Denny, if he's already making mistakes?'

'Well done. Yes, he's making mistakes but not many people know they're mistakes and definitely not the coppers. How do you know, Jimmy? I've made very sure it's been kept quiet.'

'Free information, Denny? Now there's a new idea.'

Denny relaxed.

'Okay, everyone will know soon, when I want them to. Lenny's got cancer.'

'Terminal?'

'It will be.'

'Is he getting treatment?'

'Lenny doesn't know. I made sure that when Lenny saw a doctor, I saw the doctor first. He thinks he's got a persistent infection, nothing to worry about and not too painful, yet. By the time the doctor asks for a second opinion it will be too late. Lenny's out of the frame.'

'But he still had a go at you?'

'He can see what I want and he still thinks he can stop me. But look what happened. A total balls up. Just get the word placed where it needs to go. It's not a big favour but I will be upset if you say no.'

Denny stood up but he didn't leave. 'You're sharp, Jimmy, very sharp.'

'And Harry?'

'Harry? He'll say nothing. You're going to be worth a lot more to me on the outside than you would be on the inside. And Jimmy, if we're going to work together again, get some fucking promotion. A DS is okay but Inspector or even Chief Inspector is better. You've got the talent, no reason why you couldn't go right on up.'

Jimmy shook his head.

'No thanks. I'm okay as a DS.'

'If it's the exams...'

'No, it's not the exams.'

Denny went to the door.

'Well, we'll see. Regards to Bernie,' and he left.

Jimmy sat and thought. Whatever it was, it wasn't the exams. He waited a while and then left the pub and decided to walk to the nick. He wanted to think.

The Merc pulled up like before with two men in front but this time there was no gun visible. Jimmy got in the back beside Bridie. She looked more or less the same but the coat was different. It was worse.

'Okay, Jimmy, I'm here, tell me what I want to hear.'

'That was quick, Bridie. Did you come down on your broomstick or were you already here?'

'Fuck you. The day I can't be ahead of a cripple like you I'll give up and join the Sally Ann or become a fucking nun. Now tell me what I want to hear.'

'Soon, Bridie, but I want you to come with me somewhere.'

She gave him a look and her eyes still scared the shit out him.

'Careful, Jimmy. I like you, but I don't like you that well.'

'I want to go to church, Bridie. You can say a prayer for Jamie, and maybe light a candle.'

Jimmy wasn't being funny, he meant it, Bridie could tell.

'You found him?'

He nodded.

'Then that's all I need. Fuck your candles, give me my boy.'

'Listen, Bridie, I told you you'd get the price when I knew what it was. Now I know. The price is five grand and this has to be done just how I say.'

'Or?'

'Or it doesn't get done at all.'

Bridie sat silent for a moment, then she said to the driver, 'Go somewhere quiet, Colin.'

Colin nodded and the car pulled away and joined the traffic.

'Okay, Bridie,' Jimmy was trying hard to make his voice sound calm, 'but it won't do you any good.'

'No, but it'll make me fucking feel better.' And they drove on in silence.

The Merc stopped at a derelict riverside site. Colin and the other man got out. The other man had the gun again.

'Get out,' said Bridie.

Jimmy got out, Bridie followed.

'Turn round, Jimmy, and kneel down. I don't want you to hurt yourself when you fall.'

Colin laughed. Jimmy turned round and knelt down. He felt the gun muzzle placed on the back of his head.

'Tell me where Jamie is or Bobby blows your fucking head off. There's no third way.'

'My way or not at all, Bridie.'

So Bobby blew Jimmy's head off.

When Jimmy came to and opened his eyes Bobby was standing over him still holding his gun and Colin, the driver, was putting a gun away. Bridie was getting into the car.

'Okay, Jimmy, we'll go to church and I'll listen.'

Jimmy got up and got into the car and pulled the door shut, he didn't feel well.

'Fucking hell, Bridie, every time I get into this car I need new trousers.'

Bridie laughed.

'Don't worry, that seat's been wet and worse plenty of times. But Jimmy, if I don't like what you say at church you won't be needing trousers of any sort any more. Tell Colin where to go.'

Half an hour later Jimmy and Bridie sat at the back of St Patrick's, Kilburn. They were the only ones there.

'So, Jimmy, tell me what your way is.'

'Jamie was killed about two days after he came down here. His body was doused with petrol, burned and put in a shallow grave on a farm just outside London.'

'The farm belongs to Lenny Monk?'

'I suppose so. Anyway it belongs to someone who wouldn't disturb that bit of ground for a long time.'

'You know who did it then?'

'No. I know what was done and where to find the body. Just getting that was expensive. No one wants you around here, Bridie, because you're trouble and people who poke into Lenny Monk's affairs have very nasty accidents. He may be slipping but he still pulls more weight than anyone else. Finding Jamie and staying alive while I found him cost me a lot.'

'You'll get paid. Did you say you've got him?'

'Yes, Bridie, but I had to move bloody quick. If Lenny got wind of what I wanted or who I wanted it for, Jamie would have disappeared for good. So would I. And there was a good chance Lenny would find out. If I could get the information, so could others. You know how it is, why get paid once when you can get paid twice? If the information was important to me that made it important to others.'

'So, your neck is still out and when Lenny finds you've moved Jamie he'll chop your head off. But if I was you, I'd worry about me before you worry about Lenny Monk.'

'I'll take my chances. You need me, and Lenny's got other problems at the moment.'

'Such as?'

'Cancer, stomach cancer. He'll be dead inside the year.'

Bridie was surprised. 'Cancer. Dead in a year?' She thought

about it. 'Too fucking true he'll be dead in a year, Jimmy, but it won't be cancer, it won't be that easy for him.' She looked away, then turned back. 'Thanks for that. I wasn't in any hurry before. Now perhaps I am. But Jamie first. If you've got him, I'm taking him home.'

'If you want to, Bridie, but if you do then that's all you'll do.' He knew he was on very thin ice. He was praying the "thank you" bought him something. 'Look, you can take Jamie home but what then? It's not going to be easy to square the paperwork on this one and even if you manage it how will you square the law?'

Bridie gave him a look that said squaring the law wasn't something she worried about.

'Okay, let's say you've even got enough muscle to manage that, do you have a bent priest on your payroll?' he continued.

She began to understand.

'It's up to you. You can get some of it by money and threats but how much do you want, do you want all of it? How much is a proper Requiem Mass for Jamie part of it? If it doesn't matter, say so, and you can have Jamie tomorrow.'

She sat quietly.

'Fuck off for a minute. I want to think.'

Jimmy got up, blessed himself mechanically with the holy water by the door and went out. Colin was leaning against the car. He stood up when Jimmy came out alone. Jimmy went across to him.

'Relax, Colin, she's thinking.'

Colin walked past him and went into the church. He came out again quickly.

'That's dreadful fucking language to use in a fucking church.'

They waited.

Bridie came out after about a quarter of an hour and got into the car. Colin, Bobby and Jimmy got in and the car pulled away. The smell from Jimmy's trousers was making him feel sick but no one else seemed to notice it. The car drove on for a few minutes.

'Can you get a proper Mass for Jamie?'

Jimmy nodded.

'Yes, in that church. Money will square the undertaker and the priest will be told that Jamie McDonald was a young man from Glasgow who died in a building-site accident while he was working down here.'

'What about the paperwork?'

'It won't cost much, there's nothing to it, just a young Jock's sudden death, sad but of no interest. I can make the story work around here. I can use the right people so the priest won't know any different and there's nothing for Lenny to know unless you make a fuss.'

'I want it done right, no hole-in-the-corner pissing about, a proper big Mass.'

'Sure.'

'And I don't like cremation.'

'If you can swing moving him up to Glasgow for actual burial, that's up to you. With this story it should be easy enough. But I'll need to know. The funeral's got to be soon, no more than a week.'

Bridie was silent.

'Don't be greedy, Bridie, don't lose him again.'

'Okay, Jimmy. Now take me to see him.'

'I can take you but you can only see the coffin. It's sealed.'

'Then I'll fucking open it.'

Jimmy spoke quietly.

'You can, Bridie, but what do you want your memories of him to be? I know you've seen it all, but this is your son, this is Jamie. You know how long he's been dead and what was done to him. Is that what you want to remember?'

For a second Jimmy thought Bridie would cry.

Then she said, 'So I pay you five grand for a heavy box and just take your fucking word it's Jamie? What d'you take me for, pal?'

Jimmy felt in his pocket.

'Here you are. I thought you'd want something.'

He handed her a small plastic bag. Bridie unwrapped it and took out two dirty items. One had once been an open razor with an ivory handle and elaborate decoration engraved on the blade and the other had been a cheap rosary.

'I took them off Jamie. There was nothing else to speak of, nothing I thought you'd recognise. Apart from the body that's all there is.'

She nodded. They were both presents from her to her youngest son, the rosary at his First Communion and the razor on his sixteenth birthday. He had always said they brought him luck. She had known that Jamie was dead, now she would soon know where he was.

'Okay, take me to him.'

Jimmy gave Colin the instructions and they went to an undertakers where Bridie was reunited with her son.

The funeral took place on a Wednesday morning. Father Liam said the Mass. He spoke of a young man who had died far away from home, of a young life cut short by a tragic accident, of the family's sorrow. Everything was well done, the church was full, Jimmy had seen to that, there was even a choir. Bridie and her two remaining sons were alone on the front bench. Jimmy was surprised that they all knew when to stand, sit and cross themselves. They weren't the strangers to the Mass he had expected. Colin and Bobby stayed outside across the street in the Merc.

Later, before the funeral cars pulled away from the church, Bridie came up to Jimmy and gave him an envelope.

'It wasn't what I wanted but he got sent off right. Now I'll take him home.' She stood quietly for a moment. 'Thank you, Jimmy, this was a family matter. My business with Lenny Monk will come later.'

She said it like a woman who didn't say thank you often if she ever said it at all, and she had said it twice to this man.

'Okay, Bridie.'

Jimmy pocketed the envelope without opening it.

She turned and left him.

The white Merc pulled out after the hearse and the black limo carrying Bridie and her two sons. No other cars followed. That was it, thought Jimmy. It had been risky, it still was, but it was worth it and the real payment he had received was nothing to do with the heavy packet in his coat pocket.

Chapter 9

Paddington, February 1995

NEXT MORNING WHEN Philomena came into the dining room she found Jimmy asleep at the table, his head on his arms. She made some tea and put a cup on the table beside him before gently waking him.

'Have you been here all night? There was no need for that.'

'I needed to think something out, I'm alright.'

Jimmy picked up his tea and took a drink. He needed it.

'God, Jimmy, you look dreadful. You know, when I was a young Sister, girls the same age as me used to be sorry for me, that I wouldn't have a husband, a man in my bed. They thought, what a pity, does she know what she's missing? But lots of the married women, especially the older ones, used to look at me in a way I couldn't understand back then: as if I had a secret, a lucky way that they had missed somehow. Many's the time I've envied women their husbands and children. But seeing the likes of you in the morning, Jimmy, I thank God I don't know what sex is like. Children can be a great blessing, but what a price, Jimmy, what a price. The likes of you in the same bed in the morning.'

And Philomena laughed, hid her face in her hands and laughed.

Jimmy smiled and spoke with mock seriousness.

'Well, well, if Mother Superior could hear talk like this,

what on earth would she say?'

Philomena removed her hands.

'She'd say we have the best of it. If you're built for sex, then get on with it. If you have the choice, if you can do without it, then leave it alone. It's no different from drink – ten per cent thirst and ninety per cent wishful thinking.'

'That's right,' said Jimmy, finishing his tea, 'except after a very short while it's ten per cent wishful thinking and ninety per cent habit.'

'God help us, you're a cynic, even I wouldn't say it's as bad as that.'

'Drink?'

'Sex.'

'Sorry, we're at cross purposes now. You seem to know all about sex and I know a bit about drinking. But you're the lucky one, at least you are if you got your information second-hand.'

'Which is the best way in both cases.' Philomena paused and then asked, 'Did you decide anything in your thinking, Jimmy?'

'Yes, I decided something.'

'Was it to do with us here?'

'Yes. I don't know if it will be of any help, but I'll try to find out how things stand. After that, I'm off. I can't hang about. I don't know how long I've got.'

'Don't get yourself in trouble on our account. Leave as soon as you have to.'

'The trouble's not on your account, Sister. I have a couple of days, no more. I'll do what I can.'

'What will you do?'

'Did you ever meet Mr Amhurst?'

'Once, when he first brought Lucy here.'

'Can we visit him?'

'I was going to anyway. It's the least I could do for the poor man.'

'If these killings are connected, he's the connection. As far as I can make out he's the only money in the frame and if it's not about his money, it's not about anything I can help with. These things fall into place or they don't. If they don't one ex-copper isn't any good.'

Philomena nodded. There was a ring on the doorbell. She went to answer it and came back with a detective and a policewoman.

'I gave Janine something to help her sleep. I'll bring her as quickly as I can. Would you like a cup of tea?'

'Thank you, Sister,' said the WPC.

'Make the tea, Jimmy,' Philomena said. 'We can use my office when Janine comes down.'

Jimmy knew the detective by sight.

He went into the kitchen, made the tea and brought it out.

'You're Costello?' the WPC asked him, lighting a cigarette.

Jimmy got the feeling he wasn't wanted but sat down anyway.

'That's me. Eddy Clarke not on this?'

The detective shook his head. 'He's in hospital.'

Jimmy was surprised. 'What happened?'

'Nothing that concerns you,' the WPC answered sharply.

'He took a beating.' The detective didn't mind talking. 'There was a phone call, some information for sale. Eddy went out and was found smashed up.'

'Was anybody with him?'

'A DC. They separated and the DC didn't see anything.'

'Last night?'

'What's a beaten up copper to you?' the WPC cut in.

'It's for my scrap-album, pieces of interesting information freely given. I press them when I find them, they're quite rare you know.'

'Fuck you.'

Silence settled around the table.

Despite her aggressive manner, Jimmy couldn't help noticing that the WPC was very attractive, even in uniform, and that took some doing. But he imagined how she'd be first thing in the morning with the kind of mouth she had on her. But at least coppers showed you their worst side first, he thought. If you fell in love with one it wasn't going to be because it was easy.

'Which hospital is Eddy in?' Jimmy asked, directing his enquiry to the detective.

'Central.'

At that moment Philomena came into the dining room to say that Janine was ready to speak to them, and that she would be present during the interview. It wasn't a request.

Immediately after Philomena and the officers had disappeared into her office, Jimmy left the building and headed for the Tube.

At the hospital he was directed to a small general ward and asked the nurse at the ward desk if he could visit Sergeant Eddy Clarke.

'Are you a relation?' she asked.

'A colleague.'

'Is it official?'

'No, I'm visiting as a friend. I'll just say hello and give him the station's best wishes.'

'Very well, but just that.'

Jimmy went to the side room she indicated and stood in the doorway. Sharon was sitting at the bedside. Clarke lay still, his eyes closed.

'Hello. I just came to see how Eddy is.'

Sharon turned and gave him a wan smile.

'Have you been here long?'

'Since not long after they brought him in.'

'Sharon, why don't you go and get yourself a hot drink? You look knackered. I'll sit with Eddy for a bit.'

She thought for a moment. She wasn't sure, but it was the toilet rather than the tea that persuaded her. She thanked Jimmy and left.

He took her place by the bed and put his mouth close to Clarke's ear.

'Eddy, come on, Eddy, wake up.'

He continued until Clarke's eyelids flickered opened. He turned his head painfully.

'Where's Sharon?'

He spoke with difficulty.

'Gone for a coffee, she'll be back soon.'

Clarke turned his head away and looked straight at the ceiling.

'What happened, Eddy?'

'What does it fucking look like?' Clarke answered weakly.

Jimmy knew what he meant, he could only see what was above the sheets but undoubtedly Clarke was a mess.

'You know what I mean, who did it?'

'Who do you think?'

'Why?'

'Because I gave Tommy Flavin's name to Deal.'

'Because Deal wanted to know about me?'

Clarke started to nod but stopped immediately, giving a small cry of pain.

'Why didn't you tell him yourself, why put him on to Flavin?'

'I didn't tell him the first night I saw you. After that, I had to make out I didn't know you.'

'And Flavin had this done to you?'

'Him or someone else. Why did you fucking well come back, Jimmy? Look at me, look at what they did to me just because I put Deal onto somebody who knew you.'

Tears started running from his blackened eyes, soaking into the bandages on his face.

'You'll be okay, Eddy, they've made their point. You'll get out of here and still get your pension.'

Clarke was too weak to make the appropriate reply.

'Anyway,' said Jimmy, 'it wasn't Tommy who put you in here. It was Deal, by giving Tommy your name.'

Clarke's eyes were no longer full of self-pity, something else showed there now.

'I'll say goodbye now, Eddy. Sharon will be back in a minute.'

Jimmy left the hospital. Flavin couldn't arrange it so that detective sergeants got beaten to a pulp, but he knew the people who could. Jimmy stood outside the hospital entrance, lost in thought.

When Nat had heard he was back he decided he wanted some of Jimmy's money, but now he probably knew he could do better by co-operating with the important people who were pulling strings. A hundred grand was just pocket-money to Nat and now important people wanted to be sure Jimmy wouldn't talk to anyone.

He didn't waste any time kidding himself, he was as dead as those two old ladies. He just hadn't lain down yet.

He went back into reception, found a public phone and dialled Bart's. Philomena answered.

'Hello. Yes, they've gone. She's alright, she's resting. Of course I think it's a good idea to visit Mr Amhurst today. We can be back in time to open for the night shift if Janine's up to it. I'll phone him and see what time this afternoon is best.'

Jimmy decided his next port of call was worth a cab fare. The Green Man was just off Kilburn High Road. He went to the bar and ordered a pint. Although the pub was half empty, he went and put his beer on a table that was already occupied. The man at the table ignored him and took a drink from his glass. He was wearing a dirty coat and a greasy cap. The whiskers around his mouth were stained with nicotine and his fingernails were blackened and broken. His face, what could be seen of it, was an unhealthy red.

'Hello, Father Liam.'

The old man slowly lifted his head and looked at him, gave a hacking cough and finished his drink.

'Another?'

Wordlessly, the glass was pushed towards him. Jimmy went and got another pint and brought it back to the table.

'I need two things from you, Father.'

'Don't call me Father,' came the growled response in thick West of Ireland accent.

'You were a priest when you married us.'

'Fuck off.'

The old man took another drink and sat with his head down.

'Always a priest for some things, like when a man is *in extremis*.'

'You're not fucking well *in extremis*.'

'I think I am, Father, I really think I am.'

'If I was a priest and you were as you say you are, what would you want?'

'Just for you to listen for a minute and say a few words if you can.'

'You said two things?'

'Let's get the important one over first. I'm going to kill somebody.'

'If you mean that, you're an idiot to tell anybody before you do it.'

'Not you, Father, you'll tell no one.'

'Don't be sure what I won't do for a drink. One more broken vow won't make much difference.'

'That's my chance to take.'

'Deliberate killing is always a sin, confessing in advance makes no difference.'

'Is it wrong to kill to save your own life, self-defence?'

In the dark recesses of the old man's mind something from the past stirred. 'Maybe not, not if it's the only way.'

'Is it wrong to kill to save an innocent life, somebody else's life?'

The old man took the glass from his lips and his blood-shot eyes took on a far-away look.

'In such a situation one might well apply the Just War Principle.'

Somewhere in his head the mists of alcohol began to clear. He was not a drunken, dirty derelict, he was priest-scholar, newly ordained out of Maynooth. He was a young priest asked a difficult theological question in a complex pastoral situation. He became again tall and strong, handsome in his black suit with the startlingly white Roman collar, and the words came. In his own mind he spoke clearly with confidence. Jimmy strained to make out his slurred speech.

'…damage by aggressor… only means open… reasonable chance of success… evil produced not greater than good obtained…'

Jimmy waited.

The rambling finally ceased, the old man sat still and silent.

'The next thing I want, Father, will mean a phone call. I want to meet somebody.'

'I don't know anybody any more.'

The old man's mind had clouded over again. He picked up his glass.

'You know people, it was knowing these people that got you put away.'

The old man put down his drink.

Suddenly, there was the banging in the night at the presbytery door and the respected parish priest taken away while Special Branch officers looked on.

He had upheld the just struggle of his people against a foreign tyrant and their secret police had taken him away.

It had been the beginning of his own personal Calvary and Crucifixion and it had been the beginning of the end of his priesthood. He saw again for the thousandth time the descent of the priest-scholar to the alcoholic outcast, living on the charity of the community where he had once served and been respected.

'You still know people, they keep in touch. I need them to save an innocent life. It really is a Just War this time, Father.'

The old man held out his hand.

'Give me the money for the phone and get me a Jamieson's, a big one.'

'You remember me, Father, Jimmy Costello. You know who to tell them it is?'

The old man stood up and looked at him.

'I remember you, Jimmy. You were the best boxer and the

worst fucking altar server I ever had.'

Jimmy smiled and the old man stumbled off. Jimmy waited. The old man returned after a short time.

'Take down this name and number while I can still say it.'

Jimmy took out a pen and paper and wrote a name and phone number.

'Are you sure about this?'

'I'm not sure about anything but that's all you'll get from me. That name and number won't mean anything to anyone else and I've already forgotten them.'

Jimmy stood up. He went to the bar and bought the Irish whiskey and put it on the table.

'There'll be a couple of drinks at the bar each day for the rest of the week, Father.'

But the old man had begun his drink and was already far away in the wild west country of Ireland, a young boy surrounded by beauty with a heart burning with a love of God and his native country.

Jimmy left the pub and found a phone box, where he spoke to Sister Philomena. They arranged to meet at a Tube station and go on together to see Mr Amhurst.

'By the way, Jimmy, you had another visitor.'

'Police?'

'No, not police and not the same man as before, not your businessman.'

Philomena gave a brief description.

'Yes, I know him.'

Jimmy put the phone down. Things were moving fast now. He was running out of time.

He looked at the scrap of paper and dialled the number and asked the voice that answered for the name on the paper.

Kilburn, May 1976

'Fancy a pint?'

Why not? thought Jimmy. He didn't like Eddy Clarke much but he felt like a pint. It had been a long, difficult day.

'Okay. The club?'

'No, let's go to The Sun, it'll be quiet there and no coppers, eh?'

Eddy tried to laugh but it didn't quite come off.

'Okay, have it your way. The Sun and no coppers.'

They went out of the station and walked in silence to the back street where The Sun Inn was located. It was small and clean with good beer. Jimmy had been in a few times. It was a place you could talk without being overheard. They went in.

'My shout.' Eddy made to go to the bar but Jimmy caught his arm.

'No, Eddy, when someone sells me information, I get the first round.'

Eddy tried to look surprised, but that didn't quite come off either.

'Tell me I'm wrong.'

'Alright, Jimmy, a pint.'

Jimmy brought the drinks to the table and sat down.

Eddy picked up his pint.

'Cheers.'

Jimmy took a drink, but he didn't say cheers.

'Let's have it then, and I'll see what it's worth.'

Eddy tried to look offended, but gave it up.

'I saw some papers yesterday, I thought you might be interested in what they were about. Special Branch have got that Irish priest friend of yours under surveillance.'

He stopped there and took a drink. Jimmy took a drink.

'That's it, nothing else?'

'It's enough. You know what Special Branch watching someone with an Irish connection means. It doesn't need spelling out, does it?'

Jimmy thought. No, it didn't need spelling out.

'Special Branch don't leave those sort of papers lying about.'

Eddy took a drink.

'Well, Jimmy, you know, they were sort of lying about.'

'In an unattended brief case?'

'Sort of, what's the difference? I know and now I'm telling you. It can't be bent info, what good would that do anybody? I'm telling you as a favour, stay away from him. If he goes down it will make a big splash, big enough to get serious questions asked about anybody on the surveillance pictures. Just go to another church and another priest if you need one. There's plenty about.'

Jimmy considered the advice. Eddy was right, this information was no good. The only way it could be used was to tip off the IRA or Father Liam himself and anyone would have to be mad to try to do either. Surveillance of IRA suspects was top priority and total.

'Okay, Eddy, thanks for the info but why bring it to me?'

'I know he's a friend of yours, he married you and Bernie, didn't he? I thought you'd want to know to keep out of the way.'

'And the price, Eddy?'

At first Eddy was going to laugh but he didn't and he didn't try to look surprised or offended either. He just said, 'You'll think of something, no hurry.' He finished his pint. 'Another?'

Jimmy shook his head.

'No, neither will I.'

Eddy got up.

'I think I'll be going. See you, Jimmy.'

As he left two men came in and went to the bar, got their beer, and went to a table on the other side of the room. Jimmy sat and turned over what Eddy had told him. He didn't know why he had come to him. Maybe it was because he couldn't go to anyone else. IRA info only interested Special Branch and the IRA themselves and, of course, the Security Services, who were about as trustworthy as a whore with your wallet. Poor old Eddy, some really valuable material comes his way and the only people who would pay the market price were terrorist psychos or spook psychos, and as it probably came from the spooks, it had to be the IRA or nothing. Eddy didn't have the bottle to try finding the IRA, never mind trying to sell them anything. So he has to take what he could get from me, poor sod, just a favour if and when.

Then Jimmy began to turn it all over slowly again. He didn't like it, it was wrong. Somehow it was wrong.

This kind of info was the very hardest to come by, yet according to Eddy someone had left it lying around. That didn't work. Eddy had no contacts who might let something like this slip so where did it come from? Someone had to have given it to him for a reason. If there was no one else he could go to then he brings it to me and gives it to me as a favour, because I know the priest. Now that didn't work. But if the info was true and it was given to Eddy to pass on, there had to be a reason.

What was it all about?

A light began to dawn.

What if someone, someone with real clout, was making damn sure that a humble DS didn't pick up the kind of Special Branch black mark that put the stopper on any chance of promotion. Did that work? What if whoever had given the priest to Special Branch had given the information to Eddy Clarke and pointed him straight at me. Was someone looking after him? Was he already in someone's pocket and they wanted to make sure he could move right on up? Jimmy didn't like where his thinking was taking him. He took his empty glass back to the bar and left.

That Sunday Father Liam was outside church after Mass as usual, shaking hands and talking to people. He was greatly loved by the people, he brought such a breath of joy as parish priest now that Father McGinty had finally retired. Jimmy, Bernadette and the two children regularly came to this Mass and always had a few words with him as they left church.

'Good sermon, Father, I managed to pay attention till almost halfway through.'

The priest laughed.

'It must have been good to keep your interest that long, Jimmy.'

'Special Branch are watching you.'

Jimmy's face hadn't changed, the smile was still there but his voice had dropped so only Father Liam heard clearly. The priest's face changed but Jimmy said quickly, 'I try to listen, Father, but you know how it is, the spirit isn't very willing and the flesh is worse.'

The priest laughed again, he was used to making his actions suit the occasion. You don't bury people's parents or grandparents twice a week, marry the young on Saturday and baptise babies on Sunday without learning to make your face fit the occasion and keep your own feelings to yourself.

'Next week I'll preach on football, racing and the television.'

'I'll try to listen, Father, but no promises.'

Jimmy and Bernie walked away from him and another couple took their place.

'Did you say something to him, Jimmy?' Bernadette asked.

'Nothing important, Bernie, a bit of police info he needs.'

Bernadette collected Michael and Eileen, who had been talking to friends.

She didn't like it. She didn't disbelieve Jimmy but it was all wrong. Jimmy didn't bring police work home and he would never take it to Mass on Sunday. Jimmy kept home and work very separate and home included Father Liam.

She thought about it as they walked, then she decided she didn't want to know. It was Jimmy's world not hers.

'Lunch at half past?' she asked. Sunday lunch was always at half past. It was her way of saying, 'I don't want to know.'

'Yes, lunch at half past is fine.'

It was his way of saying, 'I know you don't.'

In the darkness, an unmarked police car was cruising the busy night-time street. The two Detectives in the car were part of a squad trying to get a quick result on a series of smash and grab raids carried out around this time on jewellers in the area, which the press had decided to feature. Three armed robberies and the police with nothing to go on frightened people and made the police look foolish. Cruising the streets was a waste of police time but at least it meant the press release could say, 'our officers are out there', and that made people feel better. They had good descriptions of the robbers and there was every reason to believe they would push their luck and do another job soon. They were just idiots who had been lucky. They would push their luck one job too far.

'Pull in.'

The Detective Constable driving the car pulled into the side of the road. Jimmy, in the passenger seat, looked at his watch.

'Is it half past ten?'

'Nearly.'

'Look back there at those kids in that doorway, how old do you reckon they are?'

The DC looked.

'Eleven, twelve. Why?'

'What are they doing hanging about at this time?'

'Who cares? Leave it alone. If they're up to something, we don't want to know. Nicking kids, it's twice the time and paperwork and there's nothing at the end of it. Besides, we've got work to do.'

'Come on.'

'Not me, I told you, I'm not interested.'

Jimmy got out of the car alone and walked over to the kids. The driver watched him talking to them, then all three came back to the car. The kids got into the back and Jimmy got into the front. Closer up, the older one may have been about thirteen but the younger one was no more than eleven.

It was the older one who said, 'We going to have fun then? Cost you a tenner each.'

The DC turned to Jimmy.

'Fucking hell, what are you up to?'

'Get going, back to the nick.'

'Let us out,' shouted the older kid, 'we didn't know you was fucking coppers. You can't take us in.'

The younger kid looked frightened. Jimmy turned to them. 'We'll take you to the station till we can get you home safely. We just want to know who you are.'

'It won't do you no good, we belong to Denny Morris. Denny won't let you do anything to us,' the older boy smirked, 'not unless you pay,' and he began to giggle in an unpleasant way.

The DC shrugged his shoulders and began to drive. Jimmy radioed in. He wanted a social worker, a doctor, two WPCs and two interview rooms kept available.

When they got to the station the two boys were taken to the canteen by the WPCs. While he waited for the social worker and doctor to arrive. Jimmy began the paperwork. His partner looked on, clearly unsettled.

Quite soon, one of the WPCs came into the office.

'We've got names and addresses.' She handed Jimmy a piece of paper.

'Get on with it, then. I want the parents here as soon as you can.'

Jimmy put the paper in his pocket and the WPC left. The DC closed the door. He looked worried.

'Look, kids that age don't throw Denny's name about, not unless they really do belong to him, which means we've run into something of his. Why don't you slow down until we know what it is?'

'Don't you know what it is, Andy? Have you got to put your fucking nose in it before you can smell it's shit? Those kids are on the game.'

The DC came and sat on the edge of the desk opposite Jimmy.

'So? Since Lenny Monk joined the angels, Denny runs everything round here including the sex trade. You know that, why is this different?'

'It's different.'

Andy tried for a short while but then gave up. There was no reasoning with Jimmy when he got like this. He got up and went towards the door. Jimmy called to him.

'Hang on.'

Andy stopped. Jimmy got up from the desk and crossed the room.

'Try to leave this office and I'll put you down.'

'Don't fucking threaten me, Costello.'

Jimmy hit him once, hard, in the stomach. The DC folded and went down onto his knees.

'Okay, Andy,' said Jimmy pulling his head up by his hair so they were looking at each other, 'I won't threaten you, satisfied?'

He let go of the DC's hair.

'I said, satisfied?'

Andy nodded.

'There's going to be no phone calls. You're the only one apart from me who knows Denny Morris's name has been mentioned. I want this up and running before Denny gets told and puts the stopper on it. This time I'll nail the bastard.'

The DC got up, breathing hard.

Jimmy went back and carried on with the paperwork. It was about twenty minutes later when Detective Inspector Flavin came in.

'Hello, Jimmy. Hello, Andy.'

Jimmy was surprised.

'What brings you here?'

'Just passing, Fred on the desk tells me you've brought a couple of kids in. What's up? Found them on the street, worried about their safety?'

'Something like that.'

'Contacted the parents to come and get them?'

'A WPC's on it now.'

'Good, then they should be home before too long. That's good, nice to see kids safe. Got anything to do, Andy?'

Andy looked at Jimmy.

'Yeah, Tommy, I'll go and get on with it.'

He left the office. Tommy closed the door and turned to Jimmy.

'No point in waiting, Jimmy. There'll not be any doctor

or social worker, the kids will be taken home. The WPCs have been recalled. You should have taken advice first, once you knew this involved Denny.'

'Who told you?'

'Does it matter? That kid was shouting Denny's name all over the canteen, the whole nick knew five minutes after he got in there.'

Jimmy nodded. He should have banged the kid up instead of playing by the rules.

'So, Jimmy?'

'Tommy, those kids are on the game, at their age, for God's sake.'

'People want it, so Denny provides it, girls, boys, what's the difference?'

'Look, Tommy, the way Denny's running things now, it's no good. He takes too much in protection, the owners have to become thieves themselves so they can make the payments. He doesn't just do the ordinary trade in drugs, he makes his dealers work so hard they target fucking primary schools now. He runs girls so young that they're shagged-out slags by the time they're eighteen and now he's putting fucking little boys on the street. He's got to be stopped, Tommy. For all the real difference it would make, Denny might as well be the fucking Commissioner.'

Tommy didn't like it. Jimmy was swearing like a real copper and that was a very bad sign. He would have to reason with him. Coming the Inspector and ordering him off wouldn't work when he was like this.

'You're wrong, Jimmy, and I'll tell you why you're wrong. If we nail Denny then he still runs things from inside. Nothing would change except the coppers who sent him down would get it and maybe their families, and if Denny gets replaced it has to be by some bastard who's worse than he is. He took Lenny out because he was nastier and harder than Lenny. Replace Denny and where does that leave everybody?'

Jimmy tried not to think about it, but he knew Tommy was making some sort of sense.

Tommy, like everyone else, put Lenny Monk's recent demise down to Denny. No one except Jimmy knew about Bridie's involvement.

Tommy followed up his argument. He could see he was getting somewhere. Thank God he knew Jimmy as well as he did.

'And we do good work, Jimmy. Not everybody out there is connected up to Denny Morris. We protect a lot of people, put away some nasty sods and keep the place safe most of the time for most of the people.'

'Most of the time, Tommy?'

'Okay, some of the time. Look, don't try to change it unless you're sure you can fucking well mend it and not just make it worse.'

'What about this one, the kids?'

'It's out of my hands now. They're part of something Denny runs, more than just the street stuff, not just straight sex. I think he uses them for special clients and that puts the clients in his pocket. He probably films it or something.'

'We could have got him this time, Tommy. One kid's stupid, with a big mouth, the other's scared. We'd have got the stories and medicals so not even Denny could knot it up.'

'What you would have got would have been two dead kids. You could serve up Denny to a court on a silver plate with fucking watercress round him and he'd still beat the charge. He's too wired in. Too many people, important people, are in his pocket, or frightened, or whatever. Give it up, Jimmy, just give it up.'

So he gave it up.

He stood and went to the door.

'Okay, Tommy, let them take the little fuckers home.'

'That's right, Jimmy. Come on, let's go and have a pint at the club.'

At the club they joined Eddy Clarke, who was already sitting at a table.

'Been busy, Tommy?'

'Not really, this and that.'

'You, Jimmy?'

'No, Eddy, social work really, re-uniting lost kids with their parents.'

The conversation ran on and they were joined by another DS who Jimmy knew. They began to play cards, gin rummy. After about an hour Tommy Flavin stood up.

'Got to go, lads, got a meet at half past.'

He left the table and walked to the club door. The door opened as he reached it and a very good looking young girl walked in and looked around. She turned to Flavin.

'Which one is Jimmy Costello?'

'That table,' Tommy pointed. He couldn't swear but he got the impression she had nothing on under the coat. He would have liked to stay but the meet was important, this kids thing had to be sorted.

Late next morning Jimmy sat at his desk doing some paperwork on an arrest he had made the previous evening at the club where a drunken intruder had forced his way in and had had to be restrained. The phone rang, he answered it.

'When?' He looked at his watch. 'I can make it. Who will I meet? Why so careful? Alright.'

He got up and left. When he reached The Rose and Crown he went to the bar.

'Anyone in the back room?'

The barman looked up from the copy of *Punch* he was reading and shook his head.

'Expecting anybody?'

The barman nodded.

'So am I,' and Jimmy went into the back room.

A few minutes later another man walked into the bar.

'Morning, Mr Forester.'

The man ignored the barman and went into the back room. Jimmy looked up and recognised the man, a Chief Inspector who worked out of a West End nick.

'Hello, Jimmy,' he sat down, 'good of you to come. This is unofficial.'

'If you say so.'

'You went to visit the parents of those boys this morning, Jimmy. Why did you do that?'

'To see if they were alright.'

'It wasn't a nice thing to do, Jimmy, it made telephones ring in high places. Tommy Flavin said you were okay about this.'

'I'm still okay... maybe.'

'Maybe, Jimmy?'

'One of those kids, the older one, his mum's on the game and he would probably be as well even if Denny hadn't put him there.'

'So?'

'The other one is only just eleven, he's still at primary school. As it happens, it's the school my kids went to. His parents are respectable people. He got pulled into all this by the older kid, he's only done one trick so far. He's scared now, scared of what the other kid says Denny will do if he pulls out and scared of his mum and dad finding out.'

'What are you, a social worker?'

'These people are from where I live, Mr Forester. If they still went to church, it would be the church I go to.'

'So?'

'I want the boy off the street and the parents don't get to know it ever happened.'

'Okay, and what do you give for this service?'

'I leave it alone.'

'No, Jimmy, you'll leave it alone whatever happens.'

'Will I?'

'Unless you want to go to prison.'

Jimmy looked at him.

'You see, when that bloke you glassed last night comes up in court for assaulting a policeman the coppers who were with you will give evidence, and the story they tell will be the story I choose. It could be the drunken intruder, the assault, the struggle and his face being all cut up when he fell on the glass. Or it could be the truth, the girl you got sent, the bung you asked for and the glassing when it turned nasty.'

Jimmy put his hands on the table and looked at his thumbs.

'Denny doesn't let people go. These kids are on the game, that's it. Learn to live with it and get on with your own life.'

He got up.

'That's how it is, Jimmy. You can't make any difference, except to yourself, of course.'

He left.

Jimmy sat for a moment, then he got up and went into the bar.

'A whisky,' he said when the barman came, 'and make it a double.'

He paid for his drink and went to a table. He sipped the whisky, then took a real drink, he never liked the taste of the stuff. He left the glass on the table and went back to the bar.

'A pint of Fuller's.'

The barman pulled the pint, Jimmy paid and went back to his table. There was a man sitting at the next table reading a racing paper. He looked up at Jimmy then got up, came across and sat down opposite him. Jimmy looked at him. He was feeling angry, maybe this man might let him do something about it. Jimmy poured the rest of the whisky into the beer and took a long drink. The man watched him and then spoke with a friendly smile.

'That's a waste of good whisky, mate. If you need to do it, use gin or vodka.'

Jimmy didn't answer.

'You're Jimmy Costello.'

Jimmy looked at him, he didn't know him and he couldn't hit him yet so he waited.

'I've got a message for you, Jimmy.'

Jimmy still didn't speak. It all depended on the message. If it was from Denny Morris he'd put the man in hospital.

'I was told to say thank you and the favour will be returned when you want it.'

The man's accent was not London. Midlands, Birmingham,

maybe. Certainly not Scottish. It wasn't what Jimmy was expecting.

'I don't know what I'm being thanked for and I don't take favours.'

'Of course, but maybe you'll change your mind one day. The people I know have long memories and they never forget a favour, or anything else.'

Was that a threat? Jimmy wasn't sure. The man went back to his table and resumed his perusal of his racing paper. Jimmy watched him for a moment then got up and left the pub.

At the Station the desk Sergeant called to him as he came in.

'They found a bomb up West, Jimmy. Did you hear about it?'

Jimmy shook his head.

'It didn't go off but fucking hell, if it had! I'd like to spend half an hour in a cell with one of those bastards.'

Jimmy nodded.

'I know what you mean, Fred. I know just how you feel.'

That night Father Liam was arrested and in raids across Central London three members of an IRA bomb cell were also arrested and explosives and weapons found in two lock-up garages. They found no weapons or explosives in the priest's house but there were traces which showed explosives had been stored there. Father Liam was taken away by the police under the supervision of Special Branch officers. A priest nobody knew said the Masses on Sunday. He asked for their prayers for Father Liam, especially if he was guilty of the dreadful charges against him. He also asked their prayers for all the victims of terrorist violence and also their prayers that the men of violence would seek peaceful ways of gaining their ends. He didn't stand outside the church and nobody stayed around to chat that day.

Two weeks later a bomb did go off. The coded warning didn't give enough time and the toll of dead and injured was given out on the news.

What a fucking world thought Jimmy. He thought about

the two kids in the doorway and the man saying thank you in the pub and he thought, God forgive me for my part in making sure that it all stays that way.

Chapter 10

London, February 1995

THE UNDERGROUND TRAIN was travelling north. Jimmy and Sister Philomena had spent most of the journey with their own thoughts. Philomena looked around her. There was no one within hearing distance.

'Why are you going to see Mr Amhurst, Jimmy?'

'If the two killings are connected, his money is the only connection. If I can make that connection, I'll know where you stand.'

Philomena thought for a moment then said, 'You think I'm involved or I might be in danger?'

Jimmy nodded.

'Not nice either way, is it?'

Jimmy shook his head.

'Then I don't think I can let you ask Mr Amhurst the kind of questions you want to ask.'

'Then I'll just listen. If he wants to talk, you let him. I'll just listen.'

'If he wants to, Jimmy, but he's just lost his wife. It's what he wants and feels that matters today, not what we want.'

They left the Tube and walked out of the station into a leafy suburb. Many of the houses were mock-Tudor, mock-Georgian, or just mock, but if the architecture was mock the air of money was real enough. To live in this part of London you had to be seriously well-off.

To Jimmy's surprise, Philomena asked him to phone for a taxi. Jimmy went to the phone box outside the station. As he had expected, there were a couple of cards for taxi firms stuck above the phone. He made a call. About five minutes later a cab pulled up. Philomena gave the driver the address and they got in. They arrived at a big detached house and walked up the long gravel drive.

The front door was opened by an elderly man.

'Welcome, Sister, please come in,' Mr Amhurst looked at Jimmy, 'both of you.'

'This is Mr Costello,' said Philomena, going into the hall, 'he works with us. He knew Lucy.'

Mr Amhurst and Jimmy shook hands in that cold, formal manner which in England passes for a greeting. 'Thank you, Mr Costello, and welcome.' He stood for a second and then said, doubtfully, 'Shall we go in the living room? Would you like tea… or something else? I'm afraid I'm not very…'

Philomena stepped forward and took the old man in her arms and gave him a long hug. She made it seem the perfectly natural thing to do. Mr Amhurst slowly put his arms round her and then rested his head on her shoulder and tears began to run from his eyes. They stood for a moment. Jimmy was the only one who was at all embarrassed. They parted and Mr Amhurst stood back, took out his handkerchief and wiped his eyes.

'We'll go to the kitchen then we can make whatever we want just the way we want it.' He led the way, 'Lucy would bring people to the kitchen and ask them to make their own tea or coffee. At first I thought it rude but then she pointed out how often one is ready for a really nice cup of tea or coffee and it is made too hot or weak or sweet and one drinks it more out of politeness than pleasure.' They arrived in the kitchen. 'Everything is there, as you see, please help yourselves.' Philomena made a pot of strong tea for her and Jimmy.

'Our taste for good tea has been destroyed by the urn at Bart's. If it's strong, dark and hot then it's tea, isn't that right, Jimmy?'

Jimmy smiled and nodded. Mr Amhurst made himself a cafetière of coffee, then they all sat down at a big pine table. Mr Amhurst began to talk.

'It is very good of you to come, Sister. I do call you Sister, that is correct? I'm afraid I'm not a Catholic. I'm not anything really, although I put C of E when required to do so. My wife's faith was very important to her but it was not something we ever discussed. It is only now,' he paused, 'now that she is gone, I realise there was very little, perhaps nothing, we truly discussed.'

He looked around the kitchen.

'This kitchen is bigger than the room we lived in when we first married. And it is all due to carrier bags. That's what I manufacture, plastic bags.' He took a sip of coffee, then resumed, talking more to himself than to his visitors.

'I always thought of myself as a good provider. I thought that I gave Lucy security and comfort. When she died, it was as if somebody had removed the foundations of my whole life.' The tears began again. 'Now I realise it would all have come to nothing without Lucy. She was always there, she kept me going and kept me from going too far. She was the business, really. Looking back I see that all the real decisions were made with her. Perhaps it was her faith that caused her to be the way she was and yet I never really tried to know that part of her. I have come to realise that truly selfish people are also rather stupid. It hurts that she knew my stupidity and my selfishness so very well when I didn't know them at all, and that she loved me despite them. Now I know and it's too late.'

Suddenly he was back with them. He took out a handkerchief and wiped his eyes and cheeks.

'The priest who is looking after things is very kind, but I feel a total outsider, a stranger at my own wife's death. I don't know what to say or do… the prayers, the Masses. I can't say sorry or goodbye through the tradition Lucy found so important.' He was looking at Philomena with a kind of pleading in his eyes.

'There'll be plenty who know the prayers and get the

Masses said,' Philomena's voice was gentle but she spoke with authority. 'You say goodbye in your own way, the way Lucy would have been used to. She'll want to hear you as you always were, not trying to be someone else.'

Mr Amhurst blew his nose.

'I'm afraid I couldn't have shared her beliefs even if we had talked about them. I have always found the main propositions of Christianity vaguely absurd. But what experience has taught me is that life itself is absurd, so I suppose Christianity is quite an appropriate religion. It can produce strength through absurdity. It can produce people like Lucy.' He paused. 'Thank you both so much for coming here today. This has helped. We had few friends and no family, we had each other and that was always enough.'

'Will you be alright? Can we do anything?'

'Thank you, Sister, there is nothing to be done. One advantage of money is that everything gets done. As for myself, I don't know. I'm thinking of selling the business and giving the money to your Church.'

Philomena's voice was full of anxiety.

'This isn't the time for that kind of decision...'

'I just don't want to run the company any longer. It has all become meaningless to me. Don't worry, the money will go to your Church on my death. Through Lucy, it has given me so much. I really can't think of anything else I'd rather do with it. Lucy was very fond of what she called the missions and there was a particular project in India she and I talked about recently. Janine had told Lucy about it.'

Philomena stood up.

'Thank you for the tea, Mr Amhurst. Lucy is in our prayers and I'm sure we are all in hers.'

They all shook hands.

'We'll walk,' Philomena said. 'It will do us good.'

'Are you sure? Please let me drive you.'

'Not at all, Mr Amhurst. We'll enjoy all these lovely gardens and trees around here, even if it is mid-winter. Goodbye, and take care.'

'Good bye, Sister, and thank you again.'

As they turned into the road, Philomena said, 'I didn't want him cross-questioned, Jimmy, but I didn't tell you not to speak at all.'

'There was nothing for me to say, nothing I could think of that would help.'

'There never is. It's being there that matters.'

'You were very good with him,' Jimmy said, and added, 'Do you know where you're going, Sister?'

'If we're lost, we can always ask somebody.'

He looked at her. Hampstead, Uganda, Paddington, it was all the same to her, she was never really lost. How in hell did people like her survive? Was it luck or faith?

'I'm sorry about your questions, Jimmy.'

'That's okay. Mr Amhurst told me all I needed to know.'

Philomena stopped. Jimmy stopped beside her.

'You know what this is all about then?'

'Yes, like I said, it's all about money…'

'One minute, Jimmy. Excuse me, are we heading for the station?'

The woman walking the dog gave them their directions. They were off course, but not by much.

'Thank you.'

They crossed the road, turned right and walked on.

'Is there going to be more trouble, Jimmy? Is anyone else in danger?'

'You are, Sister.'

'Me! For God's sake, what can happen to me? I know nothing.'

'Look, Sister, you don't see things because you don't look. The police didn't see things because they didn't bother to look. You know things, but you don't know that you know. But if somebody asked you the right question, you could tell them things and that puts you in danger.'

'What do I know, Jimmy? Who am I in danger from?'

'What you call gangsters.'

'The man who came to see you?'

'Yes.'

'And the other one who came to see you today?'

Jimmy nodded.

'What would they do, Jimmy?'

Jimmy remained silent.

'I see. Well, what can I do? Should I go to the police?'

'You can if you like, it won't help.'

'You're a comfort, Jimmy.'

They saw the station sign further down the road and walked on.

As they stood on the platform Jimmy asked, 'You said Mrs Lally did jobs. What did she do?'

'She cleaned the back yard. Clients get in there and things need cleaning up and putting in bins, needles, and the like.'

'The bin yard? Where I take the bins out onto the street?'

'That's right.'

'When did she start to do that?'

'Not long ago. Is it important? Is this one of the things I know?'

'I think so.'

'It doesn't seem worth killing me for.'

A man standing nearby reading a newspaper gave them a shocked look, closed his paper and moved away.

When they began to talk again, it was more quietly.

'I won't come back right away, Sister. I have to go somewhere and then I've got to meet someone. I'll be back later.'

'Jimmy, I'm beginning to be a bit scared. I could manage this sort of thing when I was younger but I don't think I can manage so well now.'

'Nothing will happen before I get back, until then you'll be okay. I'll try to sort something out.'

The train came noisily into the station.

Central Hospital, London, October 1991

Bernadette was finally dying. The illness had not been long but it had been terrible. Only a matter of a few months had passed since she had told Jimmy of her visits to the doctor and the results from the subsequent tests. She had cancer of the pancreas. It was aggressive and untreatable, she would die quite soon and there would be a great deal of pain. The doctor was very sorry. There would be drugs that would help with the pain. She needn't worry about taking too many, the dose was to be as much as she needed. Did she take alcohol? But it didn't really matter, take whatever you like. The doctor was very sorry.

Bernadette had stayed at home for as long as possible. The Macmillan nurse had been excellent. But then the cancer had suddenly exploded and reached out rapidly. They had taken her into hospital and today or tomorrow she would die. Jimmy sat at her bed. The priest came into the private room, brought a chair and sat beside him.

'Hello, Jimmy.'

Jimmy didn't move or acknowledge him. He kept his eyes fixed on Bernadette's face. Her eyes were closed. The priest took out his rosary beads and quietly began to pray, very quietly, almost in silence. Jimmy knew the words he would be saying, the First Sorrowful Mystery, the Agony in the Garden. After about twenty minutes Bernadette opened her eyes. She looked at Jimmy, then her eyes moved to the priest. Her lips moved. The priest looked at Jimmy then came close so as to be able to put his ear close to her mouth. She was making an enormous and painful effort to speak. Jimmy could only guess at what the few words must be costing her. Then she closed her eyes again. The priest sat back in his chair, Jimmy looked at him questioningly.

'She said she wants to go home, Jimmy.'

Jimmy was shocked. He had no idea that being in hospital caused her suffering. He had just gone along with what everyone had said, he hadn't thought to ask Bernie what she wanted. He stood up. 'Then she goes home, Father. How do I do it?'

'Sit down, Jimmy.'

'Look, Father, I don't care what it costs, I can pay, whatever it takes. I can pay for doctors, nurses, equipment, whatever.'

The priest stood up and gently took Jimmy's arm. 'Jimmy,' he said quietly, 'it's not that home she wants.'

Jimmy stood, stunned.

'She wants to go home, Jimmy, to her Father's home, her Father in heaven. She wants release.'

Jimmy sat down.

'She will soon, Jimmy, she will very soon. She has had all the rites of the Church and she is ready.'

Yes, thought Jimmy. If anyone was ever ready it was Bernadette, she had kept the faith for both of them. She had passed it on to Eileen and Michael, she had taken him and the kids to church on Sundays. She had made the confessions, lit the candles and said the prayers. If he himself ever went to Heaven it would be because Bernie would get him in, somehow. Jimmy sat very still.

All these years she's looked after me when I thought I was looking after her. She made a home for me when I thought I was making a home for her. She had strength and she had faith. When I went this way and that, she went straight. What will I do without you, Bernie, who'll look after Jimmy Costello now?

The priest leaned forward and looked at Bernadette. He got up, went out and came back with a nurse. The nurse checked Bernie's pulse and then turned to Jimmy.

'I'm afraid your wife has passed away, Mr Costello. I'm sorry.'

The priest knelt by the bed and began to pray quietly. The nurse left and Jimmy looked at Bernadette. She was still the same, even though the cancer had changed her she was still the same, but now she was no longer there. I'm looking at a body, thought Jimmy, I didn't even notice her go. When Bernie died I was thinking about me. Suddenly, and with a terrible clarity, he understood the sin of pride in all its awfulness. His whole life had been centred on himself. If you had a purpose for Jimmy Costello, then fine, you fitted in, but otherwise – nothing. And even if you fitted in you had to fit the way that Jimmy wanted. He had moulded Bernie's life to fit what he saw as the right way, and the centre of everything in that right way, was always Jimmy.

The true awfulness of pride was that you didn't even stop to think about what it really was. It was the way everything was, the way it had to be, anyone who couldn't see it was wrong. And now there was no way back. Bernie's life was over. There was no way to give her anything, to see what it was that she wanted, to listen to her, to ask where she thought their lives together should go. The priest stood up.

'She's with God now, Jimmy, as sure as anything can be sure, she's at home.'

Jimmy nodded.

'Thank you, Father.'

'Is there anything I can do, anything at all?'

'No, Father, everything is taken care of. I spoke to someone at the head office of Michael's missionary order. They can't get him out of the Sudan just now. Little Jimmy's not well, Eileen will come if she can get away for the funeral. Everything is done.'

The priest quietly left.

Everything is done, everything gets done if you've got the money and I've got the money, thought Jimmy. He sat down on the bed beside Bernadette. What will I do with all that money now, Bernie? I made it for you, so one day I could surprise you. I was going to retire and say, 'Look girl, look what I've done, and it's all for you. Now you can go to Australia and visit Eileen, we can go anywhere and do anything. You can buy a really nice house, clothes, anything you want.' You were going to be so happy, Bernie. What shall I do now with all that fucking money? What's it for now?

Jimmy got up and went out to the ward desk. 'Thank you, nurse. Will you say thank you to everybody?'

'Of course, Mr Costello, I'm very sorry.'

'Everything's arranged.'

'I'm sure it is.'

He noticed a big jar on the desk with coins in it.

'What's it for?'

'Play equipment for the children's ward.'

Jimmy took out his wallet. He pulled out a note, folded it and put it through the slot in the top of the jar.

'Mr Costello,' said the nurse quickly, 'that was twenty pounds, are you sure?'

He put away his wallet.

'Sure, the kids need something when they're in here.'

She was still looking concerned. Bereavement did funny things to people.

Bernadette's Requiem Mass was very full. Jimmy hadn't realised so many people would want to come. They had never moved from Kilburn, but he knew hardly anybody other than as an acquaintance, a face you nodded to. Jimmy had said no flowers, donations to Michael's missionary order. Things had been bad in the Sudan and Michael still hadn't been able to get out.

Worrying about Michael had been something Jimmy and Bernadette had accepted as part of their lives three years ago when he was sent to Sudan. Little Jimmy was still ill, Eileen didn't know what it was, the doctors were trying to find out. It probably wasn't serious but it wouldn't go away and the poor kid had quite a bit of pain. There were two of Bernie's relatives from Ireland and a cousin of his own who kept in occasional touch, but mostly it was neighbours, colleagues and parishioners.

There had been a wedding on the previous Saturday and Jimmy had asked if the flowers could be left. Bernie liked flowers in church, she would have liked these. Only one wreath was sent. It wasn't big but it was expensive, the card said 'Bridie'. Jimmy had it put by the box in the porch where donations could be given.

A few people came back to the house from the cemetery. Most didn't stay long. Tommy Flavin and a couple of others from Jimmy's station stayed and drank whiskey together. Flavin didn't drink much but the other two drank steadily. Jimmy drank, but more for the company, he couldn't develop a taste for Irish whiskey any more than for Scotch. He was on the edge of drunk when Flavin left, taking the other two with him.

'Take it easy, Jimmy,' he said at the front door, 'take as much time as you need. Don't come in till you're ready.'

Jimmy stood steadily.

'Good night, Tommy, thanks for coming.'

'The least I could do. I'll get these two home now,' he said indicating the swaying figures standing by his car. 'Try and get to bed. Life goes on. Bernie wouldn't want you giving in.'

'No, Tommy, Bernie wouldn't want me to give in.'

Jimmy closed the door.

He went back into the living room and went to a chest of drawers and took out a small tin box. It had several keys in it. He took one, a safety deposit box key, put it in his trouser pocket, then went upstairs. On the bed was a briefcase. It had documents in it and a passport. Jimmy checked everything, then opened a wardrobe. From it he took a pick-axe handle. He carried it downstairs and picked up his car keys. He knew he was well over the limit but that was not an issue. If he was alive tomorrow morning, he would go to his safety deposit box, take his money and go. Where he went to would depend on the first available seat out of Gatwick or Luton. Heathrow would be no good. Jimmy carefully put the handle in the boot under a rug and got into his car and drove off.

Three quarters of an hour later he pulled up at a phone box, got out and dialled a number.

'Duty Sergeant.' He waited. 'There's been a break in at Hampton Flats, number 36. That's right. Occupant's badly injured. I was passing and saw the door open, so I went in... No, the door had been forced, the lock's smashed... I'm a neighbour... Look, the lad needs an ambulance. I'll wait and you can ask me all the questions you like when you get there.'

Jimmy put the phone down, got back into his car and drove off.

He parked outside The Hind. It was years since he had last been inside, but when he looked around he saw that nothing much had changed. Denny still used the same table.

'Hello, Jimmy, long time.'

'Hello, Denny.'

'Sorry about Bernie. Funeral was today, wasn't it?'

Jimmy nodded.

'You're not working then. So is this a social call or do you want something?'

'I want something.'

'Okay, Jimmy, sit down. Make room for Jimmy.'

Nat moved around and made a space. The other two men at the table shuffled round.

'What can I do for you?'

Jimmy didn't take the chair.

'I need to talk to you.'

'So talk.'

'Just you, and not here.'

'Here or nowhere.'

'You don't want me to talk here. It's you I'm thinking about, not me.'

Denny thought for a moment. He had known Jimmy a long time.

'Look him over, Nat.'

Jimmy held his arms out from his sides.

Nat looked him over very thoroughly. Nobody in the pub seemed to notice that a man was being given a body search.

'Nothing.'

Nat sat down. Denny stood up.

'Okay, Jimmy. We'll take a drive. You've got a car outside?'

Jimmy nodded.

'Give Vic the keys.'

Vic stood up and Jimmy tossed him the keys.

'Check it over, Vic. I know you, Jimmy, but Vic doesn't have my trusting nature.'

Vic left, Jimmy waited. They all sat and waited. Vic returned.

'Okay, Denny. Nothing inside and nothing in the glove box or under the seats and no wires. It'll be just you and Jimmy.'

He tossed the keys back to Jimmy.

They left The Hind and got into the car. They had been driving for a short while when Denny said, 'Come on, Jimmy, what is it you want to tell me?'

'I'm pulling out, I'm leaving. It doesn't look like we're going to work together after all.'

Denny thought about it.

'When?'

'Tomorrow.'

'A bit sudden, isn't it?'

'It needs to be sudden.'

'People after you?'

Jimmy nodded.

'Why tell me? I'm not after you.'

'I wanted you to know because if we've got any unfinished business we need to settle it now.'

Jimmy pulled the car over and parked. It was a quiet street but well lit.

'Well, Denny, have we got any unfinished business?'

Denny was thinking.

'Will you get away, Jimmy, that's the question? You know things, not much and nothing serious, but you know things. If it's the Internals that are after you, there's important people who wouldn't want to see you in an interview room.'

'No, it's not the coppers who want me.'

'Then who?'

'Ever heard of Bridie McDonald?'

'Maybe.'

'She runs Glasgow.'

'Go on.'

'I got some information from a Jock I picked up while he was down here. I thought he was nothing and the info didn't seem much but when I got in touch with a Glasgow nick they were keen to have it so I passed it on and forgot about it.'

'And?'

'And it hurt this Bridie McDonald so she sent me a message.'

'How?'

'She sent flowers to Bernie's funeral today. The message was on the card. I'm not going home tonight and I'm getting the first seat out of Heathrow tomorrow if I'm still in one piece.'

'Doesn't sound good. You're not easy to hide and I hear Bridie is good at looking.'

'I only need to get to my bank in the morning, then I'm off.'

'You won't get a pension, Jimmy.'

'Fuck the pension. I'll be okay.'

'Well, if I can help... You've got somewhere to hole up for tonight?'

Jimmy knew Denny had bitten, he was almost home. Denny was getting ready to set him up as a favour to Bridie.

'Yeah, somewhere nobody will find me, quiet and out of the way, not even the car will be noticed.'

Denny's tongue was almost hanging out. He was leaning forward and off his guard.

'Sounds good. Somewhere I know?'

'Yeah, Denny, actually it's...' and Jimmy turned and hit him hard in the throat.

Denny was hurt but he was strong. He could hardly breathe but even though Jimmy hit him again in the face, he got his gun out. Jimmy parted his fingers and jabbed them hard into Denny's eyes with one hand and pushed the gun down with the other. Denny gasped but got a shot off. The inside of the car exploded with the noise. Jimmy hit him hard on his temple. Denny was choking and blinded but he wouldn't go down. The bullet had gone past Jimmy's leg and through the car floor. Jimmy held Denny's wrist with his left hand and forced the gun towards the floor between the seats and hit Denny hard in the face again. His face was the only clear target Jimmy had to work on, so he worked on it. Denny sagged but he wasn't going out. Jimmy held his gun hand down so Denny tried to hit him with his left hand from the far side of the car or use his head. The punches landed but they were wild and awkward and from too far away and when he tried to head-butt he simply came onto the punch. Then Jimmy suddenly pulled Denny's gun arm up and broke it at the elbow.

Denny grunted with pain and dropped the gun. Jimmy picked it up and sat back.

'It's over, Denny,' said Jimmy, breathing heavily. 'I've got the gun. Move and you're fucked.'

Denny sank back. Jimmy's face was bleeding, one eye was closing. Denny was bleeding from the eyes, nose and mouth.

'I ought to top you now, and I will if you move a fucking muscle.'

Jimmy started the car and drove with one hand, the gun in the other. He turned round the first corner they came to and drove onto a building site. He got out, pushed the gun into his waistband and went round to the boot. He took out the pickaxe handle and then went round and pulled Denny's door open. Denny lunged at him but Jimmy stood back and Denny went down as the first sickening blow of the handle shattered his collar bone. The second broke his knee as he lay on the dirt. After that he just lay there as Jimmy broke his other leg and then kicked the shit out of him. Denny never made a sound and he never lost consciousness and his bloodied eyes never left Jimmy's face.

When Jimmy had finished he threw the pick-axe handle down beside Denny and got back into the car and drove to the nearest phone box. Fred was the Desk Sergeant.

'Fred? I've got Denny Morris for you. And Fred, get an ambulance and make it quick if you want him alive.' He gave the location of the building site, then he got into his car and drove off. At home he went upstairs, cleaned himself up, changed the blood-spattered clothes and picked up the briefcase and holdall. He put Denny's gun in his jacket pocket. He would dispose of it on the way to the airport. Fucking hell, Denny was tough. Anybody else would be dead but he was still conscious even at the end.

Jimmy went downstairs, picked up the car keys and went to open the front door. Then he stopped, put down the briefcase on the hall table and the holdall on the floor, turned and went into the living room and sat down.

'What the fucking hell am I doing? Where am I going?' He spoke out loud to the empty room. 'My son's in a war zone, my wife's dead, my daughter's kid is sick. Where is it I'm supposed to be going?'

And he sat there. He was frightened. He knew it would be worse than he could imagine, but after the pain there would be an end to it all. And he wanted more than anything else for there to be an end to it. Suddenly he knew he could take it, whatever it was. He would take it so long as he knew there would be an end and if there was a God and if that God was merciful, maybe he would, in time, be with Bernadette again. And if there was no God, well, he would settle for whatever had been waiting for Bernie. Jimmy sat back. He had some waiting to do. Without knowing it or meaning it the old words formed on his lips, *The first Sorrowful Mystery of the Rosary, The Agony in the Garden. Our Father...*

Chapter 11

Paddington, February 1995

IT WAS DARK when Jimmy returned to Bart's. He was carrying a bulky, heavy-duty carrier bag. He went to Philomena's office and found her working at her desk.

'Everything okay?'

'Yes, it's quiet so I decided to work. Janine's in her room. She's done some cleaning and tidying, there's not much else for her to do. I've decided we can't open if there might be trouble. I haven't mentioned anything to Janine. Should I have? Does she need to know?'

Jimmy shook his head.

'Did you get everything done that you wanted?'

'Yes, Sister, I picked up what I needed and then met a bloke I wanted to speak to.'

'And now you're back, nothing's happened yet...'

She was interrupted by the sound of someone banging on the door.

'Was that the front door, Jimmy?'

'Yes.'

'I'll go and see.'

As she got up there was a loud splintering and a bang as somebody kicked the front door open. They both stood still. Then a voice called loudly from the dining room:

'Costello.'

Philomena looked at Jimmy.

'It's okay, it's just someone for me. I was expecting them. Look after this will you? And go to Janine and both of you stay in her room.'

He put the carrier by her desk and walked away into the dining room. The man waiting was big. He wore an overcoat and had his hands in his pockets.

'Hello, Vic, I was expecting you. Sammy outside?'

Vic nodded.

'Shall we go, Jimmy?'

'Will I need anything?'

'You've got everything you need.'

'Jimmy.'

Philomena appeared in the dining room doorway. Janine stood behind her.

Jimmy looked round.

'It's okay, Sister, you and Janine go back upstairs or into your office.'

Vic didn't speak.

'I'm going out, Sister, don't worry and don't make any phone calls. Don't do anything, understand, nothing, not now, not later,' Jimmy said.

'When will you be back?'

She asked the question but she already knew the answer. Jimmy walked across and gently kissed Philomena on the cheek.

'As soon as I can, Sister. Take her away, Janine.'

Janine gently put her arm on Philomena's shoulder and they walked away together. Vic looked at Jimmy in the doorway.

'You're not going to try anything are you, Jimmy?'

'Would it make a difference?'

'Try if you like, it's all one to me.'

Vic walked to Jimmy and they went out of Bart's. On the street at the end of the alley next to the street lamp, a car waited with the engine running.

Jimmy went and stood by the car. Vic came to the back of the car to face him. The door wouldn't be between them when it opened and he could watch Jimmy all the way into the car and then get in after him.

'Open the door and get in.'

Jimmy bent to open the door, Vic moved back slightly. Jimmy could see Sammy sitting at the wheel looking straight ahead.

Jimmy opened the door and then stood looking at Vic.

'In you go, Jimmy.' Jimmy stepped forward, took him gently in his arms and lowered him onto the pavement. Sammy was out of the car very quickly, his hand already on the gun in his shoulder holster. He stopped when he saw the man on the pavement with the automatic fitted with a silencer pointing straight at him. Jimmy stood up with Vic's gun in his hand.

'Any way you want it, Sammy.'

Sammy stood still and let both his hands fall by his sides in clear view. He was good but he wasn't stupid.

'Nat isn't going to like this, Sammy. You've lost me, you've lost my money and,' looking down at the body, 'you've lost Vic, Nat's best boy.'

Sammy listened.

'Get Vic into the car, Sammy. Go and put him somewhere, and if you take my advice have a holiday yourself. Nat hasn't got a forgiving nature, he doesn't like failures and he hurts people who bring him bad news. You might make a good lesson for the others.'

Sammy thought for only a second, came round and bundled Vic's body into the back seat then slammed the door shut and got back in. The car pulled away. Jimmy turned to the man standing on the pavement, he was unscrewing the silencer.

'Thanks.'

The man spoke with a strong Northern Irish accent.

'You paid, the job's done. All I need from you now is the name you have for us, the man we owe a visit to.'

'Nat Desmond.'

The man looked surprised.

'Are you sure?'

Jimmy nodded.

'I'm sure. I got it three years ago from someone who

couldn't be wrong.'

'Well, we will have to visit Mr Desmond.'

'You know who he is?'

'Oh yes, we know Mr Desmond, but we thought he kept to his own side of the street. Okay, Mr Costello, we owed you a favour and now it's done, but one day you'll get a chance to say thanks properly. Money and one name doesn't settle this. We'll be in touch, don't you forget us now will you?'

He turned away and walked down the street.

Jimmy put Vic's gun in his pocket and went back into Bart's. Philomena was sitting at a table in the empty dining room. She looked up when he came in with surprise on her face.

'Jimmy, I thought...'

'I know, so did he.'

'What happened?'

'I persuaded them it wasn't worth it. They left.' He smiled. 'It's the blarney in me, Sister, I have a way with words.'

'Were they the danger, Jimmy? What did I know about them? I knew nothing.'

'If I hadn't come back you would have known who it was who came for me, the same man who came once before. I'd have disappeared, left the country, gone away. There would have been some story and after a while you'd have had an accident, and maybe Janine would have had one too. Then there'd be nothing and nobody to worry about. You were only a small risk, Sister, but our man doesn't take risks, not even small ones.'

'But why did they kill Mrs Amhurst and Mrs Lally, how was there anything in that for them? And why did they want to kill you?'

Jimmy looked surprised.

'They wanted me for old time's sake, it was a favour to important people. But what makes you think they killed Mrs Amhurst or Mrs Lally? What would they kill two old ladies for?'

'You said it was Mr Amhurst's money?'

'It was.'

Jimmy sat down opposite Philomena to break the bad news.

'That was Janine.'

Philomena sat in shocked silence.

'You're wrong,' she said after a while. 'You must be wrong. She couldn't.'

'I'm not wrong, Sister, she killed them both.'

'Why?'

'For some of Mr Amhurst's money. I don't know how she would have got it or how much she was to get but that's it. I could make a guess if you like.'

A voice cut into their talk.

'Make a guess.'

Janine was standing in the kitchen doorway with two cups of tea. She looked different, her eyes were different, the way she held herself was different. This was somebody Jimmy had never met. Jimmy looked at Philomena who was looking at Janine.

'Janine, did you hear what Jimmy said? You had nothing to do with this, did you?'

Janine came to the table, put down the cups of tea and sat down. She took Philomena's hands tenderly in hers.

'No, Sister, I don't know why Jimmy is saying this dreadful thing. He must know it's not true and it's upsetting you.' She looked at Jimmy. 'What makes you say such things, Jimmy?'

This was the Janine he knew, she was back.

'Because they are true, Janine, that's all.'

Philomena stood up. She looked from Janine to Jimmy, the two people she had come to care for most. She couldn't deal with it any more. She felt old and tired and beaten.

'I'll go and do some work,' she said vaguely.

'Go and lie on your bed and rest, Sister,' said Janine. 'I'll bring you some tea soon and we'll say a decade of the rosary together.' She smiled. Philomena smiled back.

'I will, Janine. I feel a bit tired. Tea will be nice, and the rosary together.'

She turned and left the dining room. Janine and Jimmy sat in silence until the sound of her feet on the stairs had gone.

'You were going to guess out loud, remember?'

The new Janine had returned.

'You visited people, Janine, you talked to them and they talked to you. You visited Lucy Amhurst and you talked about their idea for the will. You were going to make sure you got some of the money. You were going to be a good cause, probably that project in Goa, they would leave you some money for that. Once you were sure you had her you got rid of her. After a while, when everything had settled down and you had worked on Mr Amhurst and the will was made, he would go.'

Janine looked at him and smiled. It was not a nice smile.

'Not very good, Jimmy. And how did I kill her?'

It was Jimmy's turn to smile.

'I owe you for that. It saved my life tonight. You used the back yard. It opens onto the street. You spilled something in the kitchen as Mrs Amhurst was leaving and got Philomena to help clear it up. You told her you were going to get a bucket, something like that. You went to the yard. The street was clear so you slipped round to the car and knifed Mrs Amhurst. Then you're back before anyone has seen anything. You probably rehearsed it a few times with variations before everything was just right.'

Janine's manner became relaxed.

'You've got nothing.'

'I've got Mrs Lally. You were there.'

'So was the man on the stairs.'

'What man on the stairs? Your unsupported word puts a man of no description on the stairs. But you were there. You were here when Mrs Amhurst got it and you were there when Mrs Lally got it. If the same person is at two scenes of crime with the same method, that's enough for me or any copper who cares enough to notice. I don't know why you knifed Mrs Lally. My guess is she found something in the yard, maybe Mrs Amhurst's handbag. You had to put it somewhere and the bins were to hand. Maybe she told you she'd found it and asked your advice about what to do. Anyway, she had to go so you did what you did.'

'You think you're a clever man, Jimmy, but all this only exists in your head, there's no proof. Go to the police and they'll charge you with wasting their time.'

Jimmy looked puzzled.

'What are you talking about? Why would I go to the police? They've got someone for the Amhurst killing and they aren't interested in the Lally woman. What have the police got to do with any of this?'

'So what are you going to do? You have no evidence, nothing you've said will stand up in any court.'

Jimmy spoke slowly.

'I don't give a toss what happens to you but I do care about me and Philomena and perhaps I care enough about Mr Amhurst to save his life. Philomena knows you did it, I told her and I'll explain the hows and the whys so she'll be sure. I wouldn't want to read about Mr Amhurst having an accident so I'll see he knows how it is as well.' He sat back. 'There's going to be no money in this for you, Janine. You get nothing.'

Janine stood up, her face bright with anger.

'You little fucking shit, do you think your lies worry me? I want to do God's work and God is with me. I will build my school and my clinic and my orphanage because it's God's will, and God will punish you for your filthy lies.'

Jimmy stood up and faced her.

'Janine, I don't like you, you kill people. I'll take my chances with God, but if I ever meet you again, if we pass in the street, if we sit in the same restaurant, if I see you anywhere near me, I'll think the worst and I'll kill you before you kill me. There are no coincidences with you, Janine, so make no mistake, if I ever see you again I'll kill you without a second thought. Now get out.'

Janine spat full in his face, then turned and left the room.

Jimmy was sitting in the chair by the stairs when Janine

came down and swept past him. She had a small rucksack on her back.

He got up and closed the front door behind her. The lock was smashed but the bolts at the top and bottom worked.

He turned, stood for a moment and sniffed. It was a smell he recognised.

He went to his cupboard and filled a bucket with water, took it upstairs and threw it on the small fire that was beginning to burn merrily on the bed in Janine's room. He put down the bucket and went to his own room, packed his few belongings and sat for a short while on his bed looking at an envelope which was addressed to Sr Philomena. Eventually he got up, walked down the corridor and gently pushed open her door.

The light was still on but she was on the bed, fast asleep. He went into the room, put the envelope on her table in clear view, then switched off the room light and went out. He went back to his own room, tidied up, collected his bag and anorak and went down to the hall. He left his bag in the hall and went to Philomena's office and got the carrier bag with the money he had collected from his safety deposit box, then went back into the hall, put on his anorak and picked up his bag. He would have liked to have stayed for the night but he couldn't. He had done all he could. He walked through the dining room into the kitchen and opened the back door to the bin yard. He set the catch for the door to lock and pulled it shut.

Kilburn, October 1991

Jimmy was woken by the ringing of the front door bell. As he sat up on the settee where he'd eventually fallen asleep, the bell rang again. Jimmy felt stiff and awkward. Denny's gun was still in his pocket and he had been lying on it. His side hurt and he knew he was a mess. He felt it, he didn't need to look in a mirror. The bell rang again. Someone was getting impatient. Jimmy looked at his watch, seven o'clock. Whoever it was liked to be up and about early. The bell rang again. They weren't going away, soon the door would be kicked in. Jimmy went and opened it.

'Hello, Jimmy.'

'Hello, Vic.'

The big man stood with his hands in his pockets.

'Nat told me to collect you, Jimmy. You're not going to give me any trouble are you?'

Denny's gun appeared in Jimmy's hand. It was casually pointed at Vic's stomach.

'It depends what you call trouble, Vic.'

Vic didn't move, he especially didn't move his hands.

'Silly move, Jimmy, guns aren't your style. Put it away before someone gets hurt.'

Jimmy shot him in the thigh and Vic went down with an oath. Two men were out of the car and at the gate.

'Get fucking back,' shouted Vic, holding his thigh, sitting on the path. The men stopped. Curtains twitched at an upstairs window across the street.

'You're right, Vic, guns aren't my style. I might have missed you altogether or I might have blown your balls off. I wouldn't try to make me use it again.'

Jimmy was watching the two men at the gate while he spoke but the gun was still pointed at Vic. Vic pulled himself to his feet.

'Okay, Jimmy, have it your way. You know you're dead?'

'We all get dead sometime, Vic. Nobody gets out alive.'

Vic hobbled back to the car. The car drove off and Jimmy closed the door and went into the kitchen. He sat at the kitchen table, where he had so often sat with Bernadette. The remains of yesterday's funeral drinks were on the table or in the sink.

'Maybe I should have done sandwiches,' he said out loud. 'They should have had something to eat as well.'

After a while he got up, found some notepaper and a pen. He wrote a short letter, put it in an envelope, sealed it and put it in his jacket pocket. He leaned back in the chair with his hands on the table, and waited.

Jimmy sat for a long time, the untasted tea and the gun in front of him. Weird unconnected thoughts filled his head. He wasn't thinking, just watching the thoughts as they came and went.

Eventually the front door bell rang. Police or Nat? he wondered. He hoped it was Nat. It was.

'Come in, Nat. How's Vic?'

'Mad, Jimmy.'

Nat was grinning. Jimmy smiled back at him.

'Don't tell me Vic's pretending to be hurt. He's had worse than that. He walked away under his own steam, for God's sake.'

They went and sat in the kitchen.

'Pride, Jimmy, you shot him in his pride and he won't forgive you. Vic wants to be somebody one day. Letting you shoot him won't help. It encourages others to have a go.'

'Tea?'

Nat looked around the kitchen.

'Fucking hell, Jimmy, is it always like this?'

Jimmy looked around. It was never like this and especially not if there was a visitor.

'Not usually, but it's been a bit, you know, things to do so things don't get done.'

Nat took off his coat and carefully draped it over the back of a chair. Something heavy in the pocket bumped against the wood.

'Okay, Jimmy, let's get going.' He went to the sink and switched on the hot tap. 'There's not much and it's only cups and glasses. You want to wash or dry?'

'Dry. Bernie said I'm no good at washing glasses, I don't get them clean.'

Nat had rolled up his sleeves. 'That's 'cos you're a coward, like most men. If you wash up you have the water hot enough to suit your hands but not hot enough to do the job.' Nat put his fingers under the hot water then put the plug in the sink. 'Where's your washing up liquid?'

Jimmy shrugged. Nat opened a cupboard under the sink. It was there. He squirted it into the water which began to foam as his hand moved in it. He put the liquid away and plunged his hands into the sink. 'Fuck.'

'Hot?'

'No, I forgot to take my watch off.' He took off his Rolex and put it in his trouser pocket.

'Nice watch, Nat.'

'It should be, it fucking well cost enough.' He passed the first glass to Jimmy who was standing beside him with a tea towel with the Cathedrals of England and Wales on it. The glass was still hot.

Jimmy smiled. 'I'm impressed.'

'You know, Jimmy, when girls get to about twelve a strange change takes place in their bodies; it doesn't happen to boys, only girls. They develop the ability to plunge their hands into boiling water and hold red hot plates without showing pain. How many times have you burnt your fingers on a plate Bernie passed you with her bare hands?'

Jimmy smiled. Often, he thought, often.

'What about you, Nat?'

'I just don't let myself feel the pain, Jimmy, it's a knack.'

Yes, thought Jimmy, it's a knack. He slowly dried the glasses, cups and saucers which were piling up before him. Nat finished the sink-full, went to the table and picked up Denny's gun, which Jimmy had left there.

'What about this?'

Jimmy turned round, he looked at the gun pointing at him. 'I dunno, Nat, you can have it if you like, I don't want it.' And he turned back to the drying up.

'I've got one, Jimmy.'

'I know.'

Nat grinned. 'I know, I'll give it to Vic and tell him you sent it as a present, said you didn't need it any more.'

He put Denny's gun in his other overcoat pocket. Jimmy liked that, it was a nice touch.

Nat filled the sink with the last things from the table and they carried on in silence. Jimmy was very slow so Nat found another tea towel and they finished the drying up.

'Where does it all go?'

'Leave it, I'll do this later. Let's go and sit down.'

Jimmy led Nat to the living room and they sat down.

'How come you're still here, Jimmy? It was only on the off-chance Vic came, we thought you'd be well away.'

Jimmy shrugged. 'Where would I go?'

'Denny's not the bloody Mafia. There's plenty of places to be comfortable, where Denny couldn't get you. Don't tell me it's the money. Everyone knows you made it but you never fucking spent it. You must be worth a packet.'

'It's not the money. You got a family, Nat?'

'Mum and Dad.'

'See them?'

'Yeah. They live south of the river, I get round when I can.'

'They okay?'

'Sure, Jimmy. I told them they could live anywhere, I'd pay, but they won't move. I wanted them to move back to St Lucia or Ireland…'

'Ireland?'

Nat laughed.

'Surprised, Jimmy, didn't think there's any black Irishmen? My dad's from Tuam in Galway and my mum's from a little village in St Lucia. I'm half Irish, Jimmy, it's why I fit in so well here.'

Jimmy thought for a moment.

'You a Catholic, Nat?'

Nat shook his head.

'No, I got expelled.'

'How do you mean expelled? You don't get expelled.'

'I did. In my first school there weren't many black kids, lots of Irish, some Italian and the like, but not many black kids, and there was this teacher, a little bloke, dead racist. He came to the school as deputy head in my last year and set out to make my life a misery. Anyway, one day I lamped him, I can't remember why, but I was big for my age and he was a runty little guy. He liked wearing the altar boy outfit and serving at the Mass we all had to go to on Friday afternoon. Anyway, I lamped him right on that little 'tache he had.' Nat laughed at the fond memory of school days past. 'You should have seen the blood. He looked so funny. I reckon they expelled me as much 'cos I laughed as for busting his lip. After that I wasn't a Catholic anymore. Like I say, I got expelled.'

They sat in silence for a bit. Then Nat said, 'I'm going now, Jimmy. Denny will tell me what he wants to happen to you when he's ready to deal with you, so don't try to go anywhere. Vic'll be watching for you, don't give him any opportunity. Maybe he can't kill you yet, but he can hurt you.'

'I'm not going anywhere, Nat. But before you go I've got something for you.'

Jimmy took out the letter and handed it to Nat.

'This for me, Jimmy?'

Nat fingered the thin envelope. 'It's not money so it's got to be info.'

'Let's just say it calls in a favour.'

'So what will this favour do?'

'How much do you want it, Nat?'

Nat paused. 'Want what?'

'If you need to ask you don't want it.'

'Do you mean what I think you mean?'

Jimmy nodded.

'And this will get it for me?'

Jimmy nodded again.

Nat paused again. This was tricky. 'If I was interested, what would I do with it?'

'You'd take it to a pub and give it to the barman and tell him it's for Bridie.'

'Bridie McDonald?'

'That's right. Even with Denny down you couldn't take him. But you and Bridie together might.'

Nat was thinking.

'This won't get you off the hook, Jimmy. No one can do anything about you.'

'I know, I don't want anything done about me. But you better make up your mind. Denny's tough, every day you wait makes it harder, and just at the moment Vic's as slow as he's ever likely to be, so he won't stand in your way.'

'I get the picture. So what's in it for you? Nobody does something for nothing and you don't owe me a favour, so what do you get?'

'I'll tell you, Nat, you won't understand, but I'll tell you anyway. Denny's as vicious as it gets, he lives to hurt people. It's not about money with Denny, and he'll go on pushing till he's stopped. So I'm going to have him stopped.'

'And I'm going to stop him for you?'

'That's right, you and Bridie McDonald. Things will be better with you on top because it's all about money with you, Nat. You're as much a businessman as you are a villain. With you it's a career, you're really just a violent accountant. Maybe if you get on top things will get better. Everybody will make money and people will only get hurt if they have to be. That's what it's about, it's about stopping Denny by putting you on top.'

Nat was thinking hard. He wanted it, but...

'Bridie's been around a long time, maybe she's past it.'

'No she isn't. She still runs her sons and they still run Glasgow. They'll be in this.'

'What makes you so sure?'

'You remember that Scottish kid? The one you told me about and I made it so you all walked?'

Nat nodded.

'Lenny forgot to mention that he was Bridie's youngest son, didn't he? Denny pulled the trigger and you both burned and buried the body. But the only one Bridie knew about was Lenny and that's why he died like he did.'

'I thought that was down to Denny.'

Jimmy shook his head.

'Everyone did, but it was Bridie, and don't ask how he died, it wasn't nice. Give her Denny as the triggerman and she'll probably just want to keep the finger that pulled the trigger to wear round her neck on a chain. What's left she'll give to you.'

Nat was still thinking about it. It sounded right.

'Denny's down and Vic's slow. Get Bridie on board, Nat, and take your chance. Another one may not come along.'

Nat stood up.

'We'll see,' he said and he went to the kitchen and came back with his coat on. 'I'll tell you what would make it certain, Jimmy.'

'What's that?'

Jimmy was on his guard. Nat was going to try to use him, Jimmy could smell it.

'It was Denny who gave that priest friend of yours and those IRA bombers to Special Branch, and that wasn't all he gave them, he had a regular arrangement. If you were to tell your priest's friends in Belfast that...'

'Do you think I know his Belfast friends?'

'You've got a phone and maybe a couple of days. If you really want Denny stopped you could reach them. After all, whatever happens, your days as a copper are over. If you were to make that call and this all goes through before Denny's back in charge, who knows, maybe you might even get out alive.'

'You want everyone's help with Denny, Nat? How about asking the coppers as well?'

'I don't take unnecessary chances, that's all. Well, are you in?'

'Okay, I'll make the calls, but that's all I can do. They won't work with you and they'll take their own time.'

Nat smiled.

'Denny's finished. If the IRA and Bridie McDonald miss I won't. But I don't promise it will be better, Jimmy. That's in your head, not mine.'

Nat left. They didn't say goodbye.

Jimmy began turning it all over slowly in his mind.

Why would Denny give Father Liam to Special Branch? Why would Denny give anything to Special Branch? In Denny's book there were only two sides to the street, the law's side and his side, and Denny would never work with coppers, not with straight coppers, anyway. Denny thought he would live forever and always be at the top. He would never work out that money or fear was never enough insurance. He just wouldn't bother to think that everybody gets older, slower or just unlucky, and everybody goes down in the end.

But if you were someone who looked ahead and made plans for their retirement, you'd take out the right insurance policy. If you made a deal with Special Branch and you set out to be a source of info on the IRA, now that would be real insurance, that would put you on the inside, not the outside. What if you got Special Branch what they needed, not just on the IRA but on the other terrorist nutters who came to London for a bit of shopping? You would know things, because some of the people they came to deal with knew and trusted you. Now that really would be insurance, that would give you friends in very high places and buy enough immunity when the time came. But that wouldn't be Denny's way. Denny's brain wasn't a businessman's brain.

But Nat's was. If Nat was already on his way to the top he would have started a pension plan a long time ago, a nice solid government pension plan. Jimmy decided not to make any phone calls. But one day he might, one day the information might be worth making a call. One day, if he lived that long.

Chapter 12

Kilburn, February 1995

JIMMY STOOD WITH his bag and carrier in the doorway of The Liffey Lad. It was busy. By the fireplace a young red-headed man in a thick white sweater was playing good fiddle music but Jimmy didn't feel like tapping his foot. At the tables tourists looked on, happily bemused, as they ate their meals. Many tables had part-empty pint glasses of dark beer on them. The Guinness had been duly sampled but it was wine, shorts and mineral water that was being drunk. Dotted about the room were Irishesque figures with caps on and Arran sweaters. The women looked more authentic than the men, except for one man in a corner, a Catholic priest in a black suit and a Roman collar. Four years ago that same priest had a job in a bookie's not ten doors down the street. The music, the atmosphere, the rise and fall of voices was all very well done and not a bouncer in sight. Safe as well as fun, real value for money. Jimmy walked across to the bar, put his bags down.

'A pint of Directors, George, please.'

He put his hand in his pocket and pulled out a handful of change.

A local stepped to the bar, gently bumped Jimmy, turned to him and said in a loud voice, 'Sorry, y'r honour, no offence intended.' He then turned to the bar. 'Another pint, Eamon, and on the slate this time by God.'

George looked at Jimmy and then said in a equally loud

voice. 'You've had all the drink you'll get here tonight, O'Halloran. Go home to your wife while you can still walk, though it's no welcome the poor woman will give you in your state.'

The local swayed. 'You're a hard man, Eamon Doyle, with no heart at all.' You could almost hear the tears of regret in his voice, it was all very well done.

'Hard as the slate I don't write your drinks up on.'

The local flourished his cap aggressively at George. It substituted for anything that might upset the customers.

'Bad cess to you, Eamon Doyle. I will go where I am more appreciated, where a man with the drouth on him can find comfort and congenial company.' He turned and announced with a grand gesture. 'Goodnight to all here, may the blessing of St Patrick be upon you all.'

The priest in the corner looked up from his book and said, 'Amen to that,' and returned to his reading, as the local swayed accurately between the tables and left.

'Do they ever clap, George?' asked Jimmy as the tourist chatter enthusiastically resumed.

'If they did we'd have overdone it.'

'You don't call that overdoing it?'

'No, it's all nicely judged, and sorry, we've taken off the Directors. What about something else?'

Jimmy looked at the taps and handles. 'No thanks, I only really looked in to say goodbye.' Jimmy returned his money to his pocket.

'No hurry, Jimmy. Let me get you one, out of my own bottle.' George brought a bottle of Irish whiskey from under the counter.

'Okay, George, but not out of that bottle. I'll have one from any of those.' Jimmy nodded to the bottles of spirits over the back of the bar. 'Just a small one.'

George told the young barman to get Jimmy a small Irish.

'That your new barman?'

'Just temporary. Vic does it sometimes if he's on standby, it's easy work and he can get away when he's needed for anything else. He's out now but I expect him back soon.'

The barman put Jimmy's drink in front of him.

'Vic's been delayed, George. Tell the boy he'll be needed longer than you thought.'

'Have you seen Vic?'

'That's right. He was with Sammy, they paid me a visit. What's the matter, George, something upset you?'

George was looking worried.

'What's going on, Jimmy?'

'Vic's down and Sammy's running. Soon I'll be gone too.'

'I don't believe you.'

'I'm here and Vic isn't. If Vic was alive, that phone call you asked the boy to make when I came in would have had him here in... how long? How long have I got, George,' he looked at his watch, 'with Sammy driving? Is he good? How long?'

George breathed out slowly, then Jimmy took Vic's gun out of his pocket and put it on the bar.

'Fucking hell, Jimmy.'

George quickly took the gun off the bar and slipped it into his pocket. A few faces at the nearer tables turned. He lowered his voice. 'Vic and Sammy in one night? If that's kosher then it ain't good. But I can't let you just leave, Jimmy. Nat will be upset if I just let you walk away.' George's hand was still in his pocket.

'I'm going, George, no need for any trouble. I don't want trouble.'

'Like hell you don't. Nat lets you sit there for nearly four weeks, then when he wants you iced you take out his two best boys. There'll be those who say Nat's losing his touch.'

'Do you say that, George?'

'I wouldn't say it, but if someone like you, all on your own, can go up against Nat, who else might not have a go?'

'Maybe I wasn't on my own, George, maybe I had help.'

George was doing some serious thinking. 'Maybe I'll go and visit my old mum, Jimmy. She's not been well.'

'Your old mum drank herself to death years ago when she got too old and ugly to stay on the game.'

'Jimmy, you're a bastard. Three years ago you caused trouble and a lot of people got hurt. Everybody had to run for cover till things settled down. But it all got sorted and everything started running sweet as pie. Then you come back, and now...' George paused.

'You thinking about visiting your mum?'

'I'll think about it, Jimmy. I may have to think about it.'

Jimmy finished his drink and picked up his bags.

'See you, George.'

'One thing, Jimmy, why did you come back?'

'Still none of your fucking business, George, none of your fucking business.'

The faces turned again and watched Jimmy as he left. The tourists looked at each other excitedly. Now this was what they called value for money. Ten minutes after Jimmy left The Liffey Lad a man walked in and went to the bar.

'Have you seen Vic or Sammy?'

George shook his head. 'Anything up?'

'Someone's had a go at Nat. He's okay but he wants Vic and Sammy to drop what they're doing and get to him. Tell them if you see them,' and he turned and left.

George stood for a moment then turned to the young barman.

'You close up tonight, Wayne, and when you've closed up let Mr Desmond know I've just had a message, my old mum's not well. I'll have to go away for a bit.'

'Okay, George.'

And George took his coat and left.

Philomena was woken next morning by the phone ringing in the office. She awoke on her bed still fully dressed, and confused. She got up and hurried to the office to answer it. It was Inspector Deal.

'If you wait, Inspector, I'll get him.' She went to Jimmy's room. It was empty, the bed stripped, everything gone. She went back to the phone. 'I'm afraid he's gone, Inspector. No, he didn't. Either last night or this morning. No, I have no idea where he has gone.'

She put the phone down and went to check Janine's room.

Inspector Deal put the phone down with a smile. So Costello had gone, that suited him down to the ground. He sat back in his chair, there was a knock at his door which opened before he could say, 'Come in', and a man walked in.

'Inspector Deal, I'm Superintendent Smart of Internal Investigations.'

Inspector Deal got up and came round his desk. 'Nice to see you, Super, but not altogether a surprise.'

'No?'

'Well, I filed a report to A10 concerning Detective Inspector Flavin and the beating up of a Sergeant out of this nick. It was linked to an ex-officer called Costello who worked out of some North London nick some years ago. I expected a visit.'

'Your report?'

'About Inspector Flavin. You're here about my report on Inspector Tommy Flavin aren't you?'

'No. I'm here because we have received information about a recent case, the stabbing of Mrs Lucy Amhurst. You were the officer in charge.'

Inspector Deal looked shaken. 'What information?'

'That you ordered the arrest of someone knowing them to be innocent and fabricated evidence or caused evidence to be fabricated and that you obtained a confession illegally.'

'That's ridiculous, who gave you this information?'

'Your name was given to us by a fellow officer, a Detective Sergeant Edward Clarke, he co-operated fully with us. I must warn you, Inspector Deal, that these are serious charges and may result in criminal proceedings. I must ask you for your warrant card.'

He held out his hand. Deal handed over his card in a dazed way.

'Please do not leave your present address and be available for questioning when required. You are suspended from duties during our enquiries. Please leave your office and take nothing with you.'

Deal moved towards his laptop.

'Nothing, just your jacket.'

Deal noticed, for the first time, another officer standing in the doorway. He collected his jacket and went into the corridor. The other officer joined his colleague inside his office and the door closed.

Philomena found Janine's room empty and the remains of the fire on the bed. She slowly made her way back to her room and sat down, then she noticed the letter Jimmy had left. It was addressed to her, typewritten on an expensive envelope, there was no stamp.

She took it and opened it.

It was from the Duns College and the address was in the Vatican City.

She began to read.

Dear Sr Philomena,

This is to introduce James Cornelius Costello and to thank you for accepting him on a placement at Fr Lynch's recommendation. He is considering making an application to study for the priesthood at Duns College in Rome, a foundation which offers training to mature men of independent means for the Catholic priesthood.

Following initial discussions in Rome with Mr Costello, it has been agreed that he undertake a short period of pastoral work in an appropriate placement before beginning his final interviews. I have been in contact with the Superior of your Province in England who highly recommends your work.

Mr Costello is a widower with two grown-up children, one married with a family, one a missionary priest. No doubt he will give you any further information about himself you require when he gives you this letter at the commencement of his placement.

Mr Costello served for many years with distinction in the Metropolitan Police Force before retiring. I'm sure he will be as great a help to you as you will be to him. I apologise for the lack of notice in this matter but I'm sure Mr Costello will explain the circumstances.

Yours in Christ

The signature was a scrawl but underneath it was printed, Honorary Rector, Duns College.

Philomena put the letter on to the table. Why didn't you tell me, Jimmy? Why keep it secret till you were gone? But she knew in her heart that Jimmy would never tell anyone more than they needed to know. So, you've gone for a priest, Jimmy. Well I'll pray for you. I think you're going to need lots of prayers.

The front door bell rang, Philomena went down and unbolted it. On the step was Mr Amhurst.

'Excuse me, Sister, may I come in?'

'Of course, of course.' Sr Philomena led him to the kitchen after closing and bolting the door. 'Tea?'

'Coffee please.'

'Would you like to make it yourself to suit you?'

He smiled. 'Thank you, Sister.'

Philomena made her tea while Mr Amhurst made his coffee.

'I'm afraid I've come to ask a favour, Sister.'

'If it's anything I can do, I'd be delighted.'

'Would it be possible, do you think, for me to come and help here, like Lucy did? I'm afraid I don't share your faith as she did but she was happy at St Bartholomew's... Bart's.'

'It's not Bartholomew, it's named for Bartimaeus, the blind beggar.'

'Oh.'

'It doesn't matter.'

'It's probably a silly thing to ask of you, my talents outside making and selling plastic bags are as limited as my understanding of your faith, but I can make tea and wash up.'

He paused for a second. 'I think I would feel nearer to Lucy here than anywhere else and giving up business means I will have plenty of time.'

Philomena looked at him. 'You want to be a helper?'

'Very much, Sister, I know I will be of little use, but whatever I can do, and of course if money would help…'

Sister Philomena laughed. Help and finance, and people said there was no God. Wasn't there always a good soul not far off to help you on your way? 'How did you get here, Mr Amhurst?'

'Oh, I used the Skoda, that was right wasn't it?'

Philomena nodded. 'This is what we'll do…' and they sat at the kitchen table as Philomena outlined her ideas.

Endpiece

No disciplinary action was taken against Inspector Tommy Flavin, who remained in post.

Detective Superintendent Norman Forester took early retirement and obtained a senior post with a large security firm.

DS Eddy Clarke made Inspector but shortly afterwards took early retirement. He and his partner Sharon moved to Torremolinos and opened a club for expatriates.

Inspector Joe Deal resigned from the force and opened a successful string of bistro bars in several major cities outside London.

Bridie McDonald is still running her business in Glasgow but, unfortunately, has lost another son.

Bart's has re-opened another floor of the building to provide accommodation for homeless or abused women with children and is now fully refurbished. It will soon become financially self-supporting. It has two paid members of staff and Sister Philomena has been allowed by her Order to stay on for the foreseeable future.

Nat Desmond continued his business for six months but died, tragically, when his car was destroyed by a bomb. Police believe it was a case of mistaken identity.

George's old mother finally got better and he returned to The Liffey Lad when, after a period of uncertainty, a new owner was found for Nat Desmond's business. The whereabouts of Janine McIver remain unknown.

Overheard in a police station canteen some weeks later:

'If Costello ever becomes a fucking priest the confessionals will need steps for sinners to fall down so they cough to the sins Jimmy's looking for.'

It wasn't meant to be taken seriously.

Luath Press Limited

committed to publishing well written books worth reading

LUATH PRESS takes its name from Robert Burns, whose little collie Luath (*Gael.*, swift or nimble) tripped up Jean Armour at a wedding and gave him the chance to speak to the woman who was to be his wife and the abiding love of his life. Burns called one of the 'Twa Dogs' Luath after Cuchullin's hunting dog in Ossian's *Fingal*. Luath Press was established in 1981 in the heart of Burns country, and is now based a few steps up the road from Burns' first lodgings on Edinburgh's Royal Mile. Luath offers you distinctive writing with a hint of unexpected pleasures.

Most bookshops in the UK, the US, Canada, Australia, New Zealand and parts of Europe, either carry our books in stock or can order them for you. To order direct from us, please send a £sterling cheque, postal order, international money order or your credit card details (number, address of cardholder and expiry date) to us at the address below. Please add post and packing as follows: UK – £1.00 per delivery address; overseas surface mail – £2.50 per delivery address; overseas airmail – £3.50 for the first book to each delivery address, plus £1.00 for each additional book by airmail to the same address. If your order is a gift, we will happily enclose your card or message at no extra charge.

Luath Press Limited
543/2 Castlehill
The Royal Mile
Edinburgh EH1 2ND
Scotland
Telephone: +44 (0)131 225 4326 (24 hours)
Fax: +44 (0)131 225 4324
email: sales@luath. co.uk
Website: www. luath.co.uk